"You're a virgin? How is that possible?"

Paige shrugged. "Satan created me, I went through Rivka training, got caught up in a battle to save the world, then discovered I was poison to anything I touched. I've been a little busy." She paused. "So, now you see why our kissing is a bad idea? Kissing leads to sex, and then sex with you, Mr. Damned, would pretty much cancel out the last pure thing in my being." She made a face. "So, your virtue is safe with me. Which is too bad, really, because that kiss was awesome."

Jed leaned forward. "In that case, I have to warn you."

His voice had suddenly become husky, and something curled low inside her. "Warn me about what?"

"I like touching you. Kissing you, too." His gaze was dark again, his jaw tense. "I'm not going to try to seduce you, but if you throw yourself in my arms and wrap those long legs of yours around me like you did earlier . . ." His gaze settled on hers. "I'm not made of steel, sweetheart."

*Please turn this page
to find out why people are raving
about Stephanie Rowe . . .*

MUST LOVE DRAGONS

"Hilarious . . . Rowe's wacky secondary characters are back in full force: the shape-shifting Goblet with attitude; a lovesick Satan; Iris, the touch-me-not object of his affection; and Becca, Satan's right-hand woman. Rowe's blissfully bizarre paranormal romance works well on its own, but libraries will want the entire series."

—*Booklist* (starred review)

"A fun romantic fantasy . . . Stephanie Rowe writes perhaps the ultimate star-crossed romance as the dragon and dragon-slayer fall in love."

—*Midwest Book Review*

"Hilarious romp . . . hot . . . funny, and entirely satisfying. If you want sexy paranormal with a twist, this is definitely a book for you."

—WantzUponaTime.com

"Stephanie Rowe has penned another fun-filled escape into her hilarious world of imagination. Fast-paced with a marvelous cast of characters."

—ParanormalRomanceWriters.com

"4 Stars! Pure escapist fun!"

—*Romantic Times BOOKclub Magazine*

"The zany characters . . . populating *Date Me, Baby, One More Time* all reappear in *Must Love Dragons*, and they're just as much fun to read about the second time."

—CurledUp.com

more . . .

DATE ME, BABY, ONE MORE TIME

SEX
& THE
IMMORTAL
BAD BOY

Also by Stephanie Rowe

Date Me, Baby, One More Time

Must Love Dragons

He Loves Me, He Loves Me Hot

SEX
& THE
IMMORTAL
BAD BOY

STEPHANIE ROWE

FOREVER

NEW YORK   BOSTON

Copyright © 2007 by Stephanie Rowe
Excerpt from *The First Seduction* copyright © 2007 by Stephanie Rowe
All rights reserved. Except as permitted under the U.S. Copyright Act of 1976, no part of this publication may be reproduced, distributed, or transmitted in any form or by any means, or stored in a database or retrieval system, without the prior written permission of the publisher.

Forever is a division of Grand Central Publishing.

The Forever name and logo is a trademark of Hachette Book Group USA, Inc.

Cover art and design by Michael Storrings

Forever
Hachette Book Group USA
237 Park Avenue
New York, NY 10017
Visit our Web site at www.HachetteBookGroupUSA.com

Printed in the United States of America

First Printing: November 2007

10 9 8 7 6 5 4 3 2 1

For all the wonderful people at the Rose City Romance Writers. You guys are the best!

Acknowledgments

Thank you as always to my fantastic editor, Melanie Murray, for her insightful editing and her support. You rock! And thanks to my agent, Michelle Grajkowski, who never stops believing in me. And of course, my deepest thanks to JR and AR for their support, without which I couldn't possibly spend hours and hours buried in my stories. And to my mom, who is, quite simply, the best mom in the world.

One

"Hot damn! An angel!" Paige Darlington jerked upright and slammed her grande, nonfat, easy whip caramel latte down on the table as a lanky redheaded guy strode into the Starbucks she and her two best friends had been haunting for the last week. He was wearing ironed jeans and a blue oxford shirt, and he had that white aura she'd been desperately searching for. *"Finally."*

Her salvation had arrived. About time. The blackness of her soul was making her calf ache almost constantly, and it was apparent she needed some angel cleansing as soon as possible.

Paige's heart started pounding as her friends inspected the man while he sauntered up to the counter and politely ordered a double hazelnut caffè mocha with extra foam.

"Really? He's an angel?" Theresa Nichols-Siccardi, an immortal dragon with a curvaceous human body that she made sure men lusted over, sounded skeptical. "He doesn't even have a halo."

"Oh, it's there." One of the benefits of being created by Satan was that Paige could identify the occupants of heaven and hell. Or so she'd hoped. Until she'd actually seen this guy, she hadn't been certain she would know an angel when she saw one. But she had. Major relief. "He's definitely got heaven on speed dial."

Her other friend, the newly single Dani Rawlings, took a sip of her iced coffee, her brown hair shoved up in a messy ponytail. She was in an anti-man phase, which was best for all of them, given the fiasco that had occurred the last time she'd gotten involved with anyone. "He looks rather ordinary to be an angel."

"Yeah, he does, doesn't he?" Paige ran her fingers through her hair like she'd seen Theresa do and watched him move to the side to wait for his order. "How long do you think it will take to convince him to help me?"

"Well, he's a man and you've got a great rack and gorgeous blond hair that men are such suckers for, so . . ." Theresa eyed her. "Maybe one minute?"

"One minute? That's all?"

"Try to appeal to his nurturing side," Theresa suggested. "Men love to feel all manly and tough. Protect the weaker sex."

Paige frowned and tapped her foot restlessly. "I don't want to be protected. I'm way too much of a badass to be protected by some wimpy angel."

Theresa raised her eyebrows at Paige. "That kind of attitude isn't going to make him fall all over himself to help you. You have to convince him you find him wildly attractive and masculine. Men can't resist being around women who make them feel manly."

"Manly, huh?" Paige eyed the angel as he accidentally bumped into a pair of teenage girls and apologized profusely. Duh. Didn't he realize they'd bumped into him on purpose to get his attention? *Hellooo. Get some backbone, dude.* He flipped open his navy nylon wallet to count his cash. "He looks a little gentle to be manly."

Hellfire, this sucked. She didn't want a wimpy angel in her life. She wanted some hot, macho stud who would throw her up against a wall and dominate her, not being at all intimidated by the fact she could throw fireballs and turn him into a pile of ash in less than a second. Who didn't mind that she did contract work for Satan harvesting souls, or would, as soon as she reclaimed her soul.

Yep. She wanted a hottie who wore black leather and guns. One who had five-o'clock shadow and piercing blue eyes that could penetrate a woman's soul. One who could kill an innocent at a hundred yards without hesitating. A man who would love her so fiercely he'd throw himself into an acid pit just to retrieve a lock of her hair.

Yeah. That was the kind of man she wanted.

Sigh.

She drummed her fingers on the sticky tabletop and eyed the angel, inspecting his narrow shoulders and wrinkle-free polyester shirt. She *had* to find a way to convince him to help save her soul.

"Paige?"

She looked at her friends, and felt her heart tighten at the concerned expressions on their faces. "I love you guys."

They both smiled. "We love you too," Theresa said. "Now go over there and turn that angel into a lovesick wuss already, okay?"

"No problem." Paige stood up and flexed her hands behind her back, trying to ignore the throbbing pain in her left calf.

She stepped around a double stroller with screaming

twins, then eased toward the angel, trying to sway her hips across the floor in that one-hip-at-a-time seductive walk that Theresa had been teaching her for the last week. She heard Dani giggle and she abandoned the walk with a sigh. Sexy and seductive wasn't her thing. Yet. But she'd master it. Really, she would.

She sidled up to the angel and cleared her throat.

He turned his head slightly and she caught his glance at her chest. Then his gaze slowly traveled up her body to her face, and she gave him her best smile. "Hi, I'm Paige Darlington, and—"

"You're from *hell*." His eyes widened, and he took a step back.

She bristled at the look of disgust on his face. Ignorant jerk. Weren't angels supposed to be nonjudgmental and supportive and all touchy-feely? Idiot. How dare he treat her like she was pond scum? "For your information," she snapped, "I'm *not* from hell." At his disbelieving look, she added, "Anymore."

He began to back across the store toward the door. "I don't need that coffee anymore," he called out to the girl behind the counter. "I'm so sorry to inconvenience you, but I must be leaving." He glanced at Paige again, and his left eye twitched in fear.

Oh, crud. He looked like he was about to wet his pants.

You're scaring him, Paige. Be nice.

Right. Nice. She could do that. She summoned up her best smile again and injected a cheery tone into her voice as she jogged after him. "See, it's really quite simple. My life force is no longer linked to Satan so I'm a free woman, but my soul had already started to turn black before I was freed. If I don't reverse the process before I'm consumed by darkness, I'll lose the ability to love and care about all my friends, so I need you to cleanse my soul." Anxiety tugged at her chest as he reached for the door, and she grabbed for his arm. "No, please don't go. I really, *really* need your help."

He twisted out of her reach before she could touch him. "I can feel the evil in your soul already. It's too late. Stay away from me."

"No!" She was unable to keep the desperation out of her voice. "Please! You're the only angel I've managed to find, and I need help—"

He whirled to face her. "Get away from me," he growled. "You're tainted."

Paige swallowed. "That's a little harsh, isn't it? I mean, I'm trying to clean up my act . . ."

He spun around and marched out the door, slamming it in her face.

She immediately threw it open and followed him out onto the sidewalk. "What kind of an angel are you, anyway? Shouldn't you be trying to save me? Isn't that your *job*?"

He didn't even turn around, just threw up his arm to flag down a yellow cab, like she wasn't even worth his consideration. God, how insulting was that? She grabbed his arm and spun him toward her. "Listen, you arrogant—"

His face contorted into this mask of pain, and he shrieked. Then his skin turned black and he crumbled under her touch, disintegrating into a cloud of charcoal flakes, leaving her with black dust on her hand and a horrible burning sensation in her leg.

"What the heck was *that* all about?" She stared at the

remains of the angel as they mixed in with the exhaust from the New York City traffic, rubbing her right foot over her left calf to try to ease the pain that was about fifty times worse than it had been before she'd touched the angel.

"Holy shit."

Paige glanced back over her shoulder to see Theresa and Dani standing outside the Starbucks. Theresa looked startled, and Paige's gut sank. Nothing ever rattled Theresa.

But it was Dani that made her skin crawl. Dani's face was pale, her hand was over her mouth and her eyebrows were scrunched up in horror. Not blank horror. A knowing horror. The kind that said she knew what had just happened and she was scared shitless.

Paige whirled around and grabbed for Dani's arms. "What happened?"

"No! Don't touch me!" Dani jumped out of Paige's reach, tripped on the curb, and went down hard on the street. She scrambled to her feet, holding her hand out as if to ward off Paige. "Don't touch either of us. Just stand there."

A chill crept down Paige's spine. *"What?"*

Theresa frowned at Dani. "Yeah, what?"

"It's true. Holy crap. I can't believe he really did it."
"Did what?"

Dani took a deep breath, then looked at Paige. "You're in deep trouble, girl."

"For hell's sake, tell me what's going on. Last I heard, angels didn't turn into soot on a regular basis." Paige hugged herself and ran her hands up and down her arms, suddenly cold.

"When I was dating Satan Jr., he told me he'd heard a rumor that Satan was trying an experiment. A new kind of Rivka."

Paige tensed. "What do you mean, a new kind?"

"Well, they still have the ability to throw fireballs, harvest souls, and transport themselves by melting through the floor, and they still have to obey Satan's every command, but Satan wanted a better weapon. Apparently, he was getting a little intimidated by Satan Jr.'s talents and—"

"Skip the history lesson. What's different about the new Rivka?"

"Well . . ." Dani glanced at Theresa, then back at Paige. "I don't know exactly. I just know that it was bad. I wasn't really listening at the time. I was, um, you know, occupied . . ."

"For God's sake, Dani," Theresa snapped. "You have to learn to think while having an orgasm. No smart woman turns off her brain during sex! It's the best time to gather secrets on your man! Yeesh." She turned toward Paige. "Okay, girlfriend, you need to get your butt down to see Satan and find out the scoop. Capisce? No plans can be made until we know."

Paige looked at her hand, and then looked at where the angel had been. "Yeah, I guess." Then she frowned and set her hands on her hips. "You know, this is ridiculous. I couldn't have killed the angel. It was probably some fancy new thing they can do. Self-defense or something."

"You're right." Theresa marched up to Paige. "There's no way you've acquired the touch of death in the ten minutes since I last touched you." Theresa snapped her fingers. "Hold out your hand."

Dani grimaced. "I'm not so sure that's a good idea. What if she blows you up?"

Paige felt a stabbing sensation in her calf, and she had a sudden vision of launching herself at Theresa, hurting her, killing her . . . of *wanting* to hurt her. She took a step back. "I'm with Dani. There's something weird going on."

"I'm immortal," Theresa scoffed. "You know, three drinks from the Goblet of Eternal Youth and all that fun stuff. You can't hurt me." Theresa reached for her, Paige ducked, and Theresa's fingers grazed over her ear. "Squirmy little—Holy mother of hell!" Theresa jerked her hand back as the need to kill slammed through Paige's heart, and she lunged for her friend, no longer able to stop herself.

"Back off, hell girl!" Theresa stuck out her leg and swept Paige's feet out from under her, sending her crashing to the sidewalk.

Paige yelped as her chin smacked the asphalt, sending a crack through her head. She tried to stand up, but was so dizzy she crashed back to the cement again, banging her head with another smack. She groaned with relief and pain and rolled onto her back, sprawling on the sidewalk as she felt the urge to kill retreat back into her leg. "Thanks."

"No problem." Theresa leaned over her. "That's what friends are for. Need me to knock you out?"

"No, I'm good. My head hurts so much that I think I'll pass out if I stand up."

"Excellent."

Dani leaned over next to Theresa, her brow furrowed. "You should have seen your face when you were going for Theresa. You were like a total psycho from a horror movie. Creepy."

Paige groaned and rested her forearm over her throbbing head. "Did I hurt you?"

Theresa winced. "I'll be fine."

Paige frowned. "What happened?"

"Show her," Dani said. "She needs to know."

"Really, it's not a big deal." Theresa stuck her hand out. "Mona will heal it right up and—"

Paige forgot to listen to Theresa as she stared at the shriveled blackened stump that used to be Theresa's hand. "Oh, God."

"Seriously. Don't worry about it." Theresa tucked her hand back out of sight. "It's not serious enough to be permanent, and it gives me a good excuse for a new manicure."

Paige closed her eyes again and wanted to shrivel into the sidewalk. "What's happening to me? I burned up my friend?"

"I don't know, but you need to go visit your lord and master and find out."

"Satan's not my lord and master anymore."

"Still." There was a thump as Dani sat next to her on the sidewalk. "I think you need to go see him."

Paige grimaced. "I don't think that's a good idea. What if he won't let me go?"

Theresa waved her blackened stump. "A risk worth taking, don't you think? You're turning into poison, sweetie. This has to be dealt with."

Dani nodded. "You know, I agree with Theresa. There's something seriously wrong here, and you need answers. I mean, you killed an angel, Paige. That's a very big deal."

Paige pressed her lips together, trying not to think of the angel's shocked face before he'd disintegrated. Satan had barely released her from her bonded servitude to him the first time. If he'd done something to turn her into his ultimate weapon and it was working . . . he really might not let her go this time. But what choice did she have? She could feel a pulsing evil stalking her, urging her to reach out and grab Dani around the throat and choke her to death . . . *Crud.*

Dani wasn't immortal and, somehow, Paige knew for certain that if she touched Dani, her friend would die. Instantly. Like the angel. "You're right. I need to talk to Satan."

"I'll go with you," Theresa announced as she sat down next to them.

Dani winced. "You're going to see Satan with her? Aren't you afraid of him?"

"Not at all. He's no danger. You just need to know how to play him, and I've got his number." Theresa looked at Paige. "Can you do that fade-to-black thing to get to hell?"

Paige shook her head, wiping her sweaty palms on her jeans. "I dropped out of the Rivka apprenticeship program before I learned how."

Theresa pulled out her cell phone. "Then we're going to have to call on our favorite Rivka to take us down there." She grinned. "I hope she's involved in something really important. It's such fun to harass her." Theresa put her stump in her mouth and began to suck on it. "This really hurts, by the way. If you run into my ex, will you fry him? He so deserves it. I'd love to see him taken out in such a brutal and painful way."

"Yeah, sure." Paige tensed as a passerby glared at them for camping out in the middle of the sidewalk. She hissed and held her fingers up like a claw. The dude paled and bolted to the other side of the street, and her leg pulsed in anticipation of a hunt. Of prey. Of death. *I need to kill him.*

Dani sucked in her breath and scrambled backward. "You stay away from me, Paige."

Dani's shocked face snapped Paige back to reality. Oh, God. What was happening to her? She was getting out of control.

No. She wasn't out of control. She could handle this.

First thing, remove the temptation. Get away from her friends. She rolled onto her stomach to push herself up, her hand landing on a patch of grass poking out from a crack in the sidewalk. It turned black instantly, sizzled and exploded in a pile of ash. Satisfaction at the destruction thudded deep in her soul, and she felt the blackness inside her feed on the death.

Holy shit.

She glanced up and saw both Dani and Theresa staring at the remains of the grass.

"You kill anything that's alive," Dani whispered, her voice harsh with horrified awe. "You can't touch *anything.*"

Theresa spoke into the phone. "Becca. It's your favorite dragon. Call me as soon as you get this message. Your apprentice is eyeball deep in you-know-what." She slammed her phone shut and whistled softly. "You be careful, girlfriend."

Paige stumbled to her feet, wincing at the pain in her leg. "I gotta get out of here."

"I think that's a good idea. Be alone." Dani jumped up, taking several quick steps back.

Paige felt her throat tighten at the sight of Dani cringing from her, but she whirled away and started walking down the street, terrified by the knowledge she couldn't promise not to hurt her. Or kill her.

"I'll be by with Becca to pick you up as soon as I hear from her," Theresa called after her.

Paige didn't even bother to turn around, her fists clenched against her urge to hug her friends. To feel their support? Or to kill them? She didn't want to know. She just had to get away.

Two

Jed Buchanan paused on the dark terrace, listening for any sounds that might indicate he'd been spotted, but all was quiet in this ghetto of the Afterlife.

He jimmied the lock on the double doors and slipped inside, carefully shutting them behind him with a quiet *click*. He paused inside the door, giving his eyes a moment to adjust to the dim light.

The living room was small, furnished with secondhand couches. The floors were old linoleum peeling up at the corners, the plant in the corner was nylon, and the chandelier had wires covered in duct tape to prevent it from setting the place on fire.

Jed walked silently across the dusty floor, his steel-toed shitkickers making no noise as he moved through the room and down the narrow hallway toward the bedroom in the back.

Outsiders weren't welcome in the Afterlife, even in this slum.

Especially outsiders who had sold their souls to the devil's spawn.

Jed carefully turned the bedroom doorknob and eased the door open . . . and felt the prick of a blade on his neck.

He immediately faded into a gray shadow and speared for the heart of his assailant, then stopped when he realized he was wrapping himself around his brother's heart. He withdrew instantly, reforming as his brother dropped to his knees, clutching his chest as the knife clattered to the floor next to him.

"Hell, Jed," Rafi gasped. "What was that for?"

Jed cursed and squatted next to his brother, lifting his hand to pat him on the shoulder, then dropping it before he made contact. "Sorry. I didn't realize it was you." He hadn't meant to become the shadow warrior, but it had been instinct to slip into his killing form when he'd felt the blade at his neck.

"It's the middle of the night. Who else would be in my bedroom at this hour?" Rafi took a shuddering breath and sat up, his palm still pressed over his heart. "You almost killed me."

Jed scowled and stood up. "I screwed up. Get over it." Despite his words, he was as shaken as Rafi by the mistake. He'd known his job as Junior's assassin was getting to him, but he had no idea he'd become strung out enough to accidentally murder someone. His own damn brother? He rubbed the back of his neck in frustration.

"Since when do you kill first and check ID later? Hell." Rafi coughed and rubbed his chest with his palm. "Damn, you moved fast. I had no chance to stop you. You're getting good at that shit." There was both envy and resentment in Rafi's voice.

As brothers, both of them had the lineage to become shadow warriors, but only Jed had come into his powers. Rafi had died, been tortured by Satan Jr., and then locked up in his metaphysical prison ghetto instead. Oddly enough, he'd never forgiven Jed for getting him such a raw deal. Go figure. It bugged the hell out of Jed too.

Jed walked over to the window and changed the subject. "Satan Jr. ordered me to kill a woman named Becca Gibbs a few weeks ago. I failed. I'm going back tonight to finish the job, but I started thinking . . ." He nudged apart the broken slats of the venetian blind with two fingers, checking the neighborhood to make sure Satan Jr. wasn't lurking outside. The yards were overgrown, dandelions roaming freely, and there were several potholes in the street. He could hear the screeches from a nearby cat fight, and caught a whiff of stale garbage. Only one streetlight was working, but from what he could see, the psychotic son of Satan wasn't lurking in the area. "I was afraid he might decide to punish my failure by coming after you, and when you threatened me, I thought it was him and reacted before I could think."

"Junior? Here? *Shit.*" Raphael vaulted over his bed, yanked a contraband gun out from under a floorboard, then leapt to his feet, aiming his gun at the door. Beads of sweat appeared on his brow and he swung his gun around to cover the windows, and then back to the door in a frenzied, unfocused motion that bespoke of a trauma so deep that it had shaken him to his core.

Jed cursed at the frantic glaze in Rafi's eyes and grabbed for the gun, missing as his brother whirled back around to aim at the window. "Raphael! Calm down."

"Calm down?" Rafi's eyes were raging, his body vibrating, his gun dangerously uncontrolled. "I won't let him take me. Not again. Never again."

Jed ducked under the gun, then slammed Rafi against the wall so hard the wall crumbled with the impact, his forearm lodged under his brother's throat to immobilize him. "Raphael. You're free. Look at me."

Rafi blinked, and Jed saw his brother's eyes slowly focus on his face, saw the sanity return. "Get your hands off me."

Jed released his brother and reluctantly stepped back, gritting his teeth at the anger on Rafi's face.

Rafi let his head drop back against the wall, his chest heaving, sweat dripping down his temples as he fought off memories. "I can't take this anymore. I have to get out of here."

Jed locked his jaw and shook his head once. "The deal I cut with Junior to get you here is binding. There's no way out." Otherworld contracts had a power of their own. The contract controlled them both.

Rafi flicked his hand in disgust. "Screw that." Cold determination gleamed in his eyes. "I've been paying for your mistakes for eighty-five years, and I'm done." Rafi paced across the room and slammed his hands on the windowsill, staring out into the dark neighborhood.

Jed felt the tension radiating from his brother; it was like a humming. A rapid vibration with a tune of its own. Almost like the beating of an insect's wings. It felt . . . familiar. He frowned and moved closer to his brother. "What's going on?"

Rafi turned to face him, his eyes haunted. "Something's happening to me. It's like I'm being ripped apart inside. I have to get out. I need to get free."

The humming coming from Rafi increased in volume, and suddenly Jed felt an answering vibration deep inside his gut, and he knew. *God help us both.* "It's happening."

Rafi stared at him. "What are you talking about?"

"A shadow warrior is moving on. It's your time." There were twelve shadow warriors in existence at any given time. But when an existing warrior had maxed out his time as a shadow warrior and was slotted for retirement, a replacement shadow warrior was chosen. The spirit of the departing one picked the strongest receptacle and gave the power to them. But Rafi was in the Afterlife. How could he be tapped?

Rafi stared at him in disbelief, eager anticipation licking at his eyes. "I'm . . . in?"

"Well . . ." Jed glanced around the room keeping his brother hostage. "I don't think the spirit can get into this part of the afterlife. You're sealed off."

Rafi clenched his fists. "The call will rip me apart if I can't merge with it."

Jed nodded, not bothering to state what they both knew. That if Rafi died once he was in the Afterlife, he'd be truly dead. His spirit would cease to exist on any plane.

Rafi cursed and swung away, slamming his fist into the wall. Then he rested his forehead against the wall, his breath coming heavy. "My own destiny is going to kill me." Rafi lifted his head, his eyes hard. "You took your destiny and abused it. You'll pay for your choice forever, and so will I. Get out."

Jed hesitated for a moment, then turned and walked out. For the first time since he'd pulled Rafi out of Satan Jr.'s torture chamber, his brother was no longer safe.

He cursed as he swung over the balcony railing, landing with a quiet thump on the crabgrass. He hadn't been Satan Jr.'s assassin for the last sixty years just to have his brother die because some shadow warrior had the hots for him. He might not be able to free either of them from

Junior's clutches, but there was no way the shadow warrior was going to take his brother down.

Paige hadn't even made it three blocks from Starbucks and the site of her angel decimation when an inky black spot appeared on the sidewalk in front of her. A relieved smile broke out on her face as the blob rose up out of the cement, became solid, and turned into Satan's former favorite Rivka, Becca Gibbs. Theresa was hanging onto Becca's arm, catching a ride.

Theresa grinned. "Hi, sweetie. Killed any angels since I've been gone? I brought your favorite evil soul-harvester to visit. Kisses and hugs for all."

Becca was wearing a black power suit, and she looked like exactly the kind of tough chick Paige needed on her side right now.

"Oh, my God. I'm *so* happy to see you guys." Paige threw open her arms to hug Becca, then froze when Becca held up her hand to block her.

"You know I love you, Paige, but let's hold off on the hugs until we know exactly what's going on, okay? Not that Theresa's burned out stump isn't very cool," she added quickly. "I just like to get all the info first, you know?"

"Yeah, sure. That's fine." Paige's throat tightened, and she shoved her hands into her pockets. Becca was being smart. Strategic thinking by a warrior who'd stayed alive for two hundred years despite being Satan's minion. It wasn't personal or anything like that.

But it still made her feel like a leper.

Becca gave her a sympathetic smile. "Did you really blow up an angel just by touching him?"

"Apparently." Paige took a deep breath, then pulled back her shoulders and lifted her chin. "But I'm cool. Not freaking out or anything."

Theresa snorted. "You're like one big hair trigger, ready to collapse in hysteria. But that's okay. We're here for you. Break down. Sob. Hyperventilate. Whatever you need to do. I have your back."

Becca rolled her eyes at Paige. "The dragon just likes to feel needed. Ignore her and she'll go away."

"I *am* needed," Theresa announced. "You both would be lost without me."

Paige couldn't help but smile, and some of the tension eased from her chest. "You rock. You know that, don't you?"

Theresa pursed her lips in a kiss. "Stop flirting with me. We have an issue to sort out, don't we?"

"Yeah, we do." Paige and Theresa both looked at Becca. "Any ideas?"

"Not specifically, but I'm sure it's Satan's fault. He's always screwing things up with his plans for a better hell."

Paige couldn't help but wince. "Well, that's kind of a problem if Satan's really involved, isn't it? I mean, he is the ruler of the underworld. The big kahuna and all that."

Becca snapped her fingers in front of Paige's face. "Hey! Snap out of it, girl! You don't work for him anymore. He has no control over your life, remember? And even if he did, you could still outsmart him anytime you wanted. Have you learned *nothing* from me?"

Theresa leaned over Becca's shoulder to nod her agreement. "Even *I* managed to outwit him, and I'm not even related to him. You can so manage him. Don't be intimidated. You rock. We rock. We'll kick his ass to the far reaches of hell and laugh while we're doing it." She raised her hand for a high five, then lowered it right away. "Sorry. Temporarily forgot you're deadly killer girl."

Paige wrinkled her nose against the urge to plop down on her butt and cry. "I'm not deadly killer girl. I have a few issues, is all."

Becca grinned. "That's the right attitude. See? You're learning already. He'll have no chance against you." She glanced at her watch. "We'll have to be quick. I have a meeting in Amsterdam in about ten minutes to discuss expanding Vic's Pretzels to Sweden." She grinned. "Nick's coming with me to visit Markku in the area. I think we're going to stay for a few days after we're done with business. We both agreed not to bring our cell phones. Total privacy."

Paige couldn't help but smile at the look of happiness on Becca's face. Then she realized what Becca had just said and her stomach tightened. "You're going out of town for a few days? *Now?* When I'm having a crisis?"

Becca gave her a dismissive wave. "No worries, hon. You can handle this no problem." She held out her hand. "I'm going to fade us to hell. Grab my sleeve, making sure you don't touch my skin, and do it at the very last possible second."

Paige bit her lower lip. *This is only temporary. Don't freak out.* "Yeah, sure. Minimal risk and all that."

"Exactly." Becca grabbed Theresa's arm and they both began to fade through the sidewalk. At the last instant, Paige leapt up and grabbed Becca's sleeve.

She heard Becca's howl of pain even as they all faded into the asphalt.

Three

They came up through the floor of Satan's main ballroom, surrounded by hundreds of scantily clad women milling around, all of them clutching what looked like résumés and a photo layout of themselves adorned in a wide assortment of jewelry and not much else.

Becca jerked out of Paige's grip the instant they reformed, frantically trying to shrug out of her coat. "Ow ow ow ow ow." She threw the jacket on the floor and yanked up her sleeve.

Her arm was solid black, and looked like a piece of kindling that had been through a ski lodge's wood stove. She hissed and bared her teeth as she probed her arm, making little pieces of ash flake off and flutter to the white marble floor. "I've never seen anything like *this*."

"Oh, hell. I'm so sorry. I didn't mean to. I didn't think—" Cold horror crept up Paige's arms as she stared at the shriveled black twig that used to be Becca's arm. "I didn't even touch your skin."

"Thankfully." Becca grimaced. "I need to go find a way to deal with this before the meeting. I'm never going to be able to explain it away. The dragon will back you up."

She flashed a smile at Paige. "Be strong. Satan's really a pansy and he just wants someone to tell him what to do."

"But—"

Becca held up her hand to cut her off. "Paige, you don't need me for this. I know you can handle it. It's time for you to step up."

"*What?* You're the one who manipulated him for two hundred years!" She pointed at Theresa's stump. "I'm a rookie, and now isn't exactly the time for me to go solo, you know?"

"It's exactly the time to go solo. Nothing like major stakes to make a woman find her inner strength." Becca grinned. "I have total faith." She glanced at her watch, then nodded at Theresa. "You'll hang around, though?"

"You bet. We'll be great. Have fun and don't worry about her." Theresa eyed Paige just as she opened her mouth to say she wouldn't be fine at all. "Paige, you're not going to ruin Becca's first chance for a Satan-free vacation since she was created, are you? Not after she saved you from being Satan's pawn, and after you fried her arm?"

Paige snapped her lips together. Theresa was right. She owed Becca, and if Becca thought she could handle this on her own, then, well, she'd have to believe her. She pulled her shoulders back and gave a firm nod. "I'll be fine. Have fun."

Becca smiled. "See you in a few weeks."

Her confidence vanished. "Weeks? You said days—"

But Becca was already gone, disappearing through the floor.

Paige looked at Theresa. "What if she's wrong? What if we can't handle it?" Her breath started to come in short bursts. "Oh, hell. What's wrong with me? What's happening to me? Can't . . . breathe."

"Put your head between your knees," Theresa ordered. "Now."

Paige immediately bent over, trying to slow down her racing heart. "I can handle this. I'm a badass. This kind of thing doesn't scare me . . . Oh, but it does. I don't want to be the plague—"

Theresa squatted next to her, so she was level with Paige's face. "Don't stress, sweetie. Becca's not the only one who can control Satan. I mean, sure, she's got him totally wrapped around her little toe, and with me, it's a little more dicey, but it's an adventure, so we'll just see what happens, right? Between the two of us, we'll manipulate him to exactly where we want him, and then we'll get this sorted out, okay?"

Paige stared at the dragon. "You really think that?"

"Of course. I get whatever I want. So will you, by the time I'm finished mentoring you. Okay?"

Paige took a deep breath, then stood upright again, relieved to discover she was only slightly dizzy. "Yeah, right. Sure. We've got it."

"Good." Theresa rose to her feet and glanced around the room. "Would you look at all these hot chicks? I wonder what's going on here?"

"No idea." Paige looked around the room and saw Satan sitting in a golden throne on a stage at the front of the room. He was wearing a dark velvet robe with gold embroidery that was parted to reveal glossy chest hair, highly polished black Italian loafers, glittering bikini briefs, and more bling than she'd ever seen any one person wear. Weird. He wasn't usually a bling guy. He was a classy dresser, not the pimp of the Underworld. "He's over there."

Theresa eyed him. "Well, he's definitely got sex on the brain right now. Look at that erection, and the way he's eyeing all these women. He'll be in such a good mood he'll give you whatever you want." She smiled encouragingly at Paige. "You give him a try by yourself first. It'll be a good experience for you."

He did look rather aroused, and Satan aroused was always a good thing for everyone around him. "Yeah, I can handle him. Okay."

"Fabulous. I'm going to find out where that girl gets her hair done. It's fantastic, isn't it? Zeke would love it. I'll catch up in one minute." Theresa wandered off, waving at a redhead wearing an R-rated cowgirl outfit.

Paige stared after her, suddenly nervous about approaching her former boss by herself.

No. She'd be fine. Now that she wasn't linked to his life force, he didn't have control over her. She could be who she was, and she didn't have to obey him. Plus, even if she wasn't on active Rivka duty, she was still born and bred to be a Rivka, and that meant she was a total tough chick, right? Totally.

"Former Rivka apprentice? Is that you?"

She flinched as Satan's voice bellowed out over an impressive sound system. She looked at the stage and saw he was holding a microphone to his shiny lips. Was he wearing lip gloss?

"You wish to audition to be my new lover? Most excellent. To the front of the line with you." A female groan of disappointment traveled around the room, but the crowd parted, leaving nothing between Paige and Satan except for a red carpet that two gorgeous men in tuxedos were rolling across the floor straight toward her.

"Do not look at my manservants as if they were delectable fantasies," Satan ordered. "They will not be test driving you. I will test drive you myself." He waggled his brows and stood up, letting his robe fall open to reveal a gold thong that barely covered his important parts, especially since they were so obviously enjoying the view of so many breasts.

Becca had told Paige all about the love of Satan's life, Iris Bennett, former Guardian of the Goblet of Eternal Youth. He'd yearned for her for centuries, finally landed her, and then been unable to keep her. And now he was having auditions for a new woman? She felt a wave of sympathy for the leader of hell. "You miss Iris, don't you? Trying to make yourself forget about her?"

"Do not mention her name," Satan bellowed into the microphone. "I do not permit my brain to entertain thoughts of her satiny skin, her irreverent attitude, or her azure eyes that I could become lost in for many many moons! Cease or I shall have my overtly sexual manservant cut out your tongue! Do you comprehend or shall I go forward and prove my threats are not mere idle chitter chatter?"

"Oh, he is so in love with Iris," Theresa whispered from behind her. "Don't you feel so bad for him? Poor guy. Heart is broken. Overcompensation can be a bitch." She raised her voice. "Hey, big guy, how's it hanging? You getting yourself a brand-new girlfriend or what?"

Satan frowned, then lifted the microphone to his mouth. "Dragon. Why are you not naked in my presence? I thought my magnificence made your clothes fall off?"

"You get naked in front of him?"

Theresa didn't look at all embarrassed. "It happened a few times. Don't read anything into it. Now, go talk to him."

"Right." Paige straightened her T-shirt, then marched up to the stage, intentionally walking next to the red carpet instead of on it.

Theresa, however, sashayed straight along the center of the carpet, keeping a few feet behind Paige.

Paige reached the stage. "Satan. Can I have a word? No mike?"

"Say 'please.'"

She grimaced. "Please."

Satan beamed at her, and tossed the microphone over his head. One of his manservants dove across the stage to catch it before it hit the floor. "You wish to return to my services as Rivka, no? I accept. It has been much difficult since my favorite Rivka left me. I am in need of replacement. You shall suffice. You shall be my new favorite Rivka."

"No, actually, I have a question . . ."

Satan arched a brow. "You want to become my lover as well? My new man friend said you are too young for me, but if you feel strongly—"

"No. I . . . heard a rumor that you created a mutant Rivka . . . with the power to kill with their touch . . . is that true?"

Satan stared at her, then grabbed her arm and sprinted toward the back of the hall, shouting at his manservants to hold everything. He exploded them both through the wall in a flurry of golden bubbles, then flung her onto the leather couch in his office. He threw himself into his desk chair, clasped his hands in front of him and sat up straight. "You were saying?"

Paige pulled herself upright and glanced around. No Theresa. *Crud.*

"Former Rivka apprentice. You were saying?" He leaned forward ever so slightly and held his breath, his eyes fixated on her face.

"Ah . . ." She suddenly realized it had been a very bad mistake to come here. "I heard a rumor and I . . . ah . . ." She thought of how Becca used to manipulate Satan through compliments. "Someone said you couldn't do it, and I told them you could, and so I thought I'd ask, so I could defend your honor. I hate it when someone questions how great you are."

Satan's eyes flickered, then he jumped up and exploded back through his wall in a mess of golden bubbles.

He was back before Paige had time to think about what to do, dragging a young woman with him, one of the applicants to be his lover. Unlike the others, she was wearing a T-shirt that actually covered her breasts and her butt cheeks weren't hanging out of her shorts. No doubt, she hadn't even made the list of "possibles" wearing that much clothing.

Paige sat up. "What—"

Satan flung her at Paige and Paige instinctively caught her. The girl screamed, Paige leapt off the couch, stumbling over the cushions to get away from the girl, and then there was a snap and a pop and then ash floated down around them. The girl was gone.

Four

There was a delighted chortle from Satan. "Oh, my, my, my, *my*."

Paige's calf screamed with pain and she clutched it, feeling an overwhelming sense of darkness seep past her defenses, creeping into her spirit and into her soul. Death. Killing. *I want to kill.* She dragged her gaze toward Satan, fastening on the soft skin at his throat. Her hand reached for him, her vision blurred, and her head began to ring . . .

"Oh, no, no. You do not direct that look at me. Down, girl." Satan squatted beside her and laid his hands on her head. "You do not become wraith while I am in room with you."

His touch was cool, and a cold relief began to trickle down Paige's body, easing off the darkness trying to consume her. She felt the urge to kill retreat, and the pain subsided, and her mind began to clear. She blinked as Satan dropped his hands and sat back on his heels, beaming down at her. "You are a masterpiece, former Rivka apprentice."

Paige pulled herself upright and leaned back against the couch, too tired to climb back up on it.

Satan was sitting at her feet, grinning like a little kid. "I am much impressed with myself," he announced.

"What's happening to me?" Might as well lay it out there now. No more secrets.

He hopped to his feet and nearly danced over to his wall. "My scientist infected you with inner wraith." He laid his hand over a golden bust of himself, and a small door popped open. He reached inside and pulled out a bottle of Dom Pérignon and two crystal flutes. "We toast!"

"Inner wraith?" Paige pressed her palms to her forehead. "What do you mean?"

"Your touch is poison. You kill anything that has any good anywhere in its being." Satan removed the gold foil from the champagne and began to work the cork free. "Each time you kill, it feeds the inner wraith. The wraith gets stronger, compels you to kill more, which makes it even stronger. And so on, until you eventually are consumed by wraith." The cork flew off and smacked into the gold inlay ceiling. "You will be but a human shell. No emotion, no humanity, just death." He beamed. "You will become a death, kill, murder."

Paige stared at him, watching him pour the champagne as dread filled her. "Are you serious?"

"Oh, most definitely. I do not jest about issues of such importance." He swept across the floor and handed her a glass. "For short time, you will kill all that comes within reach, including me, which is why you cannot become wraith in my presence, or even in hell. But after a while, you will recognize me as your lord and savior." He sat next to her, crossed his legs, and tapped her glass in a toast. "And then fun begins! You will exist only to please me, and you will be deadly weapon." He took a sip of his champagne. "Satan Jr. will be much admiring of his father." He wagged his little finger at her, the diamond on it winking. "Even the leader of hell must continue to evolve to stay competitive. I evolve, you become poison wraith, and we kill many."

Paige felt sick. "How do I stop it?"

Satan choked on his champagne. "Stop? There is no stop. There is only go."

"But what if we wanted to stop it? Like, what you did to my head. Can that stop it?"

"That is rest only. There is no stop. It is irreversible." He took another drink of champagne. "You are close to the change. I smell the sourness of your skin. Soon. Maybe tomorrow? Tonight? Two days from now? I do not know, but I cannot wait."

She smelled sour? Fantastic. "What if I do, like, the ultimate personal sacrifice? Would that purify my soul?"

Satan snorted. "So cliché. You think I am that shallow? Please. I spit on ultimate sacrifice."

"There has to be some safety net. What if I get out of control or something?"

"Then I kill you. Is easy. Next question?" He beamed at her. "Try to stump me. You cannot, but I laugh as you try."

Paige pressed the cool crystal against her forehead, trying to think. There had to be an out. *Something.* She had a sudden idea, recalling all the souls that Becca had harvested for Satan. Experts who did Satan's work for him, who would be likely to create a back door for themselves, like all the great computer programmers were known to do. A name. She just needed a name. "Did you create me yourself?"

"I take full credit. Yes." He drained his glass and then nodded at hers. "A waste not to drink."

She handed him her glass and tried again. "But did you hire some peon to do the work for you, because you're too busy to lower yourself to that level?"

"Yes, yes, I do have peons do work for me. Expert scientist soul was quite handy. Still alive, though, so he was in mortal world. Not in hell. Unusual agreement, but worked well, did it not?" He tapped the glass against his teeth, the sound tinkling like charms.

"What's his name?"

Satan narrowed his eyes. "Why you ask?"

"So I can send him a thank-you note. I'm . . ." She choked on the words. ". . . I'm so excited about this great opportunity."

Satan studied her for a minute. "I think you lie. I think you go to kill him. I cannot permit this to occur." He stood up. "You go now. I see you when you are black wraith."

Paige climbed to her feet. "I can't go anywhere. I don't have the fade capacity." She folded her arms across her chest. "So, I guess I'll just stay here until I turn wraith, and then I'll destroy hell."

Satan winked at her, walked over to his desk, rooted around in his top drawer, and then tossed her a gold band. "Put that on your wrist."

She eyed it. "Why?"

"It gives you power to come to and from hell." He smiled. "You will need it when you come crawling back to me to be my loyal servant."

Paige stared at it, anger building in her, raging inside her like she'd never felt before. The scum dared to steal her life, rob her of the ability to love her friends, to experience the blessing of human touch, so she would *work* for him? Screw that.

She flung the bracelet at Satan. "No. I'm not leaving. If you won't save me, then I'll take you down with me. Right now." She opened her mind and began to call upon her inner wraith. It leapt in response, filling her with darkness and death and—

"No!" Satan slammed his hands down on top of her head, shoving the darkness back into its capsule. "Fine. His name is Yolanth and he has lab in Montana. Test your luck. Try to find him. Amuse yourself far away from here until you change."

She opened her eyes, hope surging in her chest. "I'll come back and turn wraith in hell if you're lying to me." She picked up the gold band. "And I can do it."

Satan scowled. "Fine. Her name is Beatrice McFleet and she has lab in Manhattan. But it will not help you."

"I'll decide that." She wrapped the gold band around her wrist. The instant she clasped it, it shrunk to fit.

"You like? I modeled it off those rope bracelets."

She held up her wrist. "Bring Theresa in here and then let us leave. I might go wraith at any second, and you wouldn't want that."

Satan grinned. "You will be most fun. Almost as manipulative as my former favorite Rivka." He bowed deeply. "I welcome you to my staff, black wraith."

And then he exploded in a mass of gold bubbles, and in his place was Theresa, who was looking a little strung out, her hair a mess, her hands morphed into dragon claws, and smoke leaking out of her nose. "What happened to you, Paige? I've been freaking out with worry! Don't *ever* scare me like that again! Dammit, I want to hug you to make sure you're okay! Can I? Did he fix it? Can I hug you?"

"No." Tears pricked at the back of Paige's eyes at the crestfallen look on the dragon's face. *Dammit. I won't let him steal my friends from me.*

"No worries, sweetie." Theresa glanced around the room and her face brightened when she saw the champagne. "I have a few ideas. All we need to do is get you into heaven long enough to get you into their cleansing moat—"

"Into heaven? I'm a Rivka. I don't get to go to heaven. The portals would fry me immediately if I even got near one."

"Oh, right. I forgot about that safeguard. You're right. Portals to heaven are out for you. Maybe there's another way in . . ." She tapped her chin. "Need to do some research on that idea . . ."

"Will you ask your husband to find Satan's scientist for me? The one who turned me into a wraith?"

"Of course. Zeke can find anyone." Theresa gave her a hopeful look. "You think this scientist will be able to reverse it?"

Paige bit her lip. "Since she's on Satan's payroll, I sincerely doubt she'd do anything to betray him, but I have to follow up every single lead on the chance I'll find something that will work. The cleansing moat sounds like a good idea, but unless we find a way for me to get into heaven, that's out. Satan won't help. So, we work on both the scientist and other access routes to heaven. I don't have time to pursue one and then the other. I could go wraith at any moment."

Theresa frowned. "That's not much of a plan."

"You have a better one? Because I'm open to any suggestions."

"Actually, I don't." Theresa sighed. "I decided you're in a bit of trouble and called Becca. Her phone's off, so I could only leave a message. I sounded frantic enough on the message that if she checks them, I'm sure she'll call." She grimaced. "I don't think she's planning to check messages, though."

"A bit of trouble?" Paige pulled her shoulders back, refusing to acknowledge the sudden surge of panic at Theresa's statement. They were on their own, and they'd have to deal with it. Her inner wraith was not going to win. One way or another, she was going to prevail. She looked around Satan's office, wondering if he had security cameras watching her. "I'll be back to take you with me, Satan, if I lose this battle."

"Lose? You can't lose, girlfriend." Theresa picked up the bottle of champagne and tucked it under her arm. "Losing to Satan's really bad."

Paige grimaced. "Oh, you have *no* idea."

Five

Paige jerked awake, clutching her hands to her chest against the searing pain crushing her body. She knew instantly that the inner wraith was trying to take over, trying to consume her while she slept and her defenses were down.

She threw herself out of the bed, slamming into the wall as she gasped for air. Dammit! She wasn't ready to give up! *You won't win.*

She dropped to her knees, her hands flat on the floor as her body recoiled, as her chest stopped working, as the air vanished from her lungs, as pain seared through her.

Trying to take her.

I am good.

I love my friends.

I. Am. Love.

Her fingers dug into the floor as a convulsion of pain knifed through her heart. Her mouth opened, no sound, no air, no anything.

No! I won't go like this!

She lunged for the night table, where an orchid sat, a gift to Becca from her true love, Nick. Representing all that was pure and alive.

She crushed the blossom in her fist and scrunched her eyes shut, shoving everything black into the plant, as fast as she could. She felt the orchid scream as she filled it with death and pain and hell, stripping it out of her body, ripping it from her spirit, shredding the life from the flower.

The plant exploded in a billow of black ash, and she felt a wave of relief even as her calf convulsed with pain, feeding on the death she'd just caused. The pressure eased off her lungs and she dropped to the floor with a moan, her cheek pressing against the soft carpet. "God, that sucked."

She closed her eyes and thought about Dani and Theresa. Embraced her love for Becca. Felt the pain recede back into her leg, settling back down to digest and build its strength. So that next time it woke up, it would be even stronger.

Next time.

What innocent thing would she have to kill next time to save herself? And how much farther would that death take her toward her future?

She rolled onto her back with a groan and draped her arm over her forehead. "There has to be a better way—" She froze, suddenly aware she wasn't alone in the room anymore.

There was another presence. A dark one. Not from hell . . . but deserving of it.

Slowly, she moved her arm so she could peek at the room. It was suddenly pitch black, too dark to see anything. But she could feel it.

Something easing up her bare leg. Something cold. Something evil. Something definitely not human.

She opened her hand, ready to flare up a fireball as she felt it creep its way along her thigh. The touch was so faint, so light, that she would never have noticed it if she weren't already so freaked out.

It inched up her belly, along her ribs to her throat, until the whole front of her body was covered with a flittering itch, like a scratchy blanket, pressing against her, like it was trying to get through her skin.

She forced herself to wait, to lie still, certain she had only one chance to take it out. No movement until she knew where to hit it. Let it think she hadn't noticed it.

But God, she wanted to twitch, to scratch, to kick the creepy feeling off her. Because that's what it felt like. Nothing more substantial than a feeling. But a really, really bad one.

Her neck tickled and she felt it creep around her throat, encircling her like a necklace.

Or a garrote.

Oh, lovely thought.

Then suddenly, instantly, the itch turned to heat, then weight and then flesh.

A human body. On top of hers. Fingers, crushing her throat.

Her eyes snapped open and she found herself looking at the face of a man, a man with the blackest eyes she'd ever seen.

Anger flashed over his face, his hands on her neck softened to a caress; she summoned up a blue fireball and slammed it into his side.

He cursed and jerked to the right. She shoved him against the wall with a fireball to the chest, then scrambled to her feet.

He was on his feet as fast as she was, his black duster swirling about his calves as he whirled to face her. She hurled another fireball at his face, wincing at the flash of pain in her leg. He ducked and the fireball slammed into the wall behind him, leaving a charred black hole through to the kitchen. Then he was on her, his body slamming into hers.

She plunged a fireball into his back as he tackled her onto the bed, and the charred smell of burned leather drifted up to her nose.

He pinned her to the bed with his knees, slammed her palms together, and crushed them between his hands so she couldn't pull them apart.

So she couldn't shoot a fireball.

Damn. Disarmed just like that.

Then again, he couldn't choke her while his hands were occupied with hers.

Impasse.

For a moment, neither of them moved. They simply stared at each other, both of them breathing heavily. Paige could make out the lines of his face in the shadowed light. His hair was dark, tousled and thick, and there was a scar on the left side of his jaw that ran down his neck and disappeared under the collar of his black leather jacket. There was the faint twinkle of something next to the edge of his dark T-shirt. A gold chain, maybe? His shoulders were so wide he positively loomed over her, and she could feel darkness vibrating off him, saturating the air around him.

He was dangerous. Deadly. And . . . she inhaled and caught a whiff of his scent. It was smoky and dark. Like a campfire. Like woods. Like man. She breathed deeper, drinking his essence into her. She'd never smelled anything like him before. He smelled . . . right. Like a bone-deep, soul-shattering *right*.

He leaned closer, his dark eyes searching hers with a desperation that startled her, his grip on her hands still so tight she knew she had no chance of breaking free. He was straddling her pelvis, and he was such a solid, immovable weight across her hips that she knew she'd never get him off.

If he were going to kill her, he'd have to let go, and then she'd act.

So, she didn't fight.

She simply waited for him to make the next move.

But then he dropped his head and he pressed his face to her throat and sniffed, his breath a warm tickle on her skin. His hair brushed across her cheek, a fragile caress that coaxed the tiniest sigh from her.

He froze for a split second, then eased himself back ever so slowly, watching her closely as he settled his weight back on her hips and brought her hands back down to her chest, so his hand rested between her breasts. Not quite touching them, but close. So close. His jaw worked . . . in frustration? "You're not her."

"Her who?"

"Becca Gibbs."

Paige frowned. "You came here to kill Becca?"

His grip tightened on her hands, the tendons in his neck tightening. "Where is she?"

"Far, far, away in a place you'll never find. Lucky for you." Paige tested his grip on her hands, tugging slightly.

His fingers squeezed hard, immobilizing her, but not hurting her. Just reminding her how strong he was. Then he leaned forward, hovering over her like a big tower of manliness. "I have to find her. Tonight." He ground the words out, each syllable precise and loaded with a threat that wasn't reflected in the bleakness of his eyes, eyes that were now violet.

Paige stared into those eyes, into those depths of pain, and suddenly realized they weren't the eyes of a killer. He wasn't going to kill her. Not now. Not ever. Whatever evil she'd felt before he'd taken his human form was simply gone. No doubt, he was dangerous, but not to her. She relaxed instantly, her body melting under his weight. "Didn't anyone ever teach you to say 'please'?"

Surprise flashed over his face. "You want me to say 'please'?"

"You invaded my bedroom, scared the daylights out of me, disarmed me, tossed me on the bed, jumped on top of me, and tempted me with your most delicious scent, all without an invite. Not that I minded, of course. I like a man who takes charge and smells good while doing it." She grinned at the confused expression on his face. "But I have to object to being bossed around. A little politeness would be nice." She breathed deeply, basking in his scent. Strangely, now that she knew he wasn't going to kill her, she actually felt even more . . . attracted to him. Was she a pathetic Rivka or what? Shouldn't she like a man with death on his mind? "So, anyway, I think I deserve a little respect, quite frankly."

He worked his jaw for a minute, and she thought maybe she saw the faintest quirk at the corner of his mouth. Finally, he said, "What's your name?"

"Paige Darlington. You want my rank and serial number too? My phone number? My birthstone? And you forgot to say 'please.' You might have the broadest chest I've ever had looming over me in bed, but you still need to say 'please'."

One eyebrow went up. "Why are you in Becca's bed?" He paused. "Please tell me."

She grinned at the reluctance in his voice, as if he'd never said "please" in his life. "I think the more important question is why you're here to kill Becca." She shifted her hips slightly, and he sank more deeply onto her, crushing her into the mattress. It felt . . . snuggly. Yeah, that was it. It felt good to have the heat of his body up against hers.

Annoyance flashed in his eyes, and suddenly they went black again . . . but more than that, they were cold. Harsh. Empty.

The eyes of a killer after all.

Well, who knew?

She felt a shiver of excitement. "You're one of those boys that doesn't get brought home to meet the parents, aren't you?"

"Call Becca. Tell her to come home."

Paige snorted. "As if." She wiggled her hips again to see if she could tempt him to press harder against her.

He did. "Stop."

"No." She wiggled again and he shifted so his legs were twisted around hers, completely immobilizing her, covering her with his body from hip to toe. He let out a barely audible groan as he settled down on her, and he closed his eyes for a split second before opening them back up and fastening those killer eyes onto her again. God, it felt good doing the twisted pretzel thing with him. She'd felt so alone and . . . She froze, staring at their entwined hands. "Holy shit."

He frowned. "What?"

"Your hands. Are they okay?"

He glanced down at his hands, which were still wrapped around hers. "What are you talking about?"

She stared at his face. "You're not in pain? You're not shriveling into a blackened pile of ash? Or exploding into dust?"

He shot her a look of annoyance. "Do I look like I am?"

"No, no, you don't. That's the thing." She tried to sit up, and he let her, still keeping her hands in his grip. She leaned forward and he didn't back up, so her face bumped his. Skin to skin.

And nothing happened to him.

"Oh, God. I can touch you." Her throat tightened up and she slumped forward, pressing her face into his neck, breathing in his scent, feeling the heat of his skin against her cheek, the bristles of his stubble against her forehead.

She felt his alarm, and he jerked back.

"No, no, don't go. Let me do this for a second, please." She was unable to keep the plea out of her voice, and she looked up at him. *"Please."*

He stilled, and for a minute she thought he was going to push her away. But then something changed in his face, something so subtle she wasn't sure what it was, but she knew he was going to let her. Her heart tightened and she moved slowly, so as not to spook him, nuzzling into the crook of his neck. She closed her eyes and drank in his humanity, his touch, his nearness. She could feel his pulse against her skin. It was so slow, so steady, so controlled. *I need this. I need to be touched.* "I thought I'd never feel this again."

He didn't move away, but she could feel his rising tension as she breathed in his scent and his essence, basked in the roughness of his stubble against her cheek, until finally he spoke.

"Enough." His voice was a low growl that made chills run down her spine.

Slowly, she lifted her face and looked up at him. He was staring down at her, the hard lines of his face drifted in shadow. His eyes were black, fathomless. Dark. Damned.

He wasn't a killer.

He was damned.

How interesting.

She knew he'd reached his limit, so she collapsed back on the pillow, basking in the feel of his hands still holding hers together, imprinting the nuzzling moment in her memory forever so she would be able to recall it at will, in case she never got to touch anyone again. . . . *Don't think like that, Paige. It's just temporary.* "So, you're not from hell, because I'd know that." She injected as much cheeriness into her voice as she could. "But you're thoroughly tainted. Nothing redeemable left inside you, anywhere. That's why I can touch you without hurting you. How'd you get that dark?"

He let go of her so suddenly that she didn't even see him move. One minute, he was on top of her, his body wrapped heavily around hers, and the next he was on his feet at the foot of the bed, his hands gripping the footboard so hard that it was creaking. "Where's Becca?"

She propped herself up on her elbows, her body screaming at the loss of human contact. *I can't let go yet. It wasn't enough.* "Touch me again."

His face grew harder. "What?"

"Touch me. Anywhere." She lifted her bare foot and pointed her toe at him, unable to keep the desperation out of her voice. "I'll answer your questions only while you're touching me. *Please?*"

Six

He stared at her for a long moment, then he peeled one hand off the footboard and wrapped it around her foot.

The instant his fingers curved around the arch of her foot, she felt her body relax. "You know, sometimes you just don't appreciate things until you lose them. Have you ever noticed that?"

"Where's Becca?"

"Okay, so you have a one-track mind. Got it." She flexed her foot, felt the roughness of his hand on her skin. "She's out of town. With her fiancé. Who's the leader of the Markku." When he didn't respond, she cocked her head at him. "You know, the Markku? The indestructible warriors that used to work for Satan before they broke free? So, really, between the two of them, you're better off that she's not here."

His thumb slid over the ball of her foot. "When's she due back?"

"A couple weeks." Paige reached over to the bedside table and tossed her phone at him. He caught it easily with his free hand, not releasing her foot. Yeah, it was a caress, but she also suspected that she no longer owned her foot. He'd taken control of it . . . was he trying to manipulate her with a little footsie? He was damned, after all. Damned people would probably tend to be sneaky like that.

She propped herself up on her elbows to watch him more closely. "She's on speed dial number two. Try it. She's got her phone off. I can't reach her, and trust me, if I could I would, even though she thinks I don't need to. I've got some issues going on."

He tightened his grip on her foot as he examined her phone, using his hand to make sure she didn't go anywhere. As if. She hadn't gotten her fix of human contact yet, and she wasn't letting him bail until she was good and sated.

Assuming she ever would be . . . which was totally just wishful thinking. She'd never have enough, not now that she couldn't have it.

He scrolled through the numbers, apparently found the one for Becca, hit SEND, and put the phone to his ear. After a moment, he frowned and tossed the phone back at her.

She caught it and let it drop on the bed next to her. "So, what's your name?"

He wrapped his other hand around her foot and began to massage it, his fingers kneading softly.

"Oh, wow," she groaned. "Do you have any idea how good that feels?" Of course he did. He was trying to work her over. *Must. Stay. Focused.*

His thumb dug into the arch of her foot. "Do you work for Satan, too?" His voice was casual, with a hint of sensual allure that made her belly curl.

She glanced at him and her lower body clenched at the

blatant sexual need on his face . . . but there was a calculating look in his eye that instantly overruled her descent
into a languid pool of sexual mush. She immediately
yanked her foot out of his grasp and flared up a fireball.
"You're not *that* good at foot massage, buddy. It'll take
more than that to turn me into a simpering pile of female
uselessness."

His jaw flexed with irritation, and she flung the fireball
at him and ordered it to stop right in front of his throat. To
her surprise, it stopped exactly where she'd wanted it to,
hovering like the kiss of death.

He shifted to the right, and it moved with him.

"Wow. That's the first time it's actually worked. Do
you have any idea how many things I've burned up prac-
ticing that?" She jumped to her feet and bounded across
the bed toward him, where he stood immobile with the
fireball at his throat. "Tell me your name."

"Jed Buchanan." There was a grudging respect in his
voice that made her grin.

"Jed, huh?" She set her chin on top of the fireball, so
the tip of her nose pressed against his. Skin to skin. *Sigh.*
"Well, Jed, why do you want to kill her? A little problem
with Satan? Pissed off that she's going to harvest you for
hell when it's your time? Because that's definitely where
you're headed, you know."

And just like that, his hands whipped out again and
hauled her against him, trapping her hands between his
corded thighs, palm-to-palm once again. The fireball hovered between them, nearly brushing against his throat.

"Damn, you're good." And well muscled. And well . . .
utterly tempting.

"Thank you." He almost smiled. "Call off the fireball."

"Or?"

He simply raised his brow and tightened his grip on her, immobilizing her against his solid body.

She was trapped, her only defenses rendered completely useless, and they both knew it. She couldn't hurt him, even if she wanted to. Which she totally didn't. She would be so happy to be trapped against the heat of his body for the rest of the millennium, assuming, of course, that she didn't have this little inner wraith to deal with . . . Oh, idea alert.

He scowled. "What?"

She leaned her head to the side so she could see around the fireball. "How much do you cost?"

His scowl deepened. "What are you talking about?"

"You're a hired assassin, right? That's why you're after Becca." When he didn't answer, she decided that was his big, strong, manly way of agreeing with her. "So, I'll pay you more. Work for me."

He was silent for a long moment.

"Hello? Earth to Jed? You with me?"

"What do you want to hire me for?"

The curiosity was evident in his voice, and she grinned. "Two things. Protect me from myself and touch me."

His body stiffened. *"What?"*

She felt her cheeks heat up at his tone. "I'm not going to hire you as a male prostitute. Geez. I just meant touching. Casual touching. Arm around the shoulder. Friendly fistfights. Stuff like that. I mean, yeah, you're totally hot and all, but merging with your black soul would send me over the edge for sure. It wouldn't be worth it. You can handle that, right? Just some casual friendly touching?"

His grip loosened slightly, and she responded by dimming the fireball and moving it to the side, so he could lower his chin without singeing his whiskers. "Protect you from yourself? What does that mean?"

"Ah, yes." She sank more deeply against him, against the heat that was him. See? Nonsexual touching was enough . . . yeah, this was so nonsexual. Not. *Give it up, Paige. You so want him.* She made herself pull back slightly and she cleared her throat. "See, I have these urges that are no good for me, and clearly, you're strong enough to keep me from doing them, as evidenced by the fact that you've disarmed me twice tonight already. So, you touch me, and make sure I'm a good girl, and I'll pay you twice what you're getting to kill Becca. Deal?"

"Urges?" There was a light in his eyes that made her lower regions flare up in blatant disregard for her non-sexual touching plan.

She rolled her eyes, unable to smack him in the chest since her hands were still anchored between his thighs. "Oh, for hell's sake. Urges to kill and maim and stuff like that. Why do you keep taking everything sexually?"

"Because you're barely wearing anything and you're pressing your body up against mine so tightly that I can feel every curve of your body." His voice sounded a little harsh. "And your hands . . . have inched up."

"Oh." She suddenly realized her breasts were smashed against his chest, and the T-shirt she'd worn to bed was hiked up over her hips, tangled in his arms where they were wrapped around her. And her thumbs were rubbing against the inseam of his jeans, right where . . . *oh.* "I . . . hadn't noticed." Too caught up in the overwhelming sensation of being held by him to notice the details.

But she was noticing now. Hoo boy . . .

He looked down at her, his face so close to hers. "Are you Satan's right hand?"

"No, I'm not. I no longer work for Satan in any form, though I'm considering hiring myself out as a contractor once I get my personal issues resolved." She cocked her head. "Is that why you want to kill Becca? Because she works for Satan? Because if that's it, then you should know she quit."

He suddenly looked so weary. So human. So . . . drained. "You're sure?"

"Of course I am. I know these things."

He sighed with visible frustration. "If I let you go, promise no fireballs?"

"Of course not. If you try to kill me, I'll fireball you. What kind of an idiot do you think I am?"

This time his mouth definitely quirked in a brief smile. "Do you promise no fireballs unless I give you a reason to use them?"

She contemplated it for a moment, then nodded. "I'm in."

He slowly loosened his grip and relaxed his thighs, and she eased her hands out from between his legs, settling back on her heels as he released her. Two steps to the right and his hand was on the bedroom door.

"You're leaving?"

"Yeah."

She jumped to her feet, feeling slightly panicky about the thought of losing the only living thing she could actually touch. "I'm serious about the offer to work for me."

His eyes were unreadable. "I know."

"So? Will you do it?" She held her breath as she waited for his answer.

She thought she saw a flash of regret in his eyes, then he shook his head. "No."

"But—"

Then he poofed out of sight. Standing in her room one second, gone the next. What?

She vaulted off the bed and ran to the door, then felt a swirling prickle on her legs, and she looked down. Darkness surrounded her legs, and then it shot away from her and down the hall, disappearing under her front door. She stared after it, awareness dawning as she realized what he was.

Of what he could offer her.

So much more than she'd thought.

So, so, so much more.

She didn't even bother getting dressed. She simply sprinted for the door.

Jed reformed on the darkened street outside Paige's apartment.

He stepped off the curb and began to stride down the darkened street, his coat swirling about his calves, the front of his jeans uncomfortably tight from being wrapped around Paige Darlington.

What the hell was she? A Rivka, yeah, but damn . . . for a minute or two, he'd actually been tempted to take her up on her offer. He had no time for things like bodyguarding or worrying about anything other than keeping Rafi alive and out of Junior's hell. Jed had had no problem maintaining his single-minded focus for the last sixty years.

Until two minutes ago when Paige had stared up at him with those hopeful eyes and that sparkle in her voice.

He stepped around one of the garbage cans set out for

the morning pickup. It was her ebullience, her unabashed declarations of what she'd wanted from him . . . yeah, that's what it had been. She'd been brimming with an enthusiasm for life that had blasted right through his shields. His hands clenched as he recalled the feel of her hips under his touch. The curves of her body while she'd grinned up at him, mischief dancing in her eyes as she used that fireball to toy with him.

He'd been in the darkness so long, he'd forgotten about what it was like to be around someone who was so alive. Who vibrated with energy, with passion.

She hadn't even cared that he was damned.

He let his breath puff out his cheeks as he stepped around a rat scurrying into a drain, even now wanting to turn around and return to her apartment.

Maybe some other time.

Maybe in another life.

Right now, it was all about Rafi.

He tried to focus on his brother's situation. First Jed had to free Rafi from the shadow warrior's grasp. Then, once he knew Rafi would live, he'd have to find a way to appease Junior for the fact he hadn't killed Becca Gibbs, because Jed's failure to kill Becca gave Junior the right to recall Rafi to his torture chamber if he chose to do so.

If tonight was any indication, Jed would never be able to kill Becca. He'd tried to get inside Paige in his shadow form, but had been unable to penetrate the Rivka shields. Yet when he'd taken his human form . . . he'd been unable to make himself kill her.

Shadow warriors didn't kill in human form, and he was no exception. Which meant he couldn't kill the Rivka in shadow form or in human form. Either way, Becca Gibbs would not die at his hands.

So, how the hell was he going to keep Junior from calling in the contract and taking Rafi back to his torture chamber? There had to be something—

"Jed!"

He glanced over his shoulder as Paige bolted out onto the street, wearing nothing but the oversized T-shirt she'd been sleeping in. Her legs were bare, disappearing under the red cotton, her chest was heaving from the exertion, and her hair was tousled around her shoulders.

Her hair was dark blond, he realized. He hadn't been able to tell when they'd been in her room, but under the streetlight, he could see the gold streaks in her hair.

"Don't leave!" She didn't even slow down, her bare feet slapping on the sidewalk as she threw herself at him.

He barely had time to brace himself for the impact before her body thudded against him. She threw her arms around him, locking her grip tight, wrapping her legs around his waist.

He caught the scent of something feminine and sweet, her skin was silky and smooth under his hands, and her legs were so tight around his hips that he could feel her feminine softness pressed up against his already hard body. *"Hell."* Before he could stop himself, he crushed her against him and slammed his mouth onto hers.

Seven

Paige froze for a split second, and then she returned his kiss with an enthusiasm that nearly dropped him to his knees. She opened her mouth for him, her tongue danced against his, and she plastered herself against him so her breasts were pressed to his chest.

A very female sound of satisfaction hummed in the back of her throat, and she kissed him deeper, meeting him thrust for thrust with every high-spirited movement of her tongue.

Her tongue flirted over his teeth, and her breath was warm in his mouth, tasting of spearmint. Her fingers twisted in his hair and she tightened her thighs around his hips, wiggling against him.

"God, you taste good," he muttered, breaking the kiss to nibble the bare skin of her neck, grinning when she whimpered. He slipped his hands under her shirt and spanned her bare back. Her muscles flexed under his hands, and he groaned at the softness of her skin. She was pure female temptation. All softness and innocence, and he wanted her so badly every muscle in his body was shaking.

He moved his right hand down over her hip, hooking his index finger over the delicate strand of lace on the sides of her underwear. He tugged it gently down, letting his thumb brush over the delicate skin on the inside of her thigh, and felt a surge of heat when Paige sucked in her breath and tightened her grip on his shoulders.

Then there was a loud catcall and a whistle, yanking him back to reality in a cold hurry. He jerked his head back from her throat, cursing himself. *Hell, Jed. On a street?*

"No, no, no! Don't stop!" Paige grabbed his hair and tried to tug him back down. "I'm not done."

He chuckled softly as he returned the lace of her underwear to its proper position. "Yeah, I wasn't either, trust me." He carefully untangled her from him, and set her back on the ground, taking a second to tug her shirt back over her hips and run his fingers down her arms, before he finally dropped his hands.

Her eyes were wide, her lips parted as she ran her tongue over them, and the flush of arousal stained her cheeks. She took a deep breath that made her breasts rise under her T-shirt. "Well. I certainly wasn't expecting *that* when I came running out here."

He cleared his throat, feeling like an ass for molesting her on a public street. "Yeah, well, sorry. I didn't mean to—"

"Oh, no." She lightly smacked his chest. "Don't be sorry. It rocked."

Something loosened in his gut and he grinned. "Yeah?"

She nodded as she fingered her lips. "That was a fantastic kiss, I'll tell you right now. I got kissed by this Markku a few weeks ago, and we were under the influence of Penha pheromones, so it was pretty intense . . ."

His grin turned into a scowl.

She smiled, her eyes twinkling as she reached up and lightly brushed her lips over his. "But this was way better."

His hands went to her hips and he held her still.

For a moment, neither of them moved, then her eyes darkened with heat as she rubbed her belly against the front of his jeans. "Seriously, Jed, you can kiss me like that anytime. I have no problem with a public street if you want to do it again?" Her voice rose hopefully at the end.

He growled, entirely unable to resist the invitation as he hauled her against him and dropped his head to—

She threw up a hand to block him just before his mouth reached hers. "Oh, hell."

He blinked and tried to focus. "Oh, hell, what?"

"Hello? Where's my brain?" She patted his cheek and gently pushed him back. "I can't kiss you."

"You can't?" He felt like an idiot repeating her words, but he was having a little trouble getting his mind off the taste of her lips and the silkiness of her skin, and the fact that her enthusiastic response to his kiss was the most erotic thing he'd ever experienced. "Why not?"

She grimaced. "Mixing your black aura with my inner wraith could be really bad news for me."

"Inner wraith?" She'd gotten his attention now. "That's what you have?"

"Yeah, kinda. Inner wraith trying to be an outer one . . . long story. No happy ending yet, so it's not worth telling." She hugged her arms to her chest and bounced in place, not dressed for the cool night air of the approaching autumn. "You're a shadow warrior, right?"

"You know what I am?" He couldn't keep the surprise out of his voice as he shrugged out of his jacket and draped it over her shoulders.

She beamed as she slid her arms into his coat. "So you are one? That's fantastic. I figured as much when you did the whole disappear-into-a-black-cloud thing before you shot out the door, totally ditching me without a good-bye. Kind of rude, just so you know—"

"Wait a sec. You know what a shadow warrior is? And you still came out here after me? Alone?" Damn. He liked the sight of her in his coat. He tugged it tight around her.

She rolled her eyes and lifted her arm so his jacket sleeve slid down her arm and exposed her hand. She waggled fingers at him. "Ooooh, big scary shadow warrior. Deadly killer guy." She dropped her hand and snorted. "Give me a break, Jed. You've got no bloodlust in your eyes right now. I'm not worried."

Damn if he almost didn't feel like laughing at her again. Her irreverence was almost contagious. "Most people realize what I am and run away screaming. Being evil and damned will do that."

She wrinkled her nose. "I know exactly how that feels. Sucks, doesn't it?"

He frowned. "I don't really pay attention—"

"Of course you do." She patted his chest. "When that angel treated me like a leper, it really upset me. Which is why I'd never treat you like that, even if I was afraid you wanted to kill me, which you don't, so we're good."

He blinked. "You met an angel?" He wasn't even sure he believed in anything that good anymore. Except possibly Paige. Inner wraith notwithstanding, there was something about her that was just so damned innocent.

Untainted. He picked up a lock of her hair and brushed his thumb over the tip.

She smiled at him and patted his hand, apparently encouraging him to keep playing with her hair.

Worked for him.

"The angel's another long story. Bad ending." She gave a dramatic shudder. "Which is why I need you to get me to a gateway. Can you do it?" She fastened an expectant gaze on his face.

"A gateway?" He had to think for a minute about what she was talking about. "You mean, a gateway between heaven and hell? One of *those* gateways?" At her eager nod, he sighed and ran his hand through his hair. "I haven't thought of a gateway in years. I can't—"

She grabbed his arm. "No, no, no. You *can*! I know the gateways are all closed up now, but they're still there, right?" Her fingers dug into the muscles in his forearm, and he caught an undercurrent of desperation that belied her carefree attitude. "I'm sure I could find my way through if you'd just point me to one. Please? It's really important."

He tangled his fingers in her hair and tugged softly. "Trust me, sweetheart, if I could, I'd jet you over to one and drop you off to have at it, but I don't know where they are. Shadow warriors haven't guarded them for almost five hundred years. Before my time."

Her shoulders sagged with a disappointment that made him feel like an ass. "I know you haven't guarded them, but you don't think you could find one? Just one?"

"Hell, Paige. I wish I did. I really do." He was surprised to realize he meant it. He just . . . something about Paige just made him want to be a better man, the kind of man who could take five minutes to give her what she wanted. Her smile would be enough to carry a man for at least a century or two, no matter how much shit he had to wade through.

She mustered a smile. Even at half strength, it still called to him. "Well, I appreciate the sentiment, even if it still leaves me completely hosed."

His eyes narrowed at the desolation in her tone, and he began to realize that she was in serious trouble, far more than her spunk would indicate. "What exactly is your problem?"

"I'm going over to the dark side. I mean, I'm going to become the dark side. The whole shebang. That's me." She sighed. "Paige the Evil Wench. It's all going to get really really ugly, trust me. I mean, I'm all about being evil, given that I'm a Rivka, but not being able to touch my friends and descending into this pit of mental depravity where I can't feel love? Rip out my heart now and spare me the pain." She plopped herself down on the curb and propped her elbows on her knees, then rested her chin in her hands. "I don't suppose you changed your mind about my offer, did you?"

It took less than a second for her dejection to penetrate his shields. With a sigh, he sat down next to her and cupped the back of her neck, kneading the tight cords of muscle. "Guarding you from yourself?"

"God, that feels good." She rubbed her right foot over her left calf and leaned against him, her shoulder fitting nicely under his arm. "And yes, guarding me from myself. Surely you could use the money for something."

"I have all the money I need—" He paused, reconsidering his words. Would money be enough to bribe Junior to leave Rafi alone? No. Though Junior craved wealth, he needed power more, enough power to dethrone his dad and take over hell.

Paige stopped rubbing her calf and looked at him, hope gleaming in her eyes. "You're considering it? You're actually *considering* it?"

He shook his head, steeling himself against his desire to help her. "I don't have time. I have . . ." He grimaced and dropped his hand from her neck. "I have my own problems to work out, and I don't think money's going to solve them."

She sat up straighter. "But it *might* solve them? What's your problem? You never know, with a little creative thinking, maybe we could both get what we want. You know, a win-win and all?"

He shot her a look. "Yeah? Well, I need a way to appease Satan Jr. since I didn't kill Becca Gibbs. I don't think money's going to be enough."

"Ohh . . . him." Paige chewed her lower lip. "Can't we just kill him?"

"No."

"You sure?"

"Trust me, I'm sure." He'd have done it long ago if it would have freed Rafi, but Junior would simply have transferred his operation into the Afterlife and tortured Rafi there.

"Okaay . . . let me think." Paige tapped her fingernails on her teeth with a faint clicking noise. "He's got all sorts of complexes about his dad, and he's obsessed with power." She sat up. "I know! Tell him that you're getting paid with money stolen from Satan. He'd love that, and it's true because Satan still funds me."

He raised his brows. "Getting closer, but still not enough. Anyone can steal money from Satan."

She rubbed her leg again. "Okay, so then, tell him that the woman you're guarding is supposed to be this big, top-secret deadly weapon of Satan's, specifically designed to bring Junior down. Tell him that by hanging out with me, you're hoping to be there when I turn into a wraith, so you can direct my loyalty to Junior instead of Satan, getting Junior the best weapon around *and* stealing it from his daddy as a bonus."

He stared at her. "Is that what's wrong with you?"

"Yeah." She wrinkled her nose at him. "Don't worry. The plan won't work because I'm supposedly hardwired to be loyal to Satan after I go insane with killing lust, but Junior won't know that. Tell him that you're pretending to try to keep me sane, but really, you're trying to push all my buttons to send me prematurely into wraith-hood." She leveled a finger at him. "But if you *do* try to push my buttons even once, the deal's off. Got it?"

He realized that she'd nailed Junior exactly. If he delivered the offer just right . . . yeah. It might work. Might buy him enough time to figure something else out. He felt a faint glimmer of hope as he studied Paige. "You're serious about all this? You're really turning into a death weapon for Satan?"

"Do I look like I'm kidding? I don't have time to be making up stories. I have to save myself and you"— she pointed at him —"are my only hope. So, what do you say? Please?"

It was the slight tremor in her voice when she said "please," that sealed it for him. He could justify it to

Junior, it bought him time, and he simply wanted to do it for her. "A hundred grand per day?"

She blinked. "Seriously?"

"It's Junior."

Paige drummed her fingers over her chin thoughtfully. "I think Satan's coffers would sustain that. Yeah, I'm in." She looked at him, hope etched on her face. "So that's it? We have a deal?"

"We have a deal. I'll touch you for money."

Eight

Paige watched the waitress set the two plates in front of Jed. Six fried eggs, two bagels, a double order of hash browns, an order of bacon, and the biggest bowl of fruit she'd ever seen.

And a pitcher of orange juice.

She looked at the granola and yogurt on her plate. "I feel so wimpy."

The man had been in overdrive since they'd agreed to the deal: rushing over to the breakfast place, telling their waitress that they were in a hurry, and now scarfing down his eggs. A man on a mission. He'd explained that doing his shadow warrior thing always depleted him and he needed to eat. It was clear from how fast he was going through his food that he considered eating nothing more than an inconvenience.

She was down with that. She didn't have time to sit around either.

Jed jabbed his fork into his hash browns. "So, you're going to turn into a wraith and you kill anything you touch—" he prompted.

"Yeah. Well, that's my destiny, apparently." She filched a piece of his bacon. "But I'm resisting. Unfortunately, since I was originally created by Satan and used to be supported by his life force, I have this natural tendency to embrace dark things. You know, like harvesting souls, killing people, violence, torture, stuff like that. It's kind of my thing, and the wraith gets off on it."

He stopped chewing and looked at her. "Seriously? You seem . . ." His gaze raked over her. ". . . more innocent than that. Pure."

"Yeah, well, I'm a virgin, so that's what you're probably reading." She picked up another strip of bacon. "So, basically—" She stopped at the startled look on his face. "What?"

"You're a virgin? How is that possible?"

She shrugged. "Satan created me only about a month ago, I went through Rivka training, got caught up in a battle to save the world, then discovered I was poison to anything I touched. I've been a little busy." She waggled the bacon at him. "But I'm thinking that maybe it's my virginity that's helping me keep this wraith at bay. I mean, it's not like there's anything else pure about me, with the whole Rivka thing and all. So, now you see why you and I kissing is a bad idea? Kissing leads to sex, and then sex with you, Mr. Damned, would pretty much cancel out the last pure thing in my being." She made a face. "So, your virtue is safe with me. Which is too bad, really, because that kiss was awesome."

He raised his brows. "Isn't that a little judgmental?"

She blinked, her cheeks getting hot with embarrassment. "Calling the kiss 'awesome'? You didn't think it was? It was just me?"

"It wasn't just you, but I was referring to the fact you think sex makes you impure." He gave her a considering look. "I seriously doubt whether or not you'd had sex makes a difference to the wraith."

Her belly tightened at his admission about the kiss. "Well, that's the only pure thing in me, so what else could be keeping it from taking over?"

Something flickered in his gaze. "Your naturally sunshiny personality?"

She snorted. "Window dressing, Jed. That's all it is." She swiped his glass of OJ and raised it. "To death, murder, and killing. Cheers."

"Huh. Well, if it is the virginity . . ." He leaned forward. "I have to warn you."

His voice had suddenly become husky, and something curled low inside her. "Warn me about what?"

"I like touching you. Kissing you too." His gaze was dark again, his jaw tense. "I'm not going to try to seduce you, but if you throw yourself in my arms and wrap those long legs of yours around me like you did earlier . . ." His gaze settled on hers. "I'm not made of steel, sweetheart, and I'm far from a saint."

The heat in his eyes sent her belly into overdrive again. "Thanks for the warning. I'll keep it in mind." Who was she kidding? She'd never forget it.

He nodded, then leaned back in his seat again, picked up his coffee cup, and drained it. He gestured for more, then turned his attention back to Paige. Heat still simmered beneath the surface, but he was focused now. "I assume you need protection 24/7, which is fine, as long as you're okay with following me around to a certain extent. I have a couple critical errands I need to run this morning, and I'm going to need to get the first payment to Junior sooner rather than later."

"I'll have to go to hell to get it. I don't keep that kind of cash on me." She tapped her fork on the table as she thought about returning to hell after Satan had told her not to return. He wouldn't be happy, but too bad for him. She'd try to avoid him, but seriously, what could he do to her? Turn her into a mindless evil wraith? Yeah, whatever.

Jed glanced at his watch, and his jaw ground with tension. "I have to make one stop first, then we'll hit hell." His gaze flicked over her shoulder, and then he sat up, his muscles bunching, his eyes narrowed as if he were preparing for a battle.

Paige spun around and tensed when she saw who was heading toward her with a determined look on his face. Anger swelled inside her and she clenched her fists, scowling as the man who'd wronged Dani approached their table. Jerome Doumani, sniveling bastard and esteemed member of the Council, which was the governing body of all things nonhuman. Jerome had nearly killed Dani after professing to love her. Paige had hated him before she'd had the black soul, but now . . . she could feel her calf swell with pain and she embraced it, directing all her anger toward Jerome.

Jerome reached the table. "Paige. Nice to see you again." He held out his hand for her to shake, and she immediately reached for it, her fingers stretching for his skin.

Jed grabbed her hand and hauled it back toward him. "Not so fast, killer."

Paige blinked as his action snapped her back into her mind.

Jerome looked in surprise at Jed. "Who are you?"

"No one relevant to you." Jed moved behind her, then

dug his fingers into her shoulder in silent warning. "Be calm, Paige," he said quietly, his breath warm against the side of her neck. He grabbed his chair with his foot and yanked it across the tile, then sat next to Paige.

She slipped her hand under the one he'd placed on her shoulder, and took a deep breath even as sharp pain began to throb in her leg and the need to kill Jerome began to build in her body. *You can do this, Paige. Don't let Jerome or the wraith lure you into self-destruction.*

Jerome eyed Jed. "I need to talk to Paige alone."

"I can't allow that." Jed's voice was hard, inflexible, not even bothering to check with Paige first to see if she wanted some private time with her visitor.

He was being completely arrogant and controlling.

And she loved it. Leather, muscles, *and* a badass attitude? This was her kind of guy.

Jerome looked at Paige. "Paige, tell him to leave—"

"He stays," she snapped. "Be glad. He won't let me fireball you."

At that comment, Jed grabbed her hands and pressed her palms together in his lap. Her fingers brushed against the inseam of his jeans and she felt that special part of him twitch under her touch. Desire pulsed through her, chasing away the anger at Jerome and replacing it with a swirling heat that made her want to lean into Jed and—

Jed's eyes darkened with desire. "Don't look at me like that," he growled.

"Well, don't press my hands up against your manly regions, then." *Duh.*

As he moved her hands to a more neutral location, she turned back to Jerome with renewed confidence, knowing that with Jed on her side, they could contain the wraith.

"What do you want?" Her voice was dripping with hostility, far more than she'd intended, and Jed pulled her onto his lap, trapping her against him. Damn wraith, making her cranky. She hated being cranky.

"Let it go," he whispered into her ear. "It's not worth it."

His hard thighs shifted beneath hers and she leaned back against his chest, trying to concentrate on the tantalizing feel of his body instead of the dark urges building inside her. "Just tell me why you're here," she said to Jerome.

Jerome shot another look toward Jed, then leaned toward her, coming within reach. All she had to do was lean forward and she'd bump his chin with her forehead . . .

She scrunched her eyes shut. *Don't kill him.*

"I got a report on my desk this morning that you killed an angel yesterday," Jerome said. "Do you have *any* idea how bad that is?"

Her eyes snapped open. "The Council's getting involved?" The Council was well known for its ruthless, arbitrary method of ruling. Yeah, the worst two members had been fired and Jerome was in charge now, but that was no comfort. Dani claimed he was a fair administrator of justice even though he couldn't be decent in his personal life, but even if he was, power corrupts and all that crap.

"There's an emergency meeting with the Council and representatives from heaven to discuss the issue. No one has murdered an angel in a thousand years. There's no precedent for dealing with this." Sympathy flickered briefly across his face. "You're in major trouble, Paige."

"It was a mistake," she said quickly. "I didn't mean to.

I didn't know I could. I just touched him and he poofed. Gone. Satan did this thing to me and now I can't touch living things that have any good in them or I kill them and—"

"I don't want to know." Jerome held up his hand for silence. "If I thought you were Satan's newest weapon, I'd have to kill you this instant, as part of my Council duties. I'm here because you're Dani's best friend, and I owe her, but once this conversation is over, I have to do my job." He straightened up and looked around the restaurant, as if checking to see if anyone was listening, then directed his attention back to her. "I found you by tracking your cell phone. Ditch it, then disappear until you fix your problem, and maybe even longer. We'll be coming for you."

She swallowed hard, all too aware of the Council's mercilessness.

Jerome nodded, apparently satisfied with whatever expression of dread he saw on her face. "I'm going to the meeting. I'll do what I can for you, but it's not going to be much." He glanced at Jed, who had leaned forward to rest his chin on her shoulder. "You kill off anything with some good in them, huh? So this guy is bad news? Let me give you some advice, Paige. Now's not the time to be aligning yourself with people like him."

Jed's body tensed, but he said nothing.

"Hey!" Sudden fury spewed through her at Jerome's attack, as if her inner wraith had been waiting for the trigger, ripping through her with all the darkness and hate it was made of. "How dare *you* insult *him*?" She sat up, her fingers curling into claws. "After what you did to Dani, you think you can insult the one guy who's sticking by me right now? He's all I've got, dammit!" Her calf twitched and she jumped to her feet, jerking out of Jed's grasp as she embraced the darkest urges gripping her. She lunged for Jerome, but Jed grabbed her and hauled her back against his chest so hard he knocked the breath out of her body.

She gasped for air; Jerome leapt backward, tripping on a chair and nearly falling into the lap of another patron, who yelped and shoved him off her.

"Calm down, Paige." Jed's voice was quiet. Steady. Utterly without inflection. Soothing . . . but not enough. "He's not worth your future."

She gripped Jed's wrists tightly, trying to breathe against the constriction in her chest. She pressed her head back against him as people stared at them. So many people. So many deaths to feed her wraith. She could sweep her arm out and get several of them at once—

She tugged at Jed's wrists, testing the strength of his grip, assessing how hard it would be to break free. At the same time, deep inside her pulsed the hope that he'd be able to hold her when she snapped, because she could feel it building. "It's coming." Her voice was raw, barely recognizable.

"Leave." Jed spoke the command at Jerome so quietly, yet Jerome knocked over another chair and crashed into a waiter in his haste to make it to the door.

Jed's breath was warm against the side of her neck. "You defended me."

"Of course." She turned her face so her cheek was against his, concentrating on the roughness of his whiskers scratching her skin. She groaned as her chest began to ache from the building pressure. "Jed," she whispered. "I can't stop it."

Jed spun her around to face him, his fingers digging into her shoulders, his face tensing when he looked at her. "Your eyes are turning black."

"Black?" she echoed. "That can't be good. Can it? No, it can't." She squeezed them shut and tried to picture Becca, tried to shove down the strengthening urges. The almost overwhelming need to kill. Anyone. Anyone would do. Just one death. To feed her wraith. "Shit, shit, shit. It's not working." She felt herself start to panic. "I can't do this. I can't. I need to get rid of it by sending it into something. Like I killed the orchid."

He cupped her face between his palms, pressed his forehead to hers, full skin-to-skin contact. "Paige," he whispered. "Build your shields. Put the urge to kill back in its box. I do it every day. You can do it. I know you can."

Her chest began to throb, her vision started to blacken. Then she snapped her eyes open, scanning the room of dining patrons for her victim, scenting out her prey. "The old lady in the corner. I'll kill her. She'll die easily." Her voice was so low she didn't recognize it, couldn't stop it, couldn't stop the image of the lady's death from blossoming in her mind. "She'll turn black, and scream and explode . . ." Her legs were shaking now, her body screaming with pain, her head hurting so much she felt like it was going to burst with the effort of keeping it at bay. "God, Jed . . . do something . . ."

Jed grabbed the wilted carnation centerpiece off the table and pressed it into her hand. "Kill this."

She immediately dropped her shields and poison

burst from her and slammed into the flower. It exploded instantly and the power surged into Jed where his hand was pressed against hers.

His eyes widened. "What the fu—" The word froze in his throat, his skin turned black, and he hit the floor.

Nine

"Jed!" Paige recoiled in horror as Jed fell to the floor of the restaurant, then she recovered and tried to yank her hand out of his grasp, but the wraith took over, forcing her fingers to dig even deeper, refusing to release its victim. "Dammit, Jed! Let go!" she screamed as she tried to stop the darkness from spewing out of her, but it poured into Jed. "Stop! God, please, stop! I don't want to hurt him!" Her legs gave out and she dropped beside him, the darkness stripping her as it screamed out of her body and into his, and smoke began rising from his shoulders. "Jed!"

Then he was gone.

And in his place was a cloud of smoke.

"Jed?" She sagged against her chair, her chest heaving as the wraith subsided, fed and satisfied. For now. "Jed? Tell me you went shadow warrior." The cloud began to dissipate and she felt herself start to panic again. "Tell me I didn't incinerate you."

And then it was gone.

It didn't zip away like it had in her apartment when he'd taken off.

It simply vanished.

Holy shit. She'd killed him. Tears welled up in her eyes. "Dammit! This wasn't how it was supposed to be!"

"Ma'am? Are you all right?"

She jerked her gaze upward as her waitress reached to help her to her feet. "No! Stay back!" She scrambled to her feet, her legs shaking so much she could barely stand up. She grabbed a butter knife and held it out, aiming it at the crowd of people who'd gathered around her. "Back off! Don't touch me!"

The manager held up his hands in a soothing motion. "It's all right, miss. Just relax. We've called an ambulance and they'll be here in a few minutes."

"No. No ambulance." Keeping the knife out, she began to back toward the door. Her lungs still hurt with each breath, and her heart ached like someone had beat it with a tire iron.

"What happened to the man?" someone asked. "Wasn't there a man with her?"

"Oh, go ahead and kick me while I'm down, why don't you?" she snapped. "Could you be any more insensitive?"

The crowd began to part, making room for her as she moved toward the door, tables of breakfast forgotten. She glanced over her shoulder, making sure no one was trying to tackle her in some asinine heroic move. "I'm leaving. If you let me leave, no one will get hurt, okeydoke? Good plan?" The manager made a move and she pointed the knife at him. "No."

He stopped.

"Good boy." Paige reached the door and yanked it open. "I'll send money for the bill, okay?"

Her waitress waved her hand. "My treat. Really. Don't worry about it."

"Thanks. Nice of you." She took one last look to make sure there was no dark cloud hovering anywhere, but there was nothing.

Jed was gone.

A sense of hopelessness slammed into her, and she threw the door shut behind her, wincing as it rattled the glass. She tossed the knife into the gutter and hurled herself into the backseat of the nearest cab, which was lined up in anticipation of the morning exodus of business-people from the nearby hotels.

"Where to?" The cab driver glanced at her in his rearview mirror.

"Hell if I know." She pressed her hands to her forehead with a soft moan. God, what now? The one man she could touch, and she'd killed him. She'd never feel the touch of a human again. Ever. No hug. No kisses. Not even the casual brush of a shoulder. Tears filled her eyes and she pressed her fists to her face, while she tried to regain control. "You can handle this," she whispered. "It's just a minor setback."

"Miss?"

She looked up just in time to see Jerome and two men in white rush into the restaurant she'd just left. Oh, God. *Heaven's enforcers* were with Jerome? The Men in White were even more ruthless than the Council, because they figured they had all the morality on their side. She shuddered and hugged herself, then took a deep breath and thought of Becca and all she'd survived. "This is nothing in comparison," she said.

"Pardon?"

She looked at the driver's registration on the glass divider, saw his name was Horvath.

Horvath was talking to her. Not afraid. See? Not everyone was afraid of her. *Baby steps, Paige.* She gave him Becca's address, and he nodded and pulled away from the curb. She'd get in, get her stuff, and then take off. To where? Anywhere that Jerome and the Men in White couldn't find her.

She leaned her forehead against the window as the cab pulled away, watching to see if her stalkers emerged from the restaurant, but she made it around the corner without seeing them.

Safe, for the moment.

She pulled out her cell phone and dialed Theresa. Her throat tightened when it went right into voicemail. She cleared her throat of anything that might sound like self-pity, then spoke briskly. "Hi, Theresa. I'm just calling to see if Zeke found Beatrice McFleet—" She suddenly remembered Jerome's warning about her phone and snapped it shut, pressing it to her temple while she tried to think.

After a minute, she shoved it between the seat cushions, wincing when her fingers hit something wet and mushy.

Then she rapped on the bulletproof divider. "Horvath? I'll get out here."

She paid, climbed out, and watched her phone drive away.

How much time had she just bought herself? Not enough, she was certain.

*   *   *

Twenty minutes later, armed with a new disposable cell phone, she huddled next to a bus stop vestibule, wearing a big straw hat and a pair of oversized sunglasses she'd pinched off a street vendor for a bargain, flinching at everyone who walked past.

She punched in the only phone number she knew by heart, and Dani answered on the fifth ring.

"It's me," she whispered.

"Paige? Where are you calling from? Are you okay? Are you . . . um . . . still yourself?"

"I'm fine." She didn't miss the hesitation, the distance in Dani's voice. She dug her fingernails into her palms, refusing to blame Dani for her wariness. "Did Zeke find Beatrice McFleet yet?"

"Hang on. Theresa's here. Her computer's on the fritz so she's using mine."

A city bus pulled up and Paige turned her back, trying to huddle deeper against the glass bus shelter as people clomped down the steps.

"Hey, sweetness, how are you holding up?"

Paige's throat tightened at the cheerful tone in Theresa's voice. At the utter lack of fear of her. See? One friend. She wasn't alone in this at all. Everything was fantastic. She could have a party with Horvath and Theresa. "Did Zeke find Beatrice McFleet yet?"

"No, not yet. Apparently Satan lied about her name, so Zeke's run into a bit of a dead end. But he's not giving up yet."

"Dead end?" Oh, God. She'd been totally counting on Zeke coming through for her.

"Satan has excellent resources for hiding people, but

Zeke's still the best missing persons expert in the world," Theresa said. "Don't judge him—"

"I'm not judging him." Paige felt someone behind her and glanced over her shoulder, but there was no one there. Just the empty bus stop. "It's just that I'm really in trouble."

"I know, sweetie. That's why I've been hitting the Internet for you. I followed up on the portal to heaven approach, and I ran into this really cool website on the cleansing moat. Turns out that it's not designed for people with your level of evil. You'd blow up heaven if you used it. And yourself, of course, which would defeat the purpose of using it. So, it's a no-go."

Paige picked up an empty coffee cup and tossed it in the trash. *Every little bit of goodness helps.* She rubbed her temples. "So, no scientist and no cleansing moat." She cursed. "So, what now? There's nothing I can do?" Dammit! She wasn't giving up!

"Not necessarily," Theresa said. "I think I found a loophole in the angel thing."

"Really? Tell me!" Paige felt a flicker of evil and she jerked her head up and scanned the area. Nothing but a few people in suits rushing by, talking on their cell phones. Two teen girls giggling over something. No one that did justice to the feeling prickling down her spine. Had the Men in White found her? Or was she being stalked by her own inner wraith? "A loophole would be really good."

"I hacked into the Council database. Apparently, that angel you killed was on probation for seducing the human he was guarding, so it's not really a big loss, though you'd never guess it from the big deal they're making of it—"

"Theresa!" She flared up a fireball and hid it by her

hip, clenching her hand around it as she searched for whatever was causing that feeling. It was getting stronger. Darker. Her calf twitched in recognition of a comrade spirit, and she felt a trickle of sweat ease down her back. She checked out the street, then ducked her head when she saw a white van screaming by with Men in White leaning out the windows, scanning the streets for her. Her heart racing, she huddled down, frozen. *Please don't let them find me.*

She waited until she heard the tires squeal as the van shot around a corner, then slid around behind the bus stop, trying to be invisible. "The loophole?" she whispered. "Talk fast."

"Okay, so this is my thought. I'm not exactly the purest girl on the planet and neither is Becca, but you fried us both. And the angel was also a seducer of innocents, so he had his bad side too. So, I think that your death touch reacts to anyone with mixed credentials. You know, a little bit of bad for the wraith to twist to its advantage, and then, of course, the good for harvesting. So, if you found an angel that was truly pure, then your death touch wouldn't do anything to him, and he could do his little thing to save you."

She cocked her head, rolling the idea over in her mind. "So, someone that was all bad wouldn't be affected either? Because there'd be no good to kill off?"

"Exactly. Which is why you could touch Satan."

And Jed. She sighed and rubbed her eyes.

"The thing is, angels are a dicey bunch," Theresa continued. "It's illegal for them to save anyone other than the being they're assigned to, and they really hate to break the rules." There was a clicking sound, as if Theresa was still hammering away on the computer keys.

Paige pressed her thumb between her eyebrows, trying to get rid of a headache that was forming as she leaned against the plastic bus station bubble shelter. "So, you think I should threaten and torture an angel into saving me, so he's blameless in the endeavor? I'm not sure that's the right approach for me to take right now."

"No, you dork. They can't be tortured into anything. They can't be vulnerable to coercion or the sanctity of heaven would be compromised. They have to do it of their own free will."

"You just said—"

"Love or lust, sweeties. Same plan as in the coffee shop, only we need to ratchet it up a level. Angels may be angels, but they're also men and ruled by their libido."

She thought briefly of Jed and his kiss. *So* not an angel. Her throat tightened. *Get over him, Paige. He's dead.* "Okay, so I assume you found out where I can find an angel on short notice? Seeing as how I can't get into heaven to find one. I don't have two weeks to hang out in Starbucks right now." Something cold touched her neck and she yelped and flung the fireball backward without even taking the time to look. She spun around in time to see it crash into the side of an office building, leaving a charred black mark in the cement.

"Of course I did. There's a club in New York where they all hang out. It's called Saving Grace. How tacky is that? Want us to meet you there? We could meet out back around ten?"

She bit her lower lip against the urge to beg Theresa to do just that. "I killed someone today by accident. I don't think you should be around me." She heard the roar of a motorcycle, and she glanced at the street, then tensed when she saw Jerome cruising by on a Harley.

Unlike the Men in White, he was going slowly, searching the crowds very carefully.

Shit! She whirled around so her back was to the street and started digging through the trash can as if she were looking for lunch or bottles to recycle. She didn't dare turn around, but she felt the skin on the back of her neck prickle as the roar of the motorcycle got louder, and she realized he was directly even with her now.

She bit her lip, forcing herself not to bolt or turn around to look at him, leaning farther into the trash can and holding her breath against the stench.

"Don't be ridiculous," Theresa said. "What are friends for, if not to pick each other up after two accidental murders? Ten o'clock in the alley behind the bar, okay?" There was a faint scuffle and Paige heard Dani protest, and Theresa muttered something about getting some backbone and being there for her friends. "Dani can't wait to see you. She sends hugs. Smooches. See you later. Try not to go over to the dark side."

"Yeah, okay." Paige kept the phone by her ear after Theresa had hung up, not moving until she heard the motorcycle engine grow more distant.

After what felt like an eternity, she lifted her head and peered over the rim of the trash can, just in time to see Jerome cruise around the same corner as the white van.

She took a deep breath and stood up. "God, I need to get out of here—" She froze as she felt a cold prickle on her skin and she whirled around, fireball up against the stalker she couldn't see. "Where are you?" she whispered.

She stared at the building behind her. Was he in there? Should she follow her natural Rivka tendencies and go in there and try to take him out, risking her wraith, or flee while she still had her own mind, hoping to get away?

"My price has doubled. Hazard pay."

Her heart jumped and she spun around to see Jed standing behind her. Alive. Unscathed. "Jed!" She started to throw her arms around him, then checked herself. "Oh, God. I can't touch you anymore."

"Bullshit." He grabbed her wrist and yanked her against him.

Ten

Paige squawked and struggled to get free, but he held her tight as he finished materializing from shadow form. "I'm okay. You can touch me. I know you need to." He steeled himself against the feel of her against him. "Go ahead."

Her body stilled, and ever so slowly, she began to relax, and her soft warmth melted into him. Her arms went around his neck and she sighed as she pressed her face against him. "I thought I'd never get to touch you again," she whispered.

He stiffened as her breath warmed the skin at the base of his throat. He knew it wasn't sexual on her part, but damn, it felt good. Her fingers twisted in his hair and she pressed herself tighter against him, her breasts flush against his chest. "I missed you," she whispered.

It was those three words, the utter lack of pretension on her part about her feelings that kicked down the wall he'd managed to rebuild after she'd shut him down on the street. The evil that consumed him while he was a shadow still tingled in his body, but her total trust in him, her need for his touch yanked him right out of the shadow and into a sense of lightness he hadn't felt in decades, if ever.

He groaned and let himself bury his face into the softness of her hair, drank in the scent that was hers, basked in how tightly she held onto him, relished in the fact that she *needed* him. Paige, with all her purity and embrace of life, needed *him,* an evil bastard with no redeeming traits at all.

She pulled back slightly and he reluctantly let her go.

But she kept one hand on his waist, and hesitantly lifted the other to touch his cheek. Her fingers traced along his jaw, and he faded into absolute stillness, so as not to scare her off. "I saw your skin turn black. And your shoulders were smoking."

"I went into shadow form to escape it. Took me a while to regroup."

Her face fell. "I *did* hurt you." She pulled away and shoved her hands in her pockets, hunching her shoulders. "Dammit. You're all bad and I still hurt you?"

"I'm fine as long as you don't slam that blackness into me. It was just getting hit that hard all at once." He rubbed his hand over her shoulder, grinning when she didn't push him away.

She bit her lower lip. "What if I can't help it? I don't have control."

"I do. If I see it coming on, I'll get out of reach. Okay?"

"You're sure?" She wrinkled her nose at him, but he saw her beginning to relax. Saw the sparkle begin to return to her face.

"Trust me, I'm capable of handling it. I'm fine." Actually, his body still ached from her touch . . . no, not his body. His soul. His soul felt like it was weighted down with lead and couldn't break free. She'd damn near killed him. Paige was powerful enough to shift the balance of power in the Otherworld . . . and the mortal world.

The Council and the Men in White would be absolutely right if they decided she needed to be eliminated before she came into her power. If he had any sense of responsibility to the greater good, he'd kill her now, before she could destroy everything.

She stood on her tiptoes and kissed his cheek. "Good. I didn't like being without you."

He stared down at her. *Screw the Council and the Men in White.* She was paying him to keep her alive, and that's what he'd do. The fate of the world wasn't his problem. He dropped his head to plant a quick kiss on her mouth, groaning when her lips parted under his instantly. Her tongue flickered into his mouth and for a moment, he kissed her back, yanking her against him.

But when she sighed and leaned into him, he clenched his jaw and pulled back. "Fuck. You're difficult to resist."

She grinned at him, her eyes sparkling. "Women love to hear that kind of thing."

"Yeah, well, I didn't mean it as a compliment."

Her smile widened. "Even better. It wasn't insincere flattery. It was from the heart, and that makes it perfect."

"You're a little bit crazy, you know that, don't you?" But hell, he liked being around her. Too damn much, he was pretty certain. He tucked his hand under her elbow, searching the street for cabs. "We need to get out of here." As he raised his hand to hail a cab, he felt her studying him. "What?"

"That was you I felt watching me, wasn't it?"

"Yeah."

"You're creepy when you're in shadow form."

He couldn't help but smile at her word choice as the cab stopped and he opened the door. "Creepy? Haven't heard that used to describe me before."

"Yeah, well, I know you were going for ominous and deadly, but it didn't quite work." She ducked under his arm and climbed into the cab and immediately tugged off her sunglasses, blinking at him. "But what's with the evil mojo? You're completely different when you're in human form."

He shoved in next to her, barely able to fit his legs in the small area in front of the seat. He gave the driver an address on the Lower East Side, tensing as he settled back in the seat and thought about where they were going. "Back when shadow warriors guarded the gateways, we went into shadow form to kill anyone who crossed the threshold. It's difficult for me not to kill the nearest being when I'm in that form."

She stared at him, her eyes wide. "So, it's like being me, then, having to resist the urge to kill."

He rubbed his jaw. "Yeah, I guess. In a way."

"So, how do you resist?" She turned sideways and draped her legs over his and let her head rest against the seat so she could watch him.

He rested his forearms on her legs, drumming his fingers on her shins while he thought. "I guess I just shut it down. I don't think about it much anymore."

"But *how* do you shut it down? Do you think about happy things? Reasons to live?"

He gave a small snort at her question. "Sweetheart, there's not a whole lot of stuff in my life that's happy. I just drill it down to discipline. I refuse to kill." He shrugged and idly traced the seam on her jeans with his index finger, enjoying being close enough to her to scent her. She smelled like woman, like some flower he had no chance of identifying but he knew he'd smelled at some point in his life.

"Discipline, huh?" She chewed her lower lip. "I don't really consider myself disciplined."

"Easy to fix."

She gave him a hopeful look. "Really? How?"

"Just decide you're going to do something, and do it. Don't think about it, don't get bogged down in the emotions of it. Just shut everything else out and do it."

She cocked her head and studied him. "If you take all the emotions out of it and shut out everything else in your life, then what's the point?"

"The point is that you don't kill anyone by mistake."

"Yeah, I guess." She sighed. "But the thing is, I like having emotions. I like my life. I wouldn't want to shut them out." She narrowed her eyes. "Oh . . . I get it. That's why you can do it. You don't want to live the life you have, right?"

He leaned his head back against the seat and closed his eyes. "My life is fine. I have a couple things to sort out, is all."

"Like what?"

"Nothing that concerns you."

"So what? I want to know. You're in my life now. That means you get to have me care about you. So, what's up? What's bugging you? It's the Junior thing, huh?"

He opened his eyes and turned his head to the side so he could see her.

She smiled at him, a smile of such genuine warmth and interest that he felt something twist in his gut. He couldn't remember anyone ever looking at him like that. Like they actually cared. He raised his fingers and traced them down her jaw, then clenched his fist in her hair. "You're for real, aren't you?"

"I'm me, if that's what you mean."

He tightened his grip in her hair and tugged gently.

She let him pull her toward him, her eyes getting wide as she neared him. "You're going to kiss me now, aren't you?"

"Yeah." He paused with his lips over hers. "Is that a problem?"

"No. As long as we don't have sex."

He smiled. "I think I can refrain from taking your virginity in the back of a cab." Then he lowered his head and brushed his lips over hers. Her mouth was warm, and she tasted like fruit. "Strawberries?"

"The lip gloss was a freebie since I bought the hat and glasses." She lifted her face to his. "Kiss me like you did on the street last night."

He brought his other hand around the back of her head and pulled her closer, and this time he didn't hold back. Her lips opened for him and he caught her mouth in a kiss that drove thought from his mind. Her tongue reached enthusiastically for his, and he caught it and suckled it, and he felt her shudder in his arms. Then he thrust deeper, and drank in all that he could take, as she offered him all that she was.

Her arm went around his neck and pulled him down toward her, her kiss getting more frantic and more demanding, and he let her take control, gave in to her needs and demands, basking in the small noises she made as she let him into everything she was.

He groaned and slid his hand down her neck, tracing her collarbone as he deepened the kiss, unable to stop himself from responding to her call, to her invitation, to her utter trust of all he was. His hand slid to her breast, and she shuddered as he flicked her nipple through her shirt and her arms tightened around him.

He felt his body respond, and he knew he was close to the edge. With a groan, he dropped his hand and broke the kiss.

Paige's eyes opened, and they were hazy with desire that made him even harder. "I hate stopping."

"Yeah, me too." He slid his fingers through her hair, not quite able to let go. "But it's dangerous. I can go only so far before I'm not going to be able to stop."

She grinned, a mischievous light in her eyes. "Because I make you so hot?"

He laughed softly. "You could put it that way."

She smiled and nestled against his chest, her fingers toying with the front of his shirt. "You almost make me forget my problems."

He wrapped his arms around her and rested his chin on her head. "That's why it's dangerous."

She sighed, and he felt some of her energy sag. "I hate to agree with such a negative statement, but you're right. I don't have time to be distracted by kisses that melt my innards into a bubbling cauldron of hormones."

He chuckled at the Paige-ism. "'A bubbling cauldron of hormones'?"

"It was the best I could do, but I'm sure it didn't do it justice." She shifted her weight so she could get closer to him. "Zeke's running up against a brick wall in the search for the scientist, so I need to go to hell to search Satan's files and see if I can find out the address of his scientist who created the wraith. I'm meeting my friend Theresa tonight to see if we can find an angel to save me, but seeing as how well that went last time, I'm not feeling confident. I'm getting a little freaked out by how much my calf hurts, so I don't want to waste my day sitting around doing nothing. I still think the scientist is my best chance if only I can find her, and it looks like I'm on my own for that. I know you said you have an errand, so maybe we should split up." Even as she spoke, her hand twisted in his shirt, as if she were anchoring herself. "You do your thing, and I'll go to hell."

Jed thought about the power he'd felt from her when she'd nearly killed him. "I don't think you should be alone."

She mustered a weary grin. "You're just saying that because you're hoping for another kiss."

He met her gaze. "I'm saying it because it's true. You're dangerous, Paige, and unless you can figure out how to manage it the way I do, you shouldn't be alone."

Her smile faded, replaced by quiet determination. "How come when everyone else says that, I feel like a leper, but when you say it, all it does is make me get serious and concentrate?"

He shrugged. "Maybe because I don't think you're a leper."

She studied him. "Or maybe it's because you get an erection when you kiss me."

He couldn't help but laugh and he hugged her. "God, I could get used to you."

She beamed at him. "You have the best hugs. I forgive you for telling me I'm too dangerous to be left alone. But how are we going to manage it? I know I said I'd go with you, but I'm kind of freaking out here."

He touched her face to calm her. "My errand will take only about twenty minutes, but it's critical. Let's take care of that, then we can go to hell and do your thing and pick up the money for Junior while we're there. I'll be with you the whole time if your wraith wakes up, okay?"

She raised her brows. "Critical? What's more critical than the fact I might turn into a wraith at any second?"

"We're going to see a shadow warrior that's retiring." He leaned forward and rested his forearms on his thighs, his knees bouncing restlessly as he thought about the importance of this visit. "He's killing my brother."

"Oh." She leaned back against the seat and folded her arms over her chest. "Okay, you win. Family should always take precedence. Family's important."

There was a wistfulness in her voice that caught his attention. "Yeah, they are. Especially when it's my fault they're in trouble."

The cab rolled to a stop at a traffic light. "How is it your fault?"

There was a sharp rap at the window and they both turned to look.

Peering at them through the window was Satan Jr. He flashed his perfect white teeth at Jed in a triumphant smile, his eyes dark with anger, his short black hair slicked back, Wall Street style. "You owed me one dead Rivka an hour ago." His gaze flicked to Paige. "And who's the girl?"

Eleven

Jed cursed and rolled down the window as Paige quickly disentangled herself from him. Junior knew perfectly well there hadn't been a deadline on Becca's death, not that there was any point in arguing with him. Not when he controlled Rafi's fate.

Junior was wearing a handmade Italian suit, dress shoes, and a monogrammed tie. Gone was the gold jumpsuit he used to wear. Ever since Junior had met up with Satan and been able to spurn Satan's paternal overtures, he'd taken it as a personal challenge to dress better than his old man.

Apparently, he'd also taken it as a personal challenge to use up the world's supply of expensive cologne.

"The girl's cash," Jed said.

"Cash?" Satan Jr. rested his forearms on the door frame, shooting a sharp glance at the cabbie to not start driving even though the light had changed to green and the cars behind him were laying on the horn. "Continue."

"She needs a bodyguard and is willing to pay me a hundred grand a day to guard her. Stolen from Satan. It's all yours." He held off mentioning the wraith, not wanting to expose Paige's issues to Junior if he could avoid it.

"Like it. This won't interfere with your services to me, I assume?"

Jed ground his teeth. "I need to put off killing Becca Gibbs for a few days, but she's out of town, so I figured that's cool. I'll kill her when she gets back, and in the meantime, you can have money stolen from your dad."

Satan Jr. narrowed his eyes. "Indeed." Then his gaze flicked toward Paige, who was muttering profanities under her breath, then he snapped his fingers at her. "Hey. Yo. You look familiar. Have I had sex with you?"

Paige leaned across Jed so Junior could see her clearly. "Not a chance."

Satan Jr.'s face darkened. "You're the bitch who fire-balled me at the Penha camp last week. My left pectoral still hurts when I go to the gym."

"You're the asshole who tried to have sex with me when I was under the influence of Penhas. That would've been rape, big guy." Paige's hand flexed as if she were readying a fireball and Jed felt dark anger rising in him.

"You tried to *rape* her?" Jed began to slide into shadow form. Into assassin mode.

"He tried. I kicked his butt, though."

Jed faded further into shadow form and embraced the darkness as it began to take over.

"Jed. Anything happens to me, your brother is mine," Junior said, his voice mild, but his eyes sharp. "It's in the contract."

Fuck. Jed closed his eyes and tried to tamp down his rage, called back his human form.

"Not my contract." Paige flared up a fireball.

Jed caught her wrist. "Don't."

She looked at him, her face softening, then she crushed the fireball in her fist. "Family first," she muttered.

He flashed her a brief smile. "Thanks."

She nodded, then scowled as Junior opened the door and started to slide into the cab. Both Jed and Paige quickly moved to the other side of the seat. Paige went for the door, but Junior stopped her with a question. "Are you Satan's new Rivka?"

She rolled her eyes. "As if I need to answer your questions. You don't have *my* brother." She opened the cab, climbed out, then slammed the door shut, stepping in front of a zooming cab that had to slam on its brakes to keep from hitting her.

"Nice rack, good ass, and an attitude to boot," Junior mused. "I want her. Get her for me."

Jed clenched his jaw so hard he felt it crack. "She wants to kill you."

"I know." Satan Jr. stroked his clean-shaven jaw, staring off into space. "I find that so sexy. Plus, she's a Rivka. I like that. Steal her from my dad. So, you failed to kill Becca Gibbs?"

Jed faced Junior and met his gaze. "Becca quit her job. She's no longer working for Satan."

Junior stared at him. "That's impossible. She can't leave him."

"She did."

Junior's eyes narrowed thoughtfully. "So, Paige must be his new favorite Rivka. Damn. She must be killed then. Kill her."

"She doesn't work for him either."

"No? She left too? How interesting." Junior leaned back in the seat and slipped his hand between the buttons on his shirt so he could stroke his stomach. He sat up suddenly, staring out the window, his eyes wide. "What is she doing? Is she right in the mind?"

Jed whipped around to see Paige working her way down the crowded sidewalk, ducking and darting and twisting to avoid brushing against anyone. Her movements were jerky and a little desperate. His fingers dug into the door handle and he had to will himself not to get out and help her. "Yeah, she's a little disturbed. You wouldn't want her."

"No, indeed. My women must be top condition in all levels—"

He stopped talking, and Jed's gut dropped as Paige tripped and bumped a small tree with her shoulder. The tree instantly turned black and exploded in a burst of ash. Paige plunked herself down on the curb and pressed her palms to her face as she took several deep breaths. Then she stretched her hands up toward the sky, as if she were trying to drink in the sunshine.

"Holy crap," Junior whispered. "He did it." Junior studied Paige, his voice breathless with excitement. "You see her fight it? She doesn't want to change." He leaned forward, nearly on Jed's lap as he watched Paige. "Convince her to be loyal to me, and then force the change."

Jed cursed to himself, but he had no choice but to play that hand now. "That was my plan. I found her when I went after Becca, and I thought she'd be a better deal. Release me from my orders to kill Becca and I'll deliver Paige to you instead. Your own personal wraith." Just saying the words ground in his throat, even though he had no intention of following through. All he needed was some time to figure out how to deal with the situation.

Junior snorted. "You think you can negotiate with me? You failed to kill Becca for a second time. By the terms of the contract, I have already recalled Rafi to my chambers."

Shock rattled through Jed. "You can't afford to call Rafi in. I have no reason to do a damn thing for you if Rafi's already . . ." He stumbled on the words. ". . . Being tortured. Even five minutes in there will kill him. Once he's dead, you lose control of me." He shimmered briefly into shadow form, unable to stop himself. "And then I come after you."

Junior held up his finger as he pulled out his phone. "Hang on." He dialed a number, then spoke into the phone. "I have someone who would like to speak to Raphael Buchanan. Put him on."

He held out the phone. "For you."

Jed grabbed the phone. "Rafi? Where are you?"

But all he heard was a horrible bellow of pain, the kind of pain that ripped a man's insides from his body and destroyed him forever. His grip on the phone tightened, until it snapped in his hand. He hucked the remains back at Junior. "You lose now, asshole." He dropped his shields to welcome his shadow state. To finally end it.

"He's still alive," Junior said quickly. "New contract. Paige for Rafi. Agree quickly and I'll return Rafi to the Afterlife while you work on Paige."

Jed cursed and slammed his shields back up again. "I need time."

Junior nodded. "You have three days to turn Paige wraith and make sure she is loyal to me. I heard she's hardwired to be loyal to my dad, so you'll have to get her to fall in love with you. Love trumps everything else when a woman is involved."

Three days? Not enough. "Five days."

Junior smiled. "Two."

"And Rafi's free?"

"Back to his holding tank the minute you agree."

Jed ground his teeth. "Deal."

Junior reached over him and opened the cab door. "There she is. Clock's ticking. And I'll be watching."

Paige was standing on the street corner, her arms folded over her chest, glaring at the DON'T WALK signal. She saw him, and her face brightened, spilling over with her natural high. He was supposed to betray her? *Hell.*

Twelve

Paige felt the tension emanating from Jed before he even made it to the sidewalk. She frowned. "What's wrong?"

He took her elbow and flagged for a cab. "Detour. I have to check on my brother."

She winced at the depth of pain in his voice. "Yeah, okay. Hell can wait for another few minutes."

The cab stopped and he practically yanked the door off he opened it so hard. She scooted inside and he landed next to her, his jaw working, his knee bouncing in agitation as he gave a new address to the driver.

Then he leaned back in his seat, pressed his palms to the top of his head, and let out a groan of frustration.

She touched his arm. "Hey, listen, I'm sorry about your brother. That sucks that Satan Jr. has him. Is that what's wrong?"

He didn't answer.

She tore open the pack of red licorice strips she'd picked up while she was waiting for Jed. "Ugly family secrets, huh? I wish I had some of those."

"No, you don't. Trust me."

She pulled out a strip of licorice and took a bite. "I do

actually. I have no family, and it sucks. I'd take bad family over no family any day. At least then, I'd have roots. I'd have some connection to something."

Jed dropped his hands to look at her, then frowned when he saw what she was doing. "You're eating candy?"

She held out the strip she'd been eating. "Want some?"

"No." He took the piece of licorice and examined it. "Candy just seems . . ."

"Light-hearted? Fun? Yeah, that's why I got some. Thought it might help my mood." She pulled out another piece and bit it. "So far, not really making a difference, though. It's just sticking in my teeth."

He tossed the licorice back on her lap. "What would you do if I said I loved you?"

Her heart stopped for a split second, this unbelievable feeling of warmth and belonging blossomed over her, and then she noticed that his eyes had faded from their lovely violet-purple to black.

Her exhilaration deflated with a thud. "That's not you talking, is it?" She realized he was looking a little peaked, and she touched his face, not at all surprised to have her finger disappear into his cheek. "You're starting to go shadow warrior, aren't you? Predator mode? For me? Why? What did I do?"

"You didn't answer my question."

"Of course I didn't. You're almost transparent. It wasn't a legit question." She could see the outline of the seat through his chest, which was now bearing a close resemblance to a rain cloud. "Even though I've got this inner wraith thing going on, I'm also a woman. And as a woman, I have fantasies. Like the first time a man tells me he loves me, or even alludes to it, it won't be when he's in evil mojo mode."

He stared at her, then his eyes turned violet, and his body began to solidify and a weird sound filled the cab.

Paige frowned, and then realized it was the sound of Jed laughing while half in specter form. "See? I knew you were insane."

But he just reached out and hugged her and kissed her forehead. "You make me laugh, killer." He groaned and rubbed his face in her hair. "I can't believe I'm laughing. I'm losing my mind."

She smiled and lifted her face so she could kiss his mouth. Because it was there and she already knew he tasted good. His lips were still curved in a smile when her mouth touched his, but the minute she flicked her tongue over his teeth, his mouth closed over hers with an intensity that smacked her in the gut.

His grip tightened on her waist, so tight it almost hurt, but not quite. His mouth was hot over hers, plunging her depths like he would never be able to kiss her deep enough or hard enough. Even if he hadn't meant what he'd said earlier when under the evil mojo, he meant *this*.

She linked her fingers behind his neck and tugged him closer as she kissed him back, felt her body arch into his. His hands slipped under her shirt, and she sucked in her breath at the feel of his bare skin on hers, at the frantic movement of his hands over her lower back, over her shoulder blades, her stomach, her breasts . . . his palm brushed over her nipples and heat exploded in her core.

Oh, hell fire. "That feels unbelievable," she whispered into his mouth. "Do it again."

He groaned and dropped his hand, pulling his mouth off hers. "We're in a *cab*."

"So? I don't care. I'm sure the driver doesn't care."

"I don't care," the driver called out.

"See? We're all on board." She tried to pull him back down. "It'll give him something to talk about over the dinner table tonight. Don't stop. Just one more kiss."

He thumbed her lip and then dropped a brief kiss on it, smiling when she tried to follow him as he pulled back. "Next time we do this, it's going to be in a place where I can finish it. When I'm not worried about my brother."

She took a deep breath and pulled herself off him, then changed her mind and snuggled against his chest. Why deprive herself? She was paying good money to be able to touch him whenever she wanted. And she wanted to touch him, so there. "You can't finish it," she reminded him. "I can't have sex with you, remember?"

His eyes darkened and he caught her face between his hands.

She held her breath at the intensity in his gaze, at the black flecks in his violet eyes. It wasn't the evil mojo exactly, but it wasn't entirely Jed, either.

"I will have you." His voice was quiet. "There is no other way."

"You won't have me." But her stomach knotted up with excitement at the determination in his voice. *But please try. I'd really like it if you tried.* "No other way for what?"

The cab rolled to a stop. "We're here," the cabbie said.

Jed dropped his hands instantly and turned away. "Let's go."

Damn. She hated it when he let go of her. She scowled as she climbed out the cab, tugging her shirt back down from where Jed had gotten it up around her armpits.

He gestured behind her, and she turned around. They were standing in front of a beautiful stone cathedral. "Your brother's in a church? Shouldn't that keep him safe from Junior?"

"I keep my portal here. No one thinks to look for it in a church."

"Because you're evil?"

He scowled. "If you want to put it that way, yeah."

"How else would I put it?" She started to walk up the stone steps, letting her hand glide along the black wrought-iron railing. "Good idea, though. I like it." She paused on the threshold, her belly suddenly flittering with nerves. "You, um, think I'll be okay in there?"

She felt him come up behind her, his presence reassuring. "If I can go in, so can you."

"Yeah . . ." She bit her lip. "What if I go up in flames or something?"

He put his arm over her shoulder, sliding her up against his side. "You may be fighting an inner wraith, but trust me, the church isn't going to hurt you. You've still got enough purity in you." He tugged her along. "Let's go."

She winced as they crossed over the threshold, then let out her breath when nothing happened to her. "So, where's your brother, anyway? Is he okay? Did Junior threaten him or something? Give you someone else to kill to keep him safe?"

When Jed didn't reply, she glanced up at him, then tensed when she realized his eyes had gone black again, and he was staring right at her, like he was about to go shadow on her. She shrugged out from under his grasp and set her hands on her hips. "What is your *problem,* right now? We're on the same team, remember?" She eyed him. "What exactly did Junior say to you?"

Jed ground his teeth, and she could tell from the look on his face that he wasn't going to tell her.

"Fine. Do your 'I'm a man and I'm an island thing.' Whatever. Maybe Dani was right to give up men. Is it so hard to return a little bit of the support I give you? Apparently so. It's not like I'm feeling a little vulnerable right now with my whole inner wraith thing going on or anything like that." She spun away from him and started to stalk across the church. "Even though Theresa can't hug me, at least she's sensitive to my fragile emotional state. Unlike you. Kiss me, mention the 'L' word to a girl who craves love, and then go all predatory on me. Yeah, sure. That's great. Like I'm not having a bad enough day—" She saw a priest at the front of the chapel, leaving through a side door. "Oh! You think a blessing by him will save me? Hello! Hello! Excuse me." She raised her voice as he disappeared through the door. "Hey! I'm in need here!"

There was a growl from Jed that sounded all too evil, so she didn't even bother to turn around. Instead, she broke into a sprint and bolted across the chapel as the door started to swing shut behind the priest. "Yo! Wait up!"

The door slammed closed just as she reached it, and she grabbed the handle and yanked.

Locked.

"No!" She yanked the door again and then kicked it. "Come on! Give me a break!" She sagged against the door, her cheek pressed against the white wood. "Ditched by a priest and an angel in the same twenty-four hours. No wonder Satan picked me—" The skin on the back of her neck prickled suddenly and she whirled around.

Jed's eyes were pitch black and he was stalking her ever so slowly, his body still solid, but fading. Even though he was still in human form, the shadow warrior had clearly taken up residence, and it looked like the only thing on its mind was her death.

"I love you," he growled. "Be mine forever."

"Um, so not believing you right now." She conjured up a fireball in her left hand, her heart starting to pound as she felt the wraith in her calf stretch and wake up, called to consciousness by the danger. It scented death, and it wanted a piece of the action. She swallowed hard, trying to shove the wraith back into its cage while she eyed Jed. "Um, Jed? Where's that discipline you were talking about? You going to back down or what?"

She didn't need him to reply to know that his answer was going to be no.

Thirteen

Rafi's vision blurred as he squatted by the end of his deck, testing the trip wire. He had to lean against the deck chair for a minute until the dizziness passed. His body was screaming in protest, but he couldn't stop. Wouldn't stop. His shirt was soaked with blood and sweat, jaw was aching; cuts all over his body from Junior's torture were still oozing, and he'd had to duct-tape makeshift splints to his shattered ankles just to be able to stand. Even his fingernails were bleeding.

Behind him was a pile of homemade weapons, made from everything useful in his home. He'd trashed the place in his mission. Furniture destroyed, windows broken, walls beaten through . . .

The gun Jed had snuck into the Afterlife for him was the only real weapon he had, but it wouldn't be enough if Junior ever tried to take him back there. He needed better defenses. Wouldn't stop until he felt safe . . . which was a bullshit concept anyway. Safe didn't exist.

He wiped the back of his hand over his brow and took a moment to steady his trembling hand before carefully tugging the trip wire. The sharp spikes made of the fireplace implements quivered slightly where they were attached to the roof, aimed to slam directly in the gut of whoever tripped the wire.

The traps were complete.

Let him come.

Rafi stood up on shaky legs, walked over to the pile of weapons, kicked them aside until there was a hole in the middle. Then he stepped into the middle of the pile, shouldered a sheaf of wooden spears made from the bed legs, slid six sharp paring knives into the belt he'd slung over his chest, checked the ammunition in his gun, and then stuck it in the back of his jeans. Strapped three butcher knives to his thigh, hoisted a stack of boards with dozens of nails protruding from each one (formerly the front door), and secured them across his back.

And then he lifted up the twenty-gallon vat of water, strapped it across his chest like a drum in a marching band, hooked a short hose and a lawn nozzle to it, and then tested it, squirting a spray of water at a nearby flower. Rumor was that water would melt Satan Jr., and he was going in prepared.

He widened his stance to take the pressure off his protesting muscles, then set his jaw. A trickle of blood and sweat dripped down his temple, and he shook it off, his entire body beginning to shake with the effort of staying vertical. His skin burned where Junior had flayed it, his throat still hurt from screaming, and his skull felt like it had been split in half.

Rafi set his shoulders and clenched his jaw. "You won't win!" he shouted. "You won't destroy me!"

No response except the harsh call of a raven.

His quads finally gave out and he dropped to his knees

with a grunt, still holding his upper body erect. "Come on. Come get me—"

He stopped suddenly as a tremor shook his body. He groaned and bent over, fighting to hold himself erect as his muscles seized for the third time since he'd been back.

What the hell was going on? What had Junior done to him? Given him brain damage?

The convulsion finally ended and he groaned, his muscles shaking with relief and exhaustion.

And then he felt it. A sudden flicker of light at the edge of his consciousness.

He opened his mind to the faint pulse, to the call.

The spirit of the shadow warrior had found him.

That's what the convulsions were. His body trying to respond to the call.

Hell.

He closed his eyes as he reached with his own spirit, trying to touch the one that was searching for him, knowing what he had to do. *You have to let me go. I can't answer the call. You must find another.*

He felt his soul break as he uttered those words, denying himself the heritage his spirit had been craving for his entire existence. The one that was his, that would make him complete.

The one that was trying to kill him.

You must leave me in peace.

There was a blinding flash of light in his head, and exhilaration rushed through him. He stumbled to his feet, dropping his weapons as his spirit leapt in response.

Yes, it's me. I can't come to you. You must come to me. Follow the link. Desperation consumed him and he reached his arms toward the invisible pull, raised his face to the sky. *I need you. I can't survive without you. We must be one.* "I'm here!" he shouted, his voice raw. "Come to me!"

The light wavered and he reached for it with his entire being, trying to draw it toward him over the fragile link that connected them. It flickered, and then it screamed his name.

Rafi's body lurched in response and convulsions seized him again, as his body fought for release that it couldn't have.

He couldn't swallow the bellow of pain that consumed his being. He crashed to the deck, oblivious to the splintered wood and nails of his own weapons driving into his flesh, knowing nothing but that he'd failed.

In the church, Jed doubled over with a sharp groan, clutching his stomach.

"Jed? What's wrong?" Paige ran to him and grabbed his arm, which was suddenly ice cold. "What the hell is going *on*?"

"Rafi," he gasped, as he went to his knees, still clutching his stomach.

"What?" She caught him as he fell over, grunting as his full weight landed on her. "God, you weigh a ton." She sank down to the marble floor, cradling his head in her lap. "Um, Jed? You're starting to scare me."

"Is he all right?"

Paige looked up to see a youngish woman in a suit peering down at them, her eyes wide behind red tortoiseshell glasses. Her hair was short and brown, a haircut that should be boyish and plain, but it actually defined her high cheekbones and made her look completely gorgeous.

Paige scowled as the woman inspected Jed. Definitely the daytime help at the church. "Low blood sugar. Do you have any chocolate around?" Paige said to her.

The woman's brows went up as she inspected the well-muscled, massive male body stretched out on the floor groaning. "*He* has low blood sugar?"

Paige wrapped her arms possessively around him. "He's mine, and he needs chocolate. Can you get some before he dies on your floor, already? If he dies because you were too busy gawking at his nice butt to get him chocolate, I'll sue your ass." Her calf twitched and she felt a sudden yearning to kill the woman. She grimaced and closed her eyes, trying to will the wraith back in its cage. *I won't kill for you.*

Fortunately for her, the church lady was already rushing across the chapel, her sensible heels clicking on the floor.

"Okay, Jed, she's gone. Time to get up." Paige patted Jed's cheeks, feeling slightly panicky when she realized how cold they were, trying to ignore the deadly urges prowling around in her body as the wraith tried to push her to kill. It had a chance with the church lady, but there was no way she was killing Jed. *Back off.* "Dammit, Jed! I can't carry you! Wake up!"

He groaned and tried to sit up. Paige shoved against the heavy muscles in his back, and that got him upright, but he let his head rest against her.

Against her breasts, to be specific.

He didn't seem to notice, but damn, it felt good to her.

"It's Rafi. My brother." His voice was raw, as if he'd been screaming for days. "Something happened to him. I can feel it."

"Oh, that's so cool. You guys are so close that you can feel it when something happens to him?" A twinge of envy made her sigh. "I would love to have a brother."

"I've never felt his pain before." He rolled onto his stomach and forced himself to his feet. "Come on."

She scrambled up next to him and couldn't help but smile when he threw his arm over her shoulders to lean on her. Then she staggered under his weight and had to concentrate on staying vertical instead of the feel of his body against hers. "Look at me, Jed."

He glanced at her as he took a deep breath, and she felt him summon strength into his body.

She relaxed. "Your eyes are violet again. What happened back there?" She wrapped both arms around his waist to support him. "You totally lost it."

He groaned and touched her cheek. "We need to talk."

"I'm guessing later, though?"

"Yeah." He pointed toward the stained-glass window off to the left. "We're heading over there."

Together, they worked their way past the rear pews to the window. When they reached it, he paused and turned toward her. "The portal lets only me through, as part of my deal when Rafi got stashed there. For you to get through, we have to be one. Trust me?"

Did she? She realized she did. "Yeah, sure."

"Since you're a Rivka, I can't get inside you unless you invite me in. Let me in, then step through the window."

"What? Why?"

But he was already gone, disappearing in a cloud of smoke that soon became invisible. She felt him tickle her skin, blanket her with a sense of pricklies, swirling around her legs, trying to get past her shields.

She shivered at the feeling of evil pressing at her, trying to get inside her. He felt like a true predator who killed for the sake of killing, who gloried in the act of death itself. Kind of like the wraith, actually.

He was like a different guy when he was in shadow form. This man would so kill her without blinking an eye. If he hadn't collapsed a minute ago, they might even be engaged in a battle to the death right now. If she'd been forced to kill him . . . it might have put her over the top. Why had he done that? Why had he been trying to pick a fight with her?

And she was supposed to let him inside her? Where he could reach her heart? When he was in his oh-so-evil state? Would he be able to resist the temptation?

The pressure intensified on the surface of her skin, and she felt like peeling it off her. Her wraith circled inside her, awakened by his darkness, prowling for prey, but there wasn't a single living thing in the church for her to kill, so Paige ignored it.

"Where he'd go?"

Paige whirled around to see the church lady standing in the doorway clutching one of those one-pound Hershey bars, and suddenly Paige felt like there was a flashing neon arrow pointing to her. *Kill this woman.* She clenched her fists and willed herself not to sprint after the woman and tackle her to the floor in a deadly skirmish. "He's, um, in the bathroom. He's waiting for you."

She brightened. "Really? I'll go take this to him." She spun and her heels clicked quickly down the hall.

Paige took a deep breath and shuddered at the

burning urge to go after the woman. She didn't know which was more dangerous: staying in the church with her hungry wraith and the juicy meal the church lady would make, or letting Jed into her body. He *could* kill her in an instant . . . but she *would* kill that woman if she stayed here.

She had to trust him. He'd told her he loved her, for hell's sake. Yeah, he'd been possessed, but still. It was a statement of faith and she was going to hold onto it. "Okay, Jed, but if you kill me, I will be severely pissed." She shook out her shoulders, flexed her fingers, and then dropped her shields.

His invasion was instant, flooding her body with a coldness that had her staggering. Her inner wraith pulsed with recognition and swarmed over to him, welcoming a kindred spirit into her soul. Then something caught inside her and pain shot through her, and she realized something was dangerously wrong. The wraith was coming alive, really and truly alive. But how? She hadn't killed anyone.

"Jed!" But she knew he wouldn't hear her, wouldn't let her go until they were through the portal, and he left her body. Her body trembling with the effort of containing the wraith, she hoisted herself up on the window ledge and let herself fall into the stained glass.

Fourteen

Paige landed with a *thud* on a patch of grass, slamming her head on a rock, the impact reverberating through her brain and shattering the last vestiges of her control over the wraith.

Then there was a shriek from inside her that had her slamming her hands over her ears. Her muscles convulsed and pain stabbed her as the wraith swelled with power and attacked Jed's shadow form inside Paige's body.

She screamed as Jed fought off the wraith, searing pain knifing through her as he battled for his freedom, as the wraith sank its claws into him to keep him from leaving her body.

Then there was a tear that felt like her soul had been cleaved in half and Jed ripped free and shot out of her. The wraith screeched in protest and spewed through Paige's body, trying to get out to follow him.

Paige curled into a ball, the pain and fury rising to a crescendo she couldn't stand until she thought she was going to be ripped apart from the pain, from the torture, from the rage—

"Paige!" Jed grabbed her shoulders and jerked her upright. "Come back to me!"

"How? Oh, God!" Her body convulsed again and tears streamed down her cheeks. "Tell me what to do!"

He cursed and then yanked her against him and slammed his mouth down on hers. Desire exploded in her and she threw her arms around his neck, attacking his kisses with all the dark energy consuming her. His mouth was hot, his tongue demanding, everything she wanted, everything she needed.

She fell onto his chest, her breasts flattened against him, heat pulsing through her at the feel of his body against hers, at his fingers sinking into her butt and hauling her against his hardness. Her mouth was desperate for his, and he met her with everything he had, teasing, caressing, thrusting, penetrating, until her body coiled up with a need and a desire so tight and so hot she felt like her body was going to snap.

Then he broke the kiss and stared down at her. "Better?"

She blinked at his abruptness. "What? Why'd you stop?"

"The wraith. It settled?"

She stared at him, trying to process the question while the desire still surged through her. All she could think about were his hands on her butt, the taste of his mouth—

"The wraith, Paige."

She finally understood what he was talking about, and she realized the wraith had indeed gone back into hibernation. "Yeah, it calmed down." She groaned, remembering what had happened, and rolled off him to flop on her back, resting her forearm over her eyes as she waited for her body to regain its strength. "What happened?"

"It fed on me." He set his hand on her belly. "You okay?"

"Ducky. Why did it feed on you?"

He was silent for a moment, and she moved her arm to look at him. His violet eyes flicked to hers. "When a shadow warrior kills outside the line of duty, a piece of the soul he's killed stays with him. Sort of a punishment for abusing our powers, I guess."

She lifted her still-trembling hand to his chest.

"What are you doing?"

"I can feel souls. It's a Rivka thing." She frowned as she felt the familiar pulse of souls in his body. Not just his soul, but others. Thousands of them. They felt different, though. Incomplete. "Everyone you've ever killed is still in you?"

"Not their whole soul."

She focused deeper, trying to untangle the web of souls in his body, and then she knew. She jerked her hand off him. "You captured their death. That's what's in you. The death of every being you've killed."

He nodded. "The wraith found them and was feeding on them." He grimaced and stroked her hair. "I have a bad feeling we just did some serious damage to your life expectancy. The wraith is going to be a hell of a lot stronger when it wakes up."

"Well, that *sucks*." She checked on the wraith again, and it was settled deep. Digesting all the deaths it had just eaten? Disgusting thought. With any luck, it would take weeks to digest such a huge meal. Or, it would wake up in an hour, so powerful that Paige would have no chance to resist it.

Ah, yes, time to stop that depressing train of thought. "So, why'd kissing me stop it?"

He shrugged. "It wasn't trying to get you to kill or anything. It was simply in a feeding frenzy, so I tried to distract it." His gaze settled on hers. "Your desire was so powerful that it worked."

"Yeah, well, good thing I have the hots for you, apparently." She sighed as she felt the strength beginning to return to her body, but she didn't move, for fear of dislodging Jed's hand from her stomach. "So, how come it doesn't try to eat all your little death friends other times? Like now?"

"Because they're deep inside my soul. Merely touching you doesn't merge our souls." His gaze flicked to her mouth. "Even a kiss doesn't. We're still separate. But when I went shadow inside you, I became a part of you. A complete merge. We can't do that again. It's much too dangerous."

"Wow." She set her hand on his and tangled her fingers with his. "So, um, what about sex? Would that merge our souls?"

"Depends."

"On what?"

His eyes got dark. "On whether it was strictly physical."

She caught her breath at the intensity on his face. "And would it be?"

"Could go either way at this point." He slid his free hand around to her hair, then bent down and kissed her.

It was a soft kiss, a kiss that said he was glad she was okay, a kiss that made her toes curl and her belly get all warm and fuzzy. She sighed when he stopped kissing her.

"Can I just tell you how much I dig your kisses? They are awesome. And not just because your kiss just saved my life." She touched his lips. "There's just something about being kissed by you that makes me happy."

He got a tortured look on his face and he cursed.

Before she could ask what was wrong, he pulled her into his arms, held her against his chest, and pressed his face into the crook of her neck. She slid her arms around his neck and held him, sensing his need to simply be held. It was a need she understood.

Finally, he lifted his head and looked at her. "You make what should be a simple decision incredibly difficult."

She frowned. "You do realize I can do nothing with a statement as vague and elusive as that, don't you? What are you talking about?"

"Come on." His voice was gruff again. "Let's go." He stood up, grabbed her, and pulled her to her feet.

He didn't let go of her hand as he headed across the wooded area they'd apparently landed in—she'd been too distracted until now to notice where they were—and emerged onto a neglected lawn that seemed to be as welcoming to dandelions and weeds as it was to grass.

She was just about to explain to him the importance of sharing in order to heal emotionally, when she caught sight of the small house they were walking toward. Broken windows, no back door, siding missing from the house, and a huge pile of garbage in the middle of the back deck. "What is this place?"

"It's Rafi's house." He broke into a run, and Paige sprinted after him, Jed's terror making her heart thud.

"Rafi!" Jed sprinted for the house, fear for his brother

stabbing deep in his chest. What the hell had happened? "Rafi!"

He grabbed the railing and vaulted up the steps, then caught his foot and pitched forward. He threw his arms up to block his fall, then grunted as something slammed into his side and blistering pain shot through him. He fell to the deck and rolled, clutching his side as he gasped in agony.

"Holy crap!" Paige landed beside him. "Are you okay?"

He gritted his teeth and felt his side. It was sticky and warm, and he could feel something lodged beneath his ribs. "Damn, that hurts."

"Yeah, I bet it does." Paige bent over him, biting her lower lip. "Um, how immortal are you?"

"This is nothing," he gritted out, trying to get a grip on whatever was sticking out of him, but his hands kept slipping in the blood. His palm hit the object and he cursed again, sucking in his breath against the pain.

She let out a breath of relief. "That's great news. Hang tight." She set her hand on his hip, and then yanked.

Pain ricocheted through him as Paige tossed a bloody fireplace poker onto the deck in front of him. "What the hell's that?" he asked.

"Homemade booby trap, apparently. Nice brother you have." She stripped off her shirt, wadded it up, and pressed it to his side. "Hold that on there. You're gushing."

Holding her shirt against his injury, he rolled to his side and willed himself to his knees, blinking when he realized she was wearing nothing but a black lace bra. She filled it out perfectly and his body surged in response. What the hell was wrong with him? He was gushing blood and she could still turn him on?

She raised her brows. "Want me to take it off so you can get a better view?"

He grimaced and rolled to his feet. "No."

"Liar." She hummed as she stood up. "Is that your brother?"

Jed turned to where she was looking and his gut froze. Rafi was sprawled on the deck, his skin shredded, his body quivering. "Rafi!"

Fifteen

Nearly forty-five minutes later, wearing one of Rafi's shirts that she'd filched from his dresser, Paige paused in the the bedroom doorway, watching Jed lean on the footboard of Rafi's bed. He was intently watching the rise and fall of Rafi's chest. Every time Rafi breathed in, Jed relaxed slightly, and then he'd tense again until the next breath.

Her chest ached as she watched them together. *I want that. I want someone to love me like that.*

She walked up behind Jed and slipped her arms around his waist, careful not to brush against his bandaged side. He stiffened as she rested her cheek against his arm. "How's he doing?"

"He seems to be stabilized. He's not as cold as he was, now that we've got him under a bunch of blankets." Sweat was beaded on Jed's brow.

"Should we call a doctor? Or a healer?"

Jed shook his head. "It wouldn't help. He's dying because a shadow warrior is trying to tap him. I was on my way to visit the shadow warrior this morning to ask him to back off when Junior intercepted us and said he'd recalled

Rafi." He grimaced. "The torture in addition to the shadow warrior is too much stress. Look at him. He's *dying*."

She tightened her arms around him at the grief in his voice. "Well, he's not dead yet, is he? We'll go find the shadow warrior and whip him into shape, and then—"

Jed shoved off the bed and turned to face her. "And then I have to keep him out of Junior's torture chamber."

She frowned. "Why do I get the feeling that's a problem for me?"

"In the cab, Junior told me that I had to convert you to wraith within two days, and make sure you fall in love with me first to ensure your loyalty to Satan Jr. through me. I have two days to do it, or Rafi goes back to Junior's hell." He ran his hands through his hair, his torment evident in his beautiful eyes.

"So what? That's what I told you to tell him in the first place."

Jed glanced at his brother. "But if I don't turn you, Rafi's dead." He cursed and looked back at her, and the pain in his eyes tugged at her heart. "Paige, he's making me choose between the two of you—"

She put her hand on his chest. "Hey, it's okay. I'd never expect my needs to trump your brother's." She forced a smile. "Why would you have loyalty to me? You just met me, and well, I'm not exactly swimming in admirers at the moment."

He frowned and didn't seem relieved by the fact she'd just given him permission to be a good brother. "I don't want to turn you, Paige, but . . ." He glanced back at Rafi. "Even his being stuck here is better than being truly dead. I can't let him die, especially not at Junior's hands."

The intensity on his face made her stomach tighten,

and she was suddenly filled with such longing to belong. To be loved. To love. "You never loved me, right? Even though you brought it up before?" Even though she knew the answer, she had to *know*.

He met her gaze. "Yes. I'm sorry for misleading you. I didn't want to . . . I just didn't know what else to do. I guess I was testing to see if I could do it. When you started asking me all those questions about Rafi in the church, I kind of lost it."

She sighed, refusing to acknowledge the disappointment in her belly. "Yeah, well, it's fine. I figured as much." She looked at him. "But what next? It's not like I'm going to fall for your nefarious plans now that you've confessed them."

"I don't know." He turned back toward Rafi and gripped the footboard again. "Since he's already died once and is in the Afterlife, if he dies again, he'll truly be dead. It might be selfish, but I'm not ready to let him go, even if it would mean Junior could never get him. That just seems like a cheater's way out, to just let him die."

The frustration in his voice, the tearing of his heart . . . her throat tightened. "Seeing how much pain you're in because of Rafi's pain . . . it's so amazing to see." She put her hand on her heart. "That's what living is all about, you know? That kind of pain is why we're alive, because that means we love, like truly love, you know?"

"The pain sucks."

"But in a good way." She leaned forward to look at Rafi. "You try to be this cold and detached assassin, you know? If you didn't have Rafi, by now you'd just be an empty shell of a man. But with him in your life, you feel pain and you're alive. I think it's beautiful."

"Beautiful? Pain is beautiful?"

"Well, of course." She sat on the bed next to Rafi, watching the rise and fall of his chest, the faded pallor of his skin, the gashes on his skin. "What's the alternative? Total emotional isolation? That sucks. Trust me, I know." She bit her lower lip to keep her eyes from getting misty. "Pain is good, because without it, you won't even notice the happiness."

Jed didn't reply, so Paige turned her head to look at him.

He was staring at her with a stunned look.

"What?"

"You did it again."

"Did what?"

He sat down next to her and picked up her hand in his. "You took everything crappy about my life, and made it sound like it was good."

"Well, it is. Even if Rafi dies, it's still good."

He wrapped his arm around her shoulder and pulled her against his chest so he could kiss the top of her head. "You amaze me."

"Because I'm insane?"

"Because you're sunshine."

She frowned. "Actually, I'm pretty evil at this point. About eighty percent wraith, one percent virgin, and the rest is all big, bad Rivka."

Jed shook his head, and touched her chest, over her heart. "In here is where it matters. You could kill a thousand people and have sex with Satan himself and you'd still have this innocence about you that draws people to your spirit." He pressed his palm more firmly, as if he were trying to tap into the light he'd claimed was there. "I want to lose myself in you so badly I can't think straight half the time."

Something tripped inside her heart and she felt herself falling. "That's so romantic," she whispered. "Say it again."

He dropped his hand and pulled back. "Shit. I didn't mean to say that."

She grabbed his hand. "No, no, no. It's okay. I didn't mind."

"I can't do this." He extricated his hand from her grasp. "This can't happen. There's too much other stuff going on. For both of us."

She took a deep breath. "Yeah, you're right." She sat back and tried to focus. *Inner wraith, Paige, remember?* "You're totally right." She stood up and walked over to Rafi and reached out with her hands, hovering just above his chest.

Jed frowned. "What are you doing?"

"Trying to distract myself from thinking about how badly I want you to kiss me by testing my Rivka abilities on your brother. I want to see whether I can find out how much time his soul has to give us an idea of— No *way*."

He was on his feet in an instant, his fists clenched. "It's bad, isn't it?"

She grinned at him. "Well, first of all, I don't know who told you that he'd died, but his soul is very much alive. He's not dead, and he never was. If he dies from the shadow warrior this time, he'll just go to the Afterlife. He'll still be around for visits and Christmas dinner."

Jed stared at her. "That's impossible. He's in the Afterlife now, and only dead people go to the Afterlife."

Paige raised her brows. "Well, I'm kind of an expert on this sort of thing, and I'm sure he's alive."

"You're sure? You're really certain?" Jed grabbed her shoulders, his fingers digging in, his eyes beginning to blossom with hope, and she felt her own eyes get a little watery for him.

"Of course I'm sure."

Jed scooped her up in a hug and nearly crushed her in his arms. "God, I can't believe this." He kissed her hard, then spun her around. "You're my goddess—" He stopped suddenly, his brow furrowing. "Shit."

"Shit?" She paused. "Ah . . . I get it. It's back to him or me again, huh? If he'd died, then you'd have had no choice to make. But now . . ."

He cursed and sat back down, then grabbed her hips and pressed his face into her belly, cursing again.

She wrapped her arms around his head, holding him against her. "I'm not going to ask you to choose me over him because I'm not stupid. Plus, I wouldn't be impressed if you chose me over your brother. Anyone who is lucky enough to have family should totally put them first."

He lifted his head to frown at her, still gripping her hips. "You *should* ask me to put you first. You're worth it. You shouldn't accept being handed over to death."

She smiled at the forcefulness of his words. "No, I'm not going to *accept* my death. I'm not going to allow you to turn me into a love-obsessed wraith. But I'm not going to ask *you* to make a choice between us. What choice would there be? He's your brother. I'm someone who's paying you to touch me. You *should* pick him."

He inhaled deeply, then he pulled back, releasing her. "How are you going to fend off the wraith without my help?"

"Well, it would be a bit of a challenge." She moved his

leg to the side so she could sit on his lap. "But I don't plan to do it alone. You're still going to help me."

He tried to shift her off his lap, but she held on. "Paige, I just said—"

"If I become a wraith, but don't fall in love with you, which I won't, then all three of us lose. So, we need to figure out another plan. A better option, you know?" She wrinkled her nose. "Some way for all of us to win."

Jed sighed. "There's no win-win here, Paige." He met her gaze, and she was startled by the bleak resignation in his eyes. "I spent years trying to figure out another option, but there isn't. I even tried to take Rafi out through the portal the way I brought you in, and the damn thing nearly killed us both. Junior's got us, end of story. I've had to accept that to stay sane. Don't try to feed me hope, Paige. I'm not going down that road again. I'm at a decent place now, one where I can get up in the morning and survive. My goal is to free Rafi from the shadow warrior and go back to the status quo."

"Status quo being me turned into a wraith?" At his curse, she leaned forward until her face was in his personal space. "My life, my future, my *soul* are inextricably tangled with yours, and I'm not giving up. Therefore, you don't have the right to abandon hope either, or to retreat into your little shell of status quo. Got it?"

As Paige stared at him expectantly, Jed felt something crack deep inside him, and suddenly he was filled with more pain than he'd felt in years. And something else . . . hope. He tried to block it, but it swelled through him, crashing down the barriers he'd worked so hard to erect.

Paige must have seen it on his face, because her face

softened with sympathy and she patted his leg. "Hope is good."

"Hope destroys." God, he couldn't go through this again. Couldn't—

Paige grabbed his chin and forced him to look at her. "Hope is a necessity of life. I want to live. I want to love. If you try to take my hope away from me, I will kick the daylights out of you, and then you will feel *real* pain for the first time in your life. *Capiche*?"

He stared into her bright blue eyes, and he wanted to believe her. For the first time in memory, he wanted to believe in something other than his own guilt for screwing up Rafi's life, he wanted to think about something other than how many lives he'd ended. "I've tried everything—"

"Not me. You haven't tried me."

There was such certainty in her voice that Jed finally caved. A little. Enough to ask, "You have an idea?"

"Who put him in the Afterlife, even though he's alive?"

Jed frowned. "It was a three-way deal that included the Council. They wanted me available to do jobs for them, so they offered a place for Rafi to stay."

"Oh, yeah. The Council sucks. Totally crooked." She brightened. "But Jerome's on the Council now. Maybe he could do something."

Jed frowned. "He's leading the hunt for you. You need to stay away from him."

She rolled her eyes. "If we don't get Rafi freed, we're screwed anyway, right? Besides, if we can get Jerome alone, we can handle him. It's the Men in White that we need to avoid." She tapped her chin with her fingers. "Oh, and Satan's an expert at breaking Otherworld contracts.

We could ask him when we go to hell later today." She glanced at her watch, and realized they still had plenty of time to make it to hell before they went to Saving Grace to recruit an angel. Surely one of those leads would work out, wouldn't they? She bit her lip and wondered if she was being naive, thinking she could really come out with a happy ending for herself, let alone Rafi and Jed. Both the scientist and the angel were a long shot, and Jerome was an incompetent who would probably let them down. . . .

"I haven't tried the Council or Satan before." True hope flickered in Jed's eyes, and she knew she wouldn't give up. For him. Because she wanted to see him believe. He deserved to believe.

"See? Hope springs eternal." She cocked her head. "Does this mean you won't try to turn me? You're still on my side?"

He nodded. "For now. I can't promise more than that."

"Understood." She snapped her fingers as she remembered. "Besides, with any luck, you only have to keep me sane until ten o'clock tonight when we find an angel to help me out. I don't have time get one to fall in love with me. It'll have to be lust."

Jed scowled. "You're going to have sex with an angel?"

"Well, yeah. Didn't I explain that?" She was startled by his growl. He sounded like he'd started to go shadow, but his eyes were still bright.

"No," he snapped. "But it sounds like a crappy idea."

She grinned at his snarl. Was he jealous? She couldn't keep the twinkle out of her voice as she patted his cheek. "Don't sound so judgmental. You were willing to become a bloodthirsty assassin to save your brother's soul. Jumping in the sack with an angel to save mine seems to be a little less drastic."

Jed scowled. "What if you save yourself and then we can't figure out how to get out of my contract with Junior? Then what? Rafi's screwed if I don't turn you wraith."

"Oh. I thought you were mad because you're jealous. Bummer." Not that she had time to be worrying about that anyway. "We'll save Rafi," she reassured him. "We have two entire days, and Junior's an idiot. There has to be a way to beat him, and we'll find it. So, don't freak about tonight if I purify myself with an angel before we save Rafi, okay? I won't abandon you." She put her hand over her heart. "I'm yours 'til the end of time. Or until all this garbage blows up in our face. Whichever comes first."

A tendon twitched in his neck. "I don't want you having sex with an angel."

She stared at him, hope flaring again at the cranky tone in his voice. "Why not? Why don't you want some hunky angel to have his hands all over my body, to ride me to the highest levels of ecstasy?" She patted her breasts to add to the effect. "Why? Does that bother you?" *Please let it bother you. I really want it to bother you.*

He stared at her, and she held her breath. Waiting. Hoping?

Finally, he cursed. "Hell, who am I to say who you have sex with? Let's go. We have a lot of shit to get through today."

She sighed. "Would a little bit of optimism in your tone be too much to ask?" At his glare, she decided that maybe it would. "Fine. Be that way. Shadow warrior first, right? Then to hell for the money and to try to find the scientist." She closed her eyes for a second and whispered a little prayer that she could find the info on the scientist, because she was still so skeptical about the angel thing.

Jed touched her arm and she opened her eyes, frowning when she realized how serious he looked. "What now?"

"If I have to choose, I'm going to choose Rafi. You know that, right? I don't want you to be under some illusion that I'm anything other than what I am. I know I already said it, but I need to make sure you really understand it."

She knew then, despite Jed's damned soul and his murderous past, he was a man of honor, refusing to mislead her and protecting his brother. So she reached up and kissed him until he stopped frowning and started to kiss her back. His hands slipped around her waist and he pulled her up against him. She enjoyed it for a few minutes, then broke the kiss and smiled up at him. "And if it comes down to Rafi or myself, I'm going to choose myself." At his frown, she kissed him again, then spun around and walked out of the room.

Dammit, but she really kind of hoped she didn't have to make that choice.

Sixteen

Paige stopped at the edge of Rafi's deck, frowning when she saw the burned-out footprints in the spotty lawn, leading back into the woods.

Jed came up behind her, and cupped the back of her neck with his hand. "You killed the grass when you were walking over it."

"Apparently." She sighed and hugged herself, suddenly cold. She hadn't even noticed murdering each blade. "Damn. I'm brutal." She couldn't bring herself to kill one more thing. Not today. "I'm thinking that maybe you should carry me back to the portal we popped out of."

His fingers continued to rub her neck. "And I'm thinking that maybe going back the way we came wouldn't be smart."

"Oooh . . . yeah. Forgot about that. Dicey moment, though the recovery was nice." She leaned back ever so slightly, so her back brushed against his chest. "I love it when you touch me."

His fingers stilled. And then he dropped his hand.

What? She was supposed to play coy and pretend she didn't notice the magic his touch was weaving? Screw coy. She didn't have time for coy. She folded her arms over her chest and tried not to sound too cranky. "Satan gave me a bracelet that I can use to take us to hell, and then we can pop right back out to the mortal world to visit the shadow warrior."

He nodded. "Then we'll go back to hell and take care of stuff there."

She held out her hand. "If you can bear to touch me, then you need to grab on."

He raised his brows. "Of course I can bear to touch you."

"Then why'd you stop when I commented on it? I liked it, I thought it would be nice to tell you that, perhaps encouraging you to continue to touch me in that way. Was I wrong? Should I pretend I hate it so that you can pretend you aren't doing something nice? Is that it? Because quite frankly, subtlety isn't my forte and if that's what our relationship is going to be based on, we're going to run into problems."

He stared at her for a minute, and then he sighed, brushing his fingers over her cheek. "I'm not used to you."

She frowned. "Question avoidance."

"Fine." He set his hands on his hips and brought his face down to her level. "You want to know why I stopped touching you?"

"Yes, I do. Didn't I make that clear?"

"I stopped because I like touching you, but I think I'm going to have to sacrifice you to save my brother." His face got darker. "Which means I need to keep distance between us."

She grinned. "That's so cute."

He frowned. "You aren't mad? I just said I was going to sacrifice you."

She gently tweaked his nose. "You already made that clear in the many pessimistic statements you've made. Why would I get mad about it now?" She grabbed his ears and pulled him even closer to her face. "I love that you like touching me. That made me feel good, and I really could use all the feel-good moments I can get right now, you know?" She let her lips hover over his mouth, not quite touching, even though every part of her was burning for the contact. To be held. To be hugged. To be *kissed*. "Do you like kissing me too?"

His face softened. "It's against my nature to disclose that information to you."

"So? Change your nature." She kissed his nose. Then his jaw. Then brushed her lips gently over his. Then pulled back ever so slightly. "Well?"

His eyes were dark again. Deep purple, not black. "Yeah. I like kissing you."

"Because you love me?" she teased.

"No. Neither of us is that stupid."

"True." She gripped his hair more tightly and tugged him down until their lips were almost touching, and she was pleased he made no effort to resist. "So, it must be lust?"

"Must be." His voice was rough.

"Mmm . . ." She kissed him again, and a shiver of excitement raced through her when she felt the flicker of his tongue against her lips. "Kissing you makes me forget that my life kind of sucks right now. I need this kind of thing to remind me that life's okay, you know?"

He deepened the kiss, and she sighed with delight and wrapped her body around his as tightly as she could without actually toppling over.

Then his hands sank into her butt and he pulled her against him, so she stopped bothering to keep her balance and just concentrated on the most delicious sensation of being kissed and touched. She opened herself and a rousing sensation of excitement crashed through her body. Her belly danced, her toes curled, and she had an almost unbearable urge to smash herself against Jed.

So she did, and he lifted her up and wrapped her legs around his waist, slipping his hands under her shirt and over the bare skin of her back. She felt his erection pressed against her and she shuddered.

"Lean back," he whispered.

"I don't take orders."

He grinned. "Please."

"Well, when you asked so nicely . . ." She leaned back and almost forgot to hold onto him when she felt his lips trail over her throat. "Holy cow. This rocks."

He chuckled and lifted his head to look at her. "Kissing you is a unique experience."

"It's all good, right?"

"Yeah." He kissed the tip of her nose, then helped her slide back down to the ground, right over a very firm and perky part of his anatomy.

Oh, *so* all good.

"How do you feel?" he asked. "Your wraith?"

She did a quick check, then nodded. "It's snuggled up asleep in its cave like a good little bottom dweller digesting all the snacks you fed it. When it wakes up, I'm sure it'll be another story, but for now, we're good."

He fingered her hair. "You let me know when it starts to wake up, okay?"

"Like there's any chance you won't notice." She held

out her hand. "Let's go visit this shadow warrior and get on with things, shall we?"

He took her hand, and she faded them out of Rafi's house.

Two fades and a taxicab ride later, Paige and Jed were running up the stairs of a very old building in Greenwich Village. Jed reached the door of an apartment on the sixth floor. It was already ajar, a musky scent and the sound of *The Price Is Right* emanating from inside. Jed was just raising his hand to knock on the door when his cell phone rang. He grimaced when he saw it was Junior. "Yeah?"

"Is she in love with you yet?"

He glanced at Paige, who gave him the thumbs-up, having apparently heard the question.

"She told me I needed a haircut and an updated wardrobe."

"Excellent! She's trying to control you. Love will soon follow. Keep me posted."

"My pleasure." Jed snapped his phone shut and rapped lightly on the door before Paige could give him grief about his haircut comment. "Hello?"

There was no reply, so he shoved the door open and stepped inside. The moment he entered the apartment, he felt a dark threat rise inside him. The territorial instincts of a shadow warrior.

"This place is way depressing," Paige said.

Jed glanced around and realized she was right. The shades were down, the furniture was stained and ratty, and there was a layer of dust on everything. A few greasy pizza boxes were on the floor, and an empty two-liter bottle of soda was on its side.

There was a creak from behind them and Jed spun toward the sound as a huge man in old jeans, a faded gray T-shirt, and black boots opened an interior door and moved into the room. His shoulders were wide, his muscles taut, but his face was gaunt, his eyes were black pits in his face, and his skin was a mottled gray.

"Whoa." Paige flared up a fireball and moved next to Jed. "Scary looking dude."

The man's gaze flicked to Paige and raked up her body, then he nodded and gestured into the room he'd just walked out of. "You'll do. Come on in."

"She'll do? For what?" Jed clamped his hand down on Paige's arm as she started to saunter toward the door. "What are you talking about?"

The shadow warrior frowned, and he finally noticed Jed. His eyes narrowed. "What do you want?"

"My brother is the shadow warrior you tapped. I want you to let him go."

The man's eyes narrowed with sudden hostility. "You're related to Rafi?"

"Yeah. You're killing him."

"Well, what the hell do you think he's doing to me? I'm supposed to be moving into my golden years of retirement, and instead, he's going to kill me. Ungrateful son of a bitch." He snapped his fingers at Paige. "Get in here. I don't know how much time I've got left. Sheets are clean—"

Paige grinned. "You think I'm here to have sex with you?" She sounded thoroughly amused, though Jed wasn't feeling the humor. "There's so little chance of that, it's not even funny. Well, it is funny, because you're so completely wrong."

The shadow warrior frowned. "You're not here to have sex with me?"

"No. Of course not. We—"

He slammed the bedroom door in their face, and they heard the creak of bedsprings as he apparently threw himself back onto the bed.

Jed shoved the door open and stepped inside, then nearly backed right out when he realized the room was packed full of shadowy, threatening figures, shimmering somewhere between life and nothingness. The shadow warrior was stretched out on the bed, watching television.

"Holy cow. These are like yours, Jed," Paige said as she leaned around him.

"My what?"

"The souls in you. These are the souls of the people he killed, waiting for the rest of their souls back." Paige stepped in the room. "Hello, everyone. Are any of you from heaven? If so, I'd like to make a deal with you."

The figures shimmered around and through her, fading when she walked through them. "No one from heaven?" She set her hands on her hips. "Chatty bunch, eh?"

The shadow warrior glanced up at her. "You sure you don't want to have sex? I'm trying to have a last hurrah before I get sucked into a deep-ass vortex in hell because I'm going to die instead of passing on the legacy."

Jed frowned and stepped in past the flickering image of a woman who was reaching out for him. "What vortex?"

The shadow warrior looked at him. "*Why* are you bothering me?"

"Because I'm trying to figure out how to save my brother."

"Oh." The shadow warrior sat up. "If you saved him, it would save me, eh?"

Jed caught a whiff of body odor that made him wince. "Yeah, probably."

"Fantastic!" The shadow warrior hopped out of the bed with sudden energy and rushed through the hovering ghosts and bolted into the bathroom. He came out squeezing toothpaste onto a bright yellow toothbrush. "My name's Bandit."

"Bandit?" Paige eyed him. "What kind of a name is that?"

Bandit shoved the toothbrush in his mouth and hucked the tube over his shoulder into the bathroom where it hit the mirror and clattered to the floor. "I named myself in honor of my illustrious career as an art thief. Do you have any idea how easy it is to steal things in shadow form?"

She glanced at the cracks in the window next to his bed. "Shouldn't you be living in some palace or something? I mean, if you're such a good thief."

"Gambling addiction. It's a bitch. Plus rent control keeps me in a nice neighborhood. Just can't afford to keep up with the knickknack crap." Bandit swept a pizza box off the dingy gray quilt on his bed and patted it. "Sit, sit. Let's talk. What's your plan?"

Jed eyed the damp spot on the bed and opted to stand. "I was hoping you'd just call off your tag and hit up another shadow warrior instead of Rafi."

Bandit shook his head. "No can do. Already tried. Next."

"Well, what's the vortex of hell thing?" Paige asked. "I'm pretty familiar with the region and I've never heard of it."

"Hyperbolic exaggeration. I was referring to the fact that if I die without passing on my legacy, then the world's one shadow warrior short, and all the gateways collapse and hell falls into heaven and it's all a gigantic mess, and I get blamed. Hence, the effort to get all the great sex I can before it's too late." He jerked his thumb at the circling specters. "And they get to eat me too. Gross, eh?"

Paige's mouth dropped open. "They *eat* you? Why?"

"To get their souls back. If I had passed on the legacy, then they would have been free to go party or whatever it is that they'd do, but if I die without freeing them first . . ." He made a face. "Like I said, vortex of hell. Not worth mentioning. It's really too depressing. So, the plan?"

Jed held up his hand. "Wait a sec. What about all the gateways collapsing? We don't guard those anymore."

"Well, duh, big guy." Bandit rolled his eyes at Paige. "The young ones think they have all the info, don't they?"

"Then we're so lucky that you do, right?" Paige asked.

"Exactly." Bandit gave a condescending sigh and turned to Jed. "We don't actually guard the gates, but we're still bonded to them. Why do you think we're all such a mess? Being deprived of our legacy has seriously screwed us all up. One shadow warrior I know runs a couple terrorist groups and another runs this cult up in Washington where they do human sacrifice and eat only spinach and pine nuts. Face it, boy, without a gate to guard, we're aimless, shiftless creatures with a hell of a lot of power and nowhere to channel it. I even heard one sorry son of a bitch actually hired himself out as an assassin to Satan Jr. Can you imagine his payback when heaven and hell collapse in the next day or two? He ought to be getting laid as much as possible, if he's got any brain." Bandit's wink said he knew exactly who Jed was.

Jed snorted. "Actually, I'm spending my time trying to save the world. I'm sort of a long-term-planner kind of guy."

"Which is why I invited you in. But I'm not hearing a plan." Bandit snapped his fingers. "Time's a-wasting. Either I need to get back to my last hurrah, or we need to stop the slide of heaven into hell."

Jed's cell phone rang, and he glanced it. Junior again? He flipped it open. "What?"

"Is she in love yet?"

"No." He snapped it shut without another explanation as Paige tapped Bandit's knee.

After touching him, she looked at her hand and wiped it on her jeans. "Have you tried to get into the Afterlife where Rafi is?"

Bandit rolled his eyes again. "Well, duh, of course I tried. Hello? Do you think I'd be sitting here on my ass waiting for all these creepy things to eat their souls out of me if I had a choice?"

Jed grimaced as one of the "creepy things" brushed a shadowy hand through Bandit's heart, as if to remind him that she was waiting for her moment.

Paige set her hands on her hips. "Well, if Jed kills you now, would that work, do you think? Preempt the slide into the vortex by having you die of unnatural causes?"

Bandit leapt to his feet, grabbed the clock radio off his nightstand, and brandished it at her. "Don't even think about it. I'll have the same result, just sooner, and I'll get no last hurrah." His pants were sagging down around his hips, revealing dingy briefs with elastic that was barely holding them up.

Jed cursed. "Pull yourself together, man. You're an embarrassment to shadow warriors everywhere."

"And no woman's going to give you a last hurrah looking like that," Paige added.

Bandit yanked his sweats up. "Women love deadly warriors."

"Not ones that smell like dead fish and have cannibalistic ghosts stalking them." Paige turned to face Jed. "We've got to talk to Jerome. If Bandit's right about heaven and hell collapsing, I'd have to think that Jerome would be willing to release Rafi long enough to get tapped."

"If they believe us." He eyed Bandit. "You willing to testify as to the truth of what you said?"

"Damn straight. It was the Council that deemed us obsolete in the first place. I'd love to go in there and—"

"You have to shower and wash your clothes," Paige interrupted. "Buy deodorant. And some cologne. Maybe a lot of cologne. Jerome won't take you seriously if you go in as a stinky, sloppy ex–art thief with a gambling addiction."

Bandit sighed and sat back down on the bed. "I'm really not a very good shopper. I don't have a sense of my color palette."

"'Color palette'?" Jed repeated. "Who cares about a color palette? Just go to any store, grab some jeans and a shirt and you'll be in much better shape than you are now."

Bandit gave them a droopy look. "If I look bad on purpose, that's me showing attitude. If I *try* to look good, and I fail, well, then, it's me being a loser." He sighed, a big belly sigh that made the dust bunnies on the floor drift several feet. "I'll just stay here."

"Oh, for hell's sake." Paige pulled out her phone and dialed it.

Dani answered on the first ring. "Hello?"

"It's me. I—"

"Oh, *Paige*. I'm so sorry about how I've been treating you. I'm such a bad friend. Theresa had a long talk with me and I realized—"

"It's okay." Paige smiled, suddenly feeling better. "I know you love me. I'd be scared of me too."

"No. It's not okay. I'm here now. I'm not going to run away."

"Good. I need a favor."

"Sure thing. Anything for you. Zeke's not having any success finding the scientist, by the way, so we have to make sure this angel thing works tonight. I think it might be your only chance."

Paige tightened her grip on the phone. "Is he giving up?"

"No, but he's not optimistic. Satan's done a great job hiding her."

Paige grimaced and Jed touched her arm. "Everything okay?" he asked.

She wrinkled her nose and shrugged.

"So, what do you need from me?" Dani asked.

Right. Focus. If they could get Jerome to free Rafi, that was one threat against her that would be taken care of. "I have a makeover project for you. I have this . . . um . . . slightly outdated shadow warrior that we need to get in shape to testify before the Council. Can you take him shopping and clean him up?"

"For sure. I'm all over it. Text me the address and I'm on my way."

"Bring your credit card. I think he's probably broke."

"Will do. Anything else?"

Paige nodded. "Just thanks for the apology. It means a lot."

"I love you, babe. I might be scared to death of you, but love trumps over terror, so I'm with you. Smooches. I'll let you know if Zeke comes up with anything."

Paige snapped her phone shut, feeling better now that she had Dani back on her side, even if she had delivered bad news about Zeke. She mustered up a smile for Jed. "She loves me."

"Why wouldn't she? You're lovable."

There was an intensity to his statement that made her breath catch for a minute. "You think I'm lovable?"

"Oh, yeah."

Oh, wow. She was suddenly feeling *much* better. "How lovable? Like throw me on the floor and ravage me, lovable? Or stand vigil over my deathbed, lovable? Or both? I'd like both. Not that I plan to die and not that we're going to have sex, but hypothetically speaking."

He met her gaze. "Hypothetically speaking—"

"Hey. Is this chick you called hot?" Bandit interrupted. "Think she'd be interested in a last hurrah?"

She glared at him. "Shut up, Bandit. Can't you see we were about to have a moment?"

"Hey, chicky. I don't even know you and I can answer the question. Of course he'd want to throw you down and ride you 'til he's got saddle sores and his horse can't move another inch. And no shadow warrior ever grieves for anyone, because we're vicious killers with no emotions whatsoever."

Jed's mouth twitched and Paige couldn't stop from laughing. "You're an idiot, Bandit. You completely blew the mood for us."

Bandit winked at her and rolled to his feet. "I gotta shower for my new lady friend. You'll call me when you want me to dominate the Council and thrash 'em 'til they weep like little babies who lost their pacifiers?"

She grinned. "I like you. You make me laugh."

He glared at her. "I'm not funny. So, you want my number or what?" And he shot another glare at Jed. "And I'm not giving it to you. I only give out my number to hot chicks, and you don't count."

Paige laughed again, and she slid her arm around Jed's waist, pleased to see he was looking amused as well. How could he not? They both had been in desperate need of a Bandit in their lives. "You have a phone?"

Bandit tugged a brand new cell phone out of the front of his pants. "Got it from a chick who thought I was hot. Traded it for great sex."

Paige raised her brows. "Really?"

"No. I stole it from a guy on the subway. I figure I've got about another hour or so before he has the service cut off. You going to call me before then?"

Paige sighed and handed him her phone. "Use this. I'll get another one."

"Great." Bandit shoved it down the front of his pants. "You can have it back after the deal's done."

"Oh, no. It's all yours," Jed said. "Our gift to you."

"Fantastic." Bandit saluted them. "Get out of my house. I got work to do." Then he whirled around and stalked into the bathroom, shouting at the ghosts to get out so he could have some privacy. They ignored him and drifted through the door to join him.

"Hey, you two!" Bandit yelled through the door as the shower came on. "In case I forgot to tell you, I'm gonna die from this shit at about two o'clock tomorrow, so don't hang around my place like you've got nowhere better to go. We're on a deadline, kids."

"Two o'clock?" Jed glanced at his watch and cursed, and Paige felt her adrenaline spike.

No! Bandit had made them both laugh! She wasn't ready to let go of it, not yet. She raised her chin. "Thinking positively," she said. "I'm sure Bandit will convince Jerome to free Rafi long enough to become a shadow warrior, then we'll find a way to get you two out of the contract with Junior without turning me wraith, then we'll win over my wraith . . ." She frowned. ". . . somehow . . ." She sighed, then lifted her chin. "So, anyway, you better start thinking about how you're going to avoid ending up like him, a major shadow warrior loser."

His brows shot up. "I'm not going to end up like him."

"I'm sure he didn't think he would either, but he did."

"I'm not—"

She faded them through the floor before he could finish his argument.

Seventeen

An hour later, Paige slammed open the door to Satan's petty cash room. "How could Satan not keep records on evil scientists hired to destroy my life? Isn't that the kind of thing that would be important enough for a paper trail? I mean, what if he lost his short-term memory and wanted to create a second deadly wraith? What then? No paper trail, no deadly wraith number two. Horrific business planning if you ask me." She stalked across the room toward Satan's petty cash stash. "You know, I'm trying to be optimistic that we're going to solve this wraith thing before it takes over me, but without that scientist, it's really difficult to be positive."

"What about sex with an angel?" Jed stood in the doorway, keeping an eye out for anyone joining them in the room. Paige was concerned about Satan showing up, since he'd apparently banned her from hell, but she'd been so certain that his files would have the information she'd needed that she'd been willing to risk it.

She'd spent the last forty-five minutes fireballing Satan's office in order to get all his safes open. The walls had shaken, flames had set off the sprinkler system, and there was smoke drifting through the air vents. She'd nearly fried two of the guards that had come running, and it had been all Jed could do to restrain her while he knocked them out. The wraith was beginning to wake, and they were both more than a little worried about how strong it would be once it came out of hibernation.

And it had all been for naught, as they'd found nothing in the files, and she was so frustrated and strung out that she was treading an edge he hadn't seen her near before.

She ran her hand through her hair. "Last time I blew up the angel, Jed. How can I be confident that it'll work this time? It could put me in a worse position than before, causing another death and giving the Men in White even more incentive to chase me down. I was so hoping we'd find the scientist and I wouldn't need to try it, but I didn't. So, I'm about to try my last hope, and I'm not even hopeful about it!"

She whirled toward a large golden cabinet. "I. Am. Freaking. Out." She yanked open the door to the gold bullion cabinet and jumped back as a pile of coins crashed onto the floor with a resounding clang. "Look at this mess. Without Becca around to keep this place running, it's going to hell." She dropped to her knees and started hurling coins back inside. "I can't believe this crap. Doesn't anyone have any organization?"

He raised his brows. "You're worried about organization?" His phone rang again and he glanced it. Junior. He sighed and answered it. "Not yet." He hung up without waiting for a response.

"No, of course not. I'm *venting*." She sat back on her heels and looked at him, ignoring the phone call. "I'm falling apart, here, Jed. Get with the program! Bandit distracted me, but then he got me to thinking how much I like to laugh, you know? And I might not get to laugh much in another day or two. And that upsets me."

Jed grimaced. "I'm sure we'll come up with something—"

"Oh, like *that* helps. You don't even believe your own words." She grabbed a duffel bag from the stack next to the cabinet, then yanked open the bag and dropped it on the floor. "At least *try* to sound convincing. I'm in need of some positive reinforcement here, Jed." She scooped up a handful of gold. "I'm taking enough to pay you for a month, so you can stuff your doom and gloom. I'm staying alive for the month. And no, I don't have a plan to get Junior to extend his deadline. But I'll come up with something!"

Jed raked his hand through his hair in frustration as she threw the coins into the bag so hard they all bounced right back out. "Listen, Paige. I *know* we'll be able to handle this. Bandit's going to be our ace and I'm sure Jerome will return the message you left for him since you explained the situation with Bandit and the vortex . . . as long as he doesn't delete it first once he realizes it came from Satan's office number. . . ." She rolled her eyes at him, but he kept going. "And if he does, we'll call again. You can't give up on this. I need your optimism, and I think your wraith might be affecting your ability to shake all this off, dragging you into a negative mind-set."

"The wraith is putting me in this bad mood? All the more reason to hate it! I hate being in a bad mood!" She hurled the handful of coins into the bag so hard they bounced out again and rolled around the floor. "Dammit. I can't believe my money is going into Junior's bank account. That's just crap too. We should rub it in poison ivy before we give it to—"

"*Your* money?"

Jed started in surprise and spun to the right.

Satan was leaning against the wall, his arms folded over his chest. *Crud.* How had he gotten in? Jed hadn't been face-to-face with Satan in at least five years, despite his numerous forays into hell to cause trouble at Junior's behest.

Paige didn't even bother to look up as she continued to scoop up gold. "It's the Rivka petty cash. I'm a Rivka. So it's mine."

"*Former* Rivka, are you not?"

Her eyes glittered with annoyance. "I didn't read any rules that said former ones lose the right to the petty cash."

Satan stared at her, then broke out into a wide grin. "Oh, you are most delightful. You have learned from my former favorite Rivka. I like spunk. I will change the rules."

Paige zipped up the bag, then hoisted it over her shoulder, staggering under the weight. "That's crap. You're the reason I have no job skills and have to continue living off the Rivka petty cash fund. You should be forced to support me in my old age."

His smile widened. "My former apprentice is in a fine mood today. I quite enjoy this. Are you feeling dark, today? A bad mood taking over your sunshiny personality, perhaps? Is a certain wraith beginning to take over your ebullient nature, turning you into bitter and cranky old maid?"

Paige blinked, and Jed saw awareness come over her

face, followed by dismay and then frustration, as Satan confirmed what Jed had already suggested. The blackness in her soul was beginning to corrupt her personality.

Dammit. He liked her personality, and he didn't want it trumped by some hostile dark side. Jed threw his arm over her shoulder and yanked her against his side. "We *will* solve this," he growled.

Paige looked at him, then broke into a smile. "Now, see? That was convincing." She stood on her toes and gave him a kiss on his cheek. "Thank you."

Satan lifted his brows at him. "You look familiar. Who are you?"

"Bodyguard."

"Bodyguard?" Satan looked at Paige, his upper lip curled in disgust. "You are so weak you need a bodyguard? You are not worthy of the title of former Rivka apprentice and you do not deserve Rivka petty cash." He went to grab the bag off her shoulder and Paige stepped back, flared up a fireball, and smacked it in his face.

Satan stumbled back, holding his hands to his face, while Jed shoved Paige behind him and braced himself for Satan's reprisal. Paige tried to move in front of him, and Jed grabbed her arm and pushed her back. "You're in no position to deal with a fight. Stay back and let me do my job. Got it?"

Her eyes widened, then a sensual heat flared in her eyes, sucker punching him in the gut. "It is *so hot* you want to protect me from Satan. I mean, yeah, I'm paying you for it, but most bodyguards would say taking on Satan went over the line."

"You fireballed me?" Satan was probing a sizzling black crater where his right cheek used to be. "With a fire-

ball hot enough to hurt me? I did not think a Rivka could generate a fireball of that power. I am much impressed."

"Of course I fireballed you! This is your fault I'm in this mess, and I'm pissed." She flared up another one and hurled it Satan, who managed to duck this time, but the fireball screeched to a halt, whirled around, and slammed into the back of his head.

Satan howled and stumbled forward, his hands bracing against the fall as his knees hit the marble floor. He jerked his head up as smoke rose from the back of his head. "What was *that*?"

"Heat sensor. I've been experimenting." She thrust the bag into Jed's stomach, then dropped to her knees in front of Satan, her face up in his grill. "How do I stop this shit from taking over me?"

He shook his head. "There is no way."

She immediately hurled a fireball at his groin. Satan crowed with delight as it screeched to a stop just before making contact. "Look how dangerous you are! I admire you muchly and I would stop if I could! I chose you as the experiment because you were too soft and I did not like your personality. But now that you fireball me, I much adore you and I would keep you if I could and put a different useless Rivka in your place as evil wraith. Why did you wait until now to develop spunk? Why?" He scowled. "This is your fault! Always yours!"

Another fireball flared up in her hand, and her vision began to blur. "There *has* to be a way. Tell me what it is!" Her voice was raspy and harsh. Not good. "Or I'll finish you now."

Jed grabbed her wrist and pried the fireball out of her hand. "Paige! You're losing it, sweetheart." He squatted next to her and grabbed her shoulders. "You need to get back in control."

She jerked her gaze to him, and he was shocked by how black her eyes were. She started to shake. "I can't stop," she whispered. "I'm so mad at him."

Shit. "Okay, it's time to get you out of here." He threw his arm around her shoulder and pulled her to her feet. Her muscles were tight, and her fists were clenched with the effort of maintaining control.

"Wait," she gritted out. "How do we break an otherworld contract?"

The contract. Jed stared at her, shocked that she was thinking about his contract when she was about to go wraith. Something warm cruised through him and he tightened his arms around her. "I'll keep you safe," he whispered. "I'll find a way."

"What contract?" Satan asked.

Jed trailed his lips over the side of Paige's neck to distract the wraith. She made a small noise and leaned into him, gripping his wrist so tightly that he was pretty sure she was drawing blood. He began to rub her back. "Stay with me, Paige."

"Satan Junior." Paige wrapped her arm around Jed, anchoring him to her, her body vibrating with tension as she fought off the wraith. "Jed needs to break a contract with him."

"Oh." Satan beamed. "That is excellent. As a proud father, I am most pleased that my progeny has trapped you by a bad contract and I do not assist your freedom. But as the leader of hell, I must take every opportunity to take down my opponent, and I must help you. I am torn about how to proceed." He frowned and was silent.

Paige closed her eyes and let her head drop back against Jed's shoulder, and he felt her darkness pulse into him. He realized she was getting darker than he could withstand. It was like at the restaurant, only worse. His soul began to ache, but he didn't release her. Not yet. "My contract with Junior will result in Paige being his servant once she turns wraith," he told Satan.

Satan stiffened. "He steals my wraith? Impossible. He cannot own her."

"Love trumps wraith-hood."

"Oh." Satan rubbed his chin. "It might. It might indeed." He marched over to Paige and leaned over her. "You will love me now."

Paige kicked Satan in the shin, and Jed yanked her back against him, wincing as his body began to go numb from her assault on him. His phone rang as he hooked his arm around Paige's upper body to hold her still, and Jed answered it by speaker phone without even looking to see who it was. "What?"

Junior's voice rang out in the room. "Is she in love yet? Have you turned her wraith? I'm so excited about stealing her from my dad. I can't stand the wait."

"You shall never steal her," Satan bellowed. "I will laugh at your failure and no longer be as impressed with you as I currently am. I do admire the plan, even though it will fail miserably."

Junior shouted a few paternal-related obscenities and hung up.

"So, how do I break the contract?" Jed ground out.

"I will not assist you." Satan stood up. "I do not believe the fruit of my loins can best me by stealing the wraith's loyalty. I welcome the battle." Then he spun around and twirled out of sight in an explosion of gold bubbles.

Jed cursed as his legs began to shake, and he knew they were out of time. "Get us out of here."

Paige groaned as she sat up in the burned-out field that used to be the green outfield at Yankee Stadium. She'd landed in left field and rolled all the way to right, killing every blade of grass along the way. It wasn't until she'd made it almost to the foul line that she'd finally felt relief and slowed down. Relief because her wraith had fed on the death of thousands of blades of grass and was digesting them.

So it could grow even stronger.

She hugged herself, realizing that she was losing control of the battle with the wraith. It would soon be stronger than she was and then even Jed wouldn't be able to stop her from killing—

"Jed?" She spun around and saw him lying on the field exactly where they'd landed. And he wasn't moving. "Jed!"

She jumped up and nearly went down as her rubbery legs gave out on her, then half-crawled her way back across the field to him. She dropped down next to him, afraid to touch him. His eyes were closed and he was still, but his chest was rising and falling gently. "Jed?"

"You would be one high-maintenance girlfriend," he mumbled. "Where's the sunshiny personality I fell in love with when we first met?"

Her eyes instantly filled up with tears. "You're okay?" Oh, God. He was *okay* . . . and he'd said he'd fallen in love with her? She blinked to clear her vision. "Jed—"

He opened one eye. "You have *got* to make more of an effort not to let people piss you off. Don't let the wraith rule you."

She bit her lower lip. "I didn't mean to hurt you—"

"Oh, hell. Come here." He grabbed her wrist and yanked her on top of him before she could resist. "I hate it when you're afraid to touch me."

She sighed and let herself relax on his chest, trying not to breathe in the smell of charred grass. Instead, she concentrated on the feel of his chest moving, his hands resting on her waist, trying to use him as her focal point to clear her mind from all the negativity.

"So, down in Satan's chambers . . . was that the Paige you want to be, or was that the inner wraith coming to take over your personality?"

She nestled tighter under his chin. "I hate being mean. Or being mad. Or being petty. I like to harvest souls that belong in hell and I enjoy a good fight with a worthy opponent." She sighed, watching his shirt ruffle under her breath. "But down there . . . that was different. I didn't like who I was. I felt . . . muddy. I felt hopeless. And angry. So unbelievably angry." She shuddered at the memory, at her loss of control with Satan.

"I'm relieved to know that it was the wraith and not you." His hands began to rub her lower back, and she felt his lips brush against her forehead. "Have you considered that maybe you don't actually want to be a heartless Rivka who tortures and destroys all comers? Maybe you just want to take out bad souls and make the world a better place. That seems like a better fit with who you are, believing you can save the world and all that."

She contemplated his words, and was surprised to realize they didn't feel wrong. "I'm not that altruistic. I'm not about saving the world. I'm just about saving myself and doing what makes me feel good."

"Are you?" There was a hint of amusement to his voice, and his hands continued to caress her back, sliding under her shirt to her bare skin. "Which is why you asked about my contract with Junior when you were on the verge of snapping?"

She frowned. "Did I? It's all kind of a blur."

"You're better than you want to be," he whispered into her mouth as his hand snuck around to the back of her neck, anchoring her right where she was. "I really want to kiss you right now."

"Really?" She looked thrilled. "Do it."

He thumbed her lip. "I can't be good for you."

"In the big picture, I totally agree." She fisted the front of his shirt and tugged him down to her. "But for now, I think you're exactly what I need." She lifted her head and kissed him, his mouth warm under hers. She sighed as he responded instantly, slipping past her tongue, tasting her teeth.

He lifted his head. "You're like . . ." Then he kissed her again, and didn't finish.

She pulled back, her heart racing. "I'm like what? Tell me."

His eyes were dark. "You're like sunshine. My own personal angel."

Her stomach fluttered at the growl in his chest; then he caught his leg around hers, flipped her under him, and let his hips drop on top of hers, while he propped his upper body up on his hands. "You're like a drug."

She swallowed at the intensity on his face, at the delicious feel of him pressed between her legs. "The kind that will save you or kill you?"

"Kill me, definitely." His face darkened. "And I don't care."

And then he kissed her like he really didn't.

Eighteen

Jed's phone rang as Paige's lips parted to welcome him, and he cursed and tossed it aside without answering it. He felt her body arch up under him and he groaned under a sudden blast of need. For her. Her spirit was hot, alive, and brimming with enthusiasm, and she was reaching for *him*. He, who was damned. So black that she couldn't hurt him with her touch, and she didn't care.

Her fingers gripped his hair so tightly he could feel the pain reverberating down his back, and he basked in it. Basked in the fact that she could want him so much that she'd hold on that desperately. He kissed her deeper, and she kissed him back just as hard, her breasts pressing up against his chest.

Her breasts . . . He slid his hand along her waist, along the silken softness of her skin, traced her ribs—

"Do it," she whispered. "Please, just do it."

Heat flared in him and he covered her breast with his hand, and she let out a small moan that went straight between his legs. "God, Jed, this feels so amazing." Her hands were suddenly at his back, sliding beneath his jeans, her fingers tentative and careful.

"You can't hurt me," he mumbled as he slid his lips

down the side of her neck, tasting her skin, sweet and salty and perfect. She tasted like . . . he grazed her collarbone with his teeth . . . sunshine. He didn't know how he knew what sunshine tasted like, but Paige was it.

She sighed and tilted her head back as her fingers dug into his butt. Her hips twisted under him as he trailed his lips lower, tugged down the collar of her shirt as something stirred deep inside him, something that was waking up that he'd kept hidden for years.

Something soft.

Something . . . "Paige," he whispered. "Oh, my sweet, sweet Paige . . ." He tugged her shirt up and then paused. Her skin was perfect. Exquisite. Her breasts . . . He bent down and gently brushed his lips over the tip as his phone rang again.

Paige sucked in her breath. "Oh, *wow*. Theresa wasn't exaggerating. This . . ."

Jed swallowed her words with a kiss, cupping her face with his hands, desperate to get closer, to drink in more of her, to feel her kissing him back with such reckless need.

She knew what he was, and *she wanted him anyway.*

And not because she wanted the thrill of getting it on with a bad guy, or because he was wrong for her, and was a danger to her . . . she wanted him because she couldn't help herself. . . .

Suddenly he couldn't get enough. He crushed his mouth over her breasts, yanked at her jeans, desperate to be inside her, to be closer, for one minute to just feel her complete and total acceptance of him, and to let the brightness of her soul consume him.

Her hands met his and she unbuttoned her jeans and

unzipped them, because his fingers had suddenly started trembling too hard to manage her pants. Her hands dropped from his and went to his hair again as he slipped his hand beneath the silken material, to the softness of her core.

Paige's hips jerked under his touch. "Holy hell," she whispered. "Jed—"

She was ready for him, hot and pulsing, and heat roared into his brain, slamming him so hard he could barely see. "You want me." He couldn't believe it. "But I'm *damned.*"

"Jed!" She yanked his hair so he had to look at her. Her cheeks were flushed and her mouth was parted, and she looked like she'd been thoroughly loved, and was still eager for more. "When are you going to get that I don't care about that? You aren't some flawed beast! You're the most amazing man I've ever met and I want you to make love to me until my body is nothing but a weak puddle of mush on the burned-out patch of grass we're lying on—"

He groaned, yanked his hand out of her pants, and rolled off her.

She propped herself up on her elbows, not even bothering to pull her shirt and bra back down over her breasts. "What? What did I say? What happened?"

He reached over and tugged her bra back down, tucking her safely out of sight. "I can't make love to you. It'll push you over the edge if our souls merge." He glanced around. "And we're in the middle of a burned-out baseball stadium. Anyone could come by and catch us." He felt like growling at the thought of anyone spying on Paige. "Your first time can't be here. It should be surrounded by candles, on a four-poster mahogany bed with white silk sheets, champagne and strawberries, with something romantic playing on the CD player, with a guy who you love who will love you forever . . . or some shit like that."

She stared at him, her mouth open.

"What?" He eased her shirt back down and pushed her hair out of her face, tucking it behind her ear.

"You're a romantic. I can't believe it!"

He scowled as he rubbed dirt off her cheek. "Screw that. I'm damned."

"A damned romantic."

He retrieved his phone, stood up, and held out his hand to her. "Come on. We need to get out of here before we're arrested for destroying the outfield. We don't have time to be arrested."

She grabbed his hand and let him pull her up, intentionally rubbing her body against his as she rose.

He scowled and pushed her back. "Don't push it. I'm not made of stone."

She grinned. "No, you're hard muscles and sexuality."

He turned and started walking toward the dugout as his phone rang again. He scowled and answered it. "I was in the middle of seducing her and you ruined the moment by calling. Stop calling and I'll get it done sooner."

"Damn. Sorry. I'm just so excited. I know she's my key to taking over hell," Junior bubbled. "I'll stop calling, I promise."

Jed snapped his phone shut and shoved it in his pocket. "Ten to one he calls back within five minutes."

"Why do you keep answering?" She caught up to him

and settled in next to him, grabbing his hand and entwining her fingers with his, and he couldn't bring himself to push her away.

"Because if I don't, I'm afraid he'll get pissed off and take it out on Rafi. It's not worth the risk." They reached the door to the dugout, and it was locked. He cursed, then dissolved into shadow and slipped under the door. He felt the darkness consume him as soon as he took the shadow form, and he instinctively checked the hall for a victim. For someone to take.

He forced himself to reform before finding release, and dropped his head against the door as Paige knocked on it, reminding her not to forget about him.

"Hang on," he muttered. "I still want to kill you. Need a sec."

He closed his eyes and waited for the call of evil to subside. After a minute, he stood back up and opened the door from the inside. Paige was sitting on the floor, leaning against the wall with her eyes closed.

He frowned. "You okay?"

She opened them. "I'm worried about the fact Jerome hasn't called us back yet. He should be all over stopping the vortex of hell thing, right?"

"Yeah, well, it's the Council. They aren't always predictable. Jerome probably got the message, and now his team's probably trying to figure out a way to use the vortex as a way to increase their power." He flicked his hand. "Let's get out of here. The Yankees are out of town, but I can't imagine this place is deserted."

She didn't move, staring out over the field. "If we broke the contract, and Rafi was free, and you were no longer bound to Satan Jr., what would you do with your life?"

He grabbed her wrist and tugged her to her feet, set his hands on her shoulders, and began propelling her toward the door. "I'd never go shadow warrior again."

She glanced back over her shoulder. "But that's your destiny. You'd walk away from it?"

"Yep."

"But won't that leave you feeling empty and lost?"

He shrugged as they came up a ramp to a main hallway. "I'd find a way to live with it, I'm sure." He pointed. "Exit sign. Let's go."

There was a sudden shout and they both looked back to see a security guard standing at the end of the hallway.

"Damn. I wish I could just fireball him."

He raised his brows. "And I don't believe you really want to kill him."

"Well, if it weren't for my wraith I would—"

"Really? Or is it all talk because you're trying to prove you're something that you think you have to be?" He touched her face. "It's okay to be who you are."

The guard started running toward them, his feet pounding on the cement as he spoke into his radio, giving their location. Jed glanced at him, then back at Paige. "Run?"

"Fine. Let's go." She pushed past Jed and started sprinting toward the exit, him close on her heels.

"Just so you know . . . ," she huffed as she ran, "we can no longer think . . . about dating . . . because . . . I can't . . . be with . . . a man . . . who tries to keep . . . me . . . from . . . my destiny . . . as a badass Rivka. . . . Hell, I'm . . . out of . . . shape. . . ."

"Your destiny is to harvest the souls of people who

deserve hell," he shot back as he jogged next to her, not even remotely out of breath. They ran through a doorway, then Jed paused to shut the door and throw the bolt. He wedged a row of metal footlockers across the door and then turned to face her. "Not slaughter innocents."

"Well . . . yeah . . . that's my destiny . . ." She turned and started walking down the hall, confident that no human would be able to open the door with the lockers wedged across it. "But I want to expand and kill innocents."

"Bullshit." They reached a metal fire door and stopped. It was locked and solid steel.

"I'm a Rivka. If I'm not bad, then what am I? Nothing. I'm like a gateless shadow warrior, but worse, because I walked away on my own. It's who I am, Jed. Without it . . . I don't have meaning." She flared up a fireball and threw it into the metal door, then rolled her eyes when it ricocheted back at her and slammed her in the chest. "Yeah, fire door. Duh."

They heard shouts and then pounding against the door they'd locked behind them as the guards failed miserably at getting through it.

Jed grabbed her and slammed her up against the fire door, pressing her shoulders against the cold metal. "Who the hell cares if you don't follow the Rivka path? It doesn't define you. You don't need to slaughter innocents to have meaning in your life. You've got friends, you care about people. Goodness oozes out of every pore of your body and it's so appealing I can barely keep myself from throwing you down right here and losing myself in all that you are."

She closed her eyes and let her head drop back against the metal with a clunk. "I'm so confused."

He softened his grip on her shoulders. "Don't be confused. Just listen to who you are."

She opened her eyes to look at Jed. "But how do you know who you really are? How am I supposed to know if what I think I am or supposed to be isn't me at all?"

He brushed the back of his hand against her cheek. "It's in you. Just listen."

"I'm trying. It's a little crazy in there right now."

There was a sudden shout of triumph and they both tensed as the sound of running feet echoed through the halls. Jed cursed and glanced around to find another way out, but before they could move, five security guards rounded the corner, guns out.

"Freeze!"

"Put your hands up," another one ordered.

Paige bit her lip, her gaze flicking to the security guards as they eased closer, yelling orders. "If they grab me . . ."

"I'm on it." Five deaths on her soul would do her in. Unacceptable.

He whirled around and slammed into the front guy.

Thirty seconds later, there were five bodies on the floor, and none of them were his. "Let's go."

Paige stared at him, her cheeks flushed with excitement. "That was amazing. Why were we running if you're that tough?"

He started walking back down the hall. "I'm in human form."

"Ah." Paige jumped over a couple of the bodies and

trotted next to him. "Have you ever killed in human form?"

"No."

"Have you ever hurt anyone in human form before this?"

"No."

"How did it feel?"

"Sucked."

"But you did it anyway? For me?"

He said nothing.

She smiled and tucked her arm though his. "Thanks."

Nineteen

By the time they got back from Yankee Stadium and dodged the Men in White posse which had caught sight of them outside Jed's apartment, it was time to meet Dani and Theresa at Saving Grace to recruit angelic help. Jerome hadn't called back yet, and there was no word from Zeke on the scientist. The deadline for Bandit's vortex was fast approaching, plus Satan Jr. had called Jed six more times, each time promising it was his last. Paige had finally answered it the last time, and Junior had hung up without saying anything, like a little boy caught with his pants down.

He was becoming a joke between them, but his constant calls were an ugly reminder that time was running out for both of them, and so were options.

When Paige finally walked into the alley behind Saving Grace and saw Dani and Theresa, her eyes filled up and she almost threw herself at them. "You came! I was so worried you'd be too afraid of me to show up."

"No way," Dani said. "We're here for you."

"Amen to that, sister." Theresa put her arm over Dani's shoulder and beamed at Paige. "This is going to go great, I promise."

Dani smiled with genuine warmth, though there was still a bit of wariness in her gaze. "I took care of Bandit. He cleaned up well. He's hilarious."

Paige grinned. "Isn't he? Did you give him a last hurrah?"

"I was tempted after I got him cleaned up."

"You were? Seriously? That's great." Maybe he'd really be presentable enough to convince Jerome of the truth of his words. If Jerome ever called back.

Theresa's grin faded and she gave Paige an appraising look. "How are you doing, sweetie?"

"Great. Fine." *God.* She felt such an aching sense of loss that she couldn't hug her friends. Her calf was a steady pulse, but her inner wraith was quiet, digesting its meal of Yankee Stadium outfield grass. "Did Zeke find the scientist?"

Theresa shook her head. "No. Sorry. He's still searching, but I think you stumped him."

Paige bit her lip against the surge of panic. Without the scientist, her only chance was the angel. "So, I guess I have to do this, huh?" Jed stiffened against her, and she peeked up at him.

He gave her a grouchy look as Theresa handed Paige a Neiman Marcus bag. "It'll be fine, Paige. Here. Put this on."

Paige reluctantly released Jed to open it. She held up a lacy white dress that was both demure and sensual. "This will attract an angel? I was thinking of a nun's outfit."

"Men are men. You look like a woman, and they'll come crawling."

Jed took the dress from her and held it up. He scowled, then handed it back to her without another word.

"Well?" Theresa set her hands on her hips and looked at Jed. "You'd do her in that dress, wouldn't you?"

"I'd do her in a nun's outfit." His face was dark, his voice darker, edged with a sensuality that made her insides curl.

Paige suddenly felt better.

"Oh." Theresa's eyes widened. "*Oh.* So *that's* how it is."

"It isn't any way," Jed growled.

But Dani grinned. "Who exactly *are* you?"

He fisted his hands. "Bodyguard."

"Jed Buchanan. He's protecting me from myself," Paige added. "What about my feet?"

Theresa held up a pair of white satin stilettos, and Paige frowned. "How am I supposed to fight in those?"

"You're here to seduce, not fight," Dani pointed out.

Theresa spun one of them around in her hand and pressed the tip of the heel into Paige's chest. "See? Lethal weapons."

"Oh, I like those." Paige took it and flicked her finger over the tip. "Is that a metal stud in the end?"

"Specially made in case you run into trouble. Nice, huh?"

"Yeah. Really nice."

"Get dressed." Theresa clapped her hands. "I have a table reserved starting at a quarter after, right down in front next to the dance floor. Puts you in prime viewing position."

"Right." Paige glanced around for a place to change, realized that they were in an alley, and short of climbing into a Dumpster, there was nowhere to go. She sighed and yanked her shirt over her head, smiling to herself at the grunt from Jed as she exposed her bra.

"I'll watch to make sure no one's coming." Dani jogged over to the end of the alley and peered around the corner as Paige started to slide the dress over her head.

"You *cannot* wear that black bra with that dress! Are you crazy?" Theresa grabbed the dress back and held out a sheer lace bra. "Put it on."

She felt her cheeks flush as she took it, and she couldn't help but glance at Jed. He was staring at the new bra with such heat that her legs almost got wobbly. "This isn't my style," she said. "I'm not into the nipple-viewing thing."

His gaze jerked to her face, and then he turned away, giving her privacy.

What? No sneak peeks?

Damn.

"Do it anyway," Theresa ordered. "You can't wear that nun bra you have on."

"It's not a nun bra," Jed said. "I like it just fine."

She grinned at Theresa. "*He* likes it."

"But you're not trying to seduce *him* . . . or are you?"

"Um . . . I guess not." She was totally unable to keep the disappointment out of her voice, and she saw Theresa eye Jed with renewed interest as he scowled at the bra.

Then he turned away again.

"Fine. I'll change bras." She yanked her existing bra off and traded it for the new one, and Jed didn't even try to turn around. Too much the gentleman. Sigh. Theresa took one look at her old bra, then tossed it in the Dumpster. "For someone descended from Satan, you have a serious lack of good lingerie. If you survive this whole thing, I'm so going to take you shopping."

"I *will* survive."

"Sure. Of course. I know."

She glanced at Theresa as she tugged her jeans down over her hips.

"Good God, Paige! No wonder you're still a virgin. Haven't you heard of granny panties?"

Jed coughed.

"I know what they are, and these aren't granny panties." She eyed the white silken thong dangling from Theresa's hand. How uncomfortable did that look? "I really don't think I need that to be sexy."

"Of course you do."

"Jed? Opinion, please."

He cautiously turned to look at her, his gaze dropping instantly to her body, and she belatedly remembered that she was wearing only the see-through bra and her own silk bikini underwear, and her socks. His face darkened and she held up the thong. "Do I need this to be sexy?"

"Hell, no." His gaze flickered over her again. "I think you should wear overalls and a heavy sweatshirt."

She grinned. "Because I'm so naturally sexy?"

"No. Because he's jealous and he doesn't want anyone else touching you."

Jed snapped a sharp gaze at Theresa. "She's too good for the shit you're trying to dress her in. She doesn't need it. She's perfect the way she is. Any angel would see it."

Paige grinned and twirled the thong around on her finger, just to tease him a little bit.

Jed glared at Paige. "Do what you want." He turned his back on them for a third time, watching the alley, his arms folded across his broad chest.

Paige decided to go with the thong. Just for fun. "He's got some issues going on," she whispered to Theresa as she pulled the dress over her head. "He's a little stressed."

Theresa arched her brows. "Yeah, I'm sure that's all it is. He's stressed."

Jed swung back as the dress slipped over Paige's hips. She couldn't believe how the cool silk felt sliding over her hips. It was so soft, like a caress. His eyes darkened as his gaze swept over her, and she felt heat pool in her belly.

Theresa cleared her throat, and Paige immediately felt her cheeks turn red. She glanced at Theresa and tried to distract her before she could make any more suggestive comments that completely embarrassed Paige. "You know any loophole experts?" She briefly explained Jed's issue about needing a way to void his contract with Junior.

"Sure," Theresa said. "My old roomie, Justine Bennett. As Guardian of the Goblet of Eternal Youth, she had to do some major loophole jumping. And her husband's hot brother is great at the detail stuff too. He's a brilliant mathematician, great at decoding. You have a copy of the contract, Jed?"

He jerked his gaze off Paige with a visible effort that made Paige smile. "Yes, I do."

Paige gave him her back. "Will you do up the buttons?"

Theresa winked at her and ambled off to the end of the alley to stand with Dani.

He grunted, and started to work on the several dozen pearl buttons that went from the cleft of her bottom to her shoulder blades. His fingers brushed the bare skin of her lower back. And again. "You trust these people?"

"I trust Theresa. She's extremely loyal."

"So are you." He lifted the hair off her back and tucked it in front of her shoulder, his fingers slow to release it.

"Of course I am. Friends are what matter in life." She sighed as he went back to buttoning. "I need the people I care about." *I need you.* She blinked. Had she said that out loud? She didn't think so.

He brushed his fingers over her upper back. "You're set."

She took a deep breath and turned to face him. "What do you think?"

He studied her. "I don't like what you're doing." He reached out and grabbed her wrist, gently tugging her until she was against him. He hooked his hands loosely around her waist. "There has to be another way, other than having sex with an angel."

She rested her cheek against his chest, feeling his heart beating steadily. "My leg hurts all the time now, and I can even feel pain in my hip. It's building, and I'm constantly afraid it's going to explode and I'm not going to get another chance. It's going to take an angel to fix this, and one of them is going to have to willingly break the rules to do it. I'm a little short on angel friends right now."

He cursed softly and pressed his face to her hair.

After a moment, he dropped his hands and stepped back. "Let's go."

"Right." She tucked her cell phone in the bodice of the dress, then lifted her chin and clenched her fists. "It's about time I had sex anyway. I'm too old to be a virgin."

He held out her shoes, a grim look on his face. "Spoken like a true descendant of Satan."

Jed sat back in his seat, watching Paige search the club. The place was packed, and it seemed to be like any other meat market. Dark lighting, pulsing music, men and women prowling around, getting it on on the dance floor, throwing back the drinks and trading suggestive looks.

Except . . . there was lightness in the air. A place like

this usually felt dark, and his shadow warrior usually reacted. But here . . . his other self was quiet. If he went shadow warrior here . . . would it still be the same? Or would all the angels soothe his savage beast?

He was almost tempted to try. To find out if it was possible to embrace that side of himself without becoming murderous.

But tonight was about Paige. Not about him.

He turned his attention to the table. Paige was between him and Theresa, with Dani on the other side. Dani had clearly not wanted to get too close to Paige, and he'd seen the hurt on Paige's face, and it had pissed him off. The three women were checking out the angels and debating about which one Paige should approach.

Theresa had already warned off three who'd approached the table, not wanting Paige to waste time with one she couldn't manipulate.

"They don't look like angels," Theresa said. "They look normal."

"They have halos."

He looked at Paige in surprise. "You can see their halos? Really?"

She nodded, and took another handful of peanuts. "It's this sort of yellowish white glow that looks like it's coming out of their ears."

"Ears?" He squinted at a couple dancing in front of him. Ears looked normal to him.

"Ears. Maybe it's the 'hear no evil' thing."

Jed raised his hand to catch the attention of the dancing couple, then shouted, "What time does this place close?"

"When the last person leaves," the girl yelled back.

Jed gave her a thumbs-up then returned to the table. "They heard me, so they can hear evil. Guess again."

Paige giggled and whacked him on the arm, but Theresa gave him a thoughtful look. "You're evil?"

"Damned. Why do you think she can touch me?"

"Damned? Really?" She scooted her chair closer. "How's that work?"

"Long story."

"So, you hoping to ride Paige's coattails to purity so you can go to heaven?"

He narrowed his eyes. "No. I'm not worried about my soul. It's pretty much a done deal."

"He made a deal with Satan Jr.," Paige added.

"Junior?" Dani suddenly leaned forward. "You know him? I used to date him. How's he doing?"

"Dani! How can you possibly care how he is?" Theresa smacked her in the temple. "He trapped you in a death blister! Have you no pride?"

Dani ignored the dragon. "Jed? How is he?"

Jed eyed the girl. "He's an ass."

"But he's doing okay? Not lonely? Is he seeing anyone?"

"Excuse me." Theresa stood up, walked around the table, and grabbed Dani by the hair. "I have to go plunge her head into a toilet as a gentle reminder that there are bad boys, and then there are Bad Boys. My God, girlfriend, what is your *problem*? I know Jerome did a number on you, but that's no excuse for prostituting yourself to that sick bastard—"

Her voice faded as she dragged Dani through the crowd, Theresa shoving right through anyone who was in her way.

Paige stood up. "I'll go help beat some sense into her—"

Jed grabbed her wrist. "How's your leg feel?"

She hesitated, then cursed and sat back down. "The same."

"You need to learn how to meditate."

"I need to get laid by an angel." She propped her chin up on her hands and surveyed the room. "So, who's your pick for tonight?"

He felt his shadow warrior stir. "You're asking me?"

"Yeah. You're a guy. You know what it looks like when guys are checking out the goods. Who looks the most in need of me?"

He scowled, well aware that he hadn't been able to scare off every guy who'd looked at her. He'd tried to make eye contact with each one of the bastards, but some of them had been so enraptured by Paige that they hadn't noticed his hostile glare. Yeah, it wasn't helping Paige's goal, but he hadn't been able to help himself. "No one."

She rolled her eyes and scanned the bar, then broke into a smile. "Him."

Jed followed her gaze, and saw a well-muscled, attractive man in an expensive suit, holding a martini. He was giving Paige an inspection that made Jed want to drill right into the guy's heart. "He's too good looking," he snarled, letting his shadow warrior into his eyes long enough for the guy to pale and turn his back on Paige.

Paige shot him a hopeful look. "Jealous? You should know, you're way better looking than any guy here."

Jed felt some of the ice around his heart soften. "The problem with that guy is that he can get any chick he wants. It won't be worth it for him to break the rules for you, since you'll be easily replaceable by someone who doesn't come with strings."

"Oooh . . . good point." She pursed her lips and scanned again, then nodded. "The guy at the other end of the bar."

The guy in question was skinny, short, had bad skin, and looked totally uncomfortable with the bar scene. Jed's fists clenched, as he acknowledged that that guy was the perfect choice. Could he really stand back while she did this? Yes. He had to. They had a deal. He gritted his teeth, and forced his voice to be calm. "He'd work."

She touched his shoulder. "Just so you know, if I had the choice . . . I'd pick you all day long."

He couldn't keep himself from looking at her, from searching her face to see if she was telling the truth. When she met his gaze with a steady look, with her chin jutted out, he knew she was being completely honest.

"Hell."

She smiled, then stood up, and smoothed out her dress. "Wish me luck."

Jed had to avert his gaze from her, or he'd be down on his knees, begging her not to go.

Begging.

Him?

Sure as hell, yeah.

He ground his teeth. "If you run into trouble, just yell. I'll be there."

"I know you will. Thanks."

"Good luck," he managed.

He felt her gaze on him, then saw her walk away out of the corner of his eye. When her back was to him, he allowed himself to study her openly. Watched the sway of her hips as she crossed the floor, saw her fiddle with the dress, scratch her earlobe, then come to a complete stop several feet away from her quarry, shifting her weight restlessly.

Hell, she was nervous. He cursed and stood up to go after her.

Then she lifted her chin and squared her shoulders, and started moving forward again.

Jed hesitated as she walked up to the guy and said something. The guy looked at her, his eyes widened in shock, and then he gave her an awkward smile and started talking.

Darkness swirled around Jed, and he slammed his ass back into the chair.

Twenty

Three virgin daiquiris and two hours later, Paige was exhausted. It had taken her almost an hour to get Ralph Mullins, as her man was named, relaxed enough to actually talk to her without stuttering and another hour to get him out on the dance floor.

Jed's dark gaze had been tracking her the whole time, and he was totally stressing her out. Dani had been talking to Jed most of the time, no doubt trying to get the goods on Satan Jr., and Theresa had been sending Paige obscene gestures for the last twenty minutes, until Jed had grabbed her arm and apparently ordered her to leave. After a hostile argument in which Jed had actually begun to go into shadow form, the women had left, and Jed was her only backup.

He was enough.

"Paige? Did you hear me?"

She looked back at Ralph, who was dancing too close for her comfort. "I'm sorry. What were you saying?"

"I . . . um . . . was wondering if you had plans later tonight. I mean, if you wanted, we could, um, you know, like I don't live too far and my cleaning people came today, so it's not dusty or anything."

She smiled. "You know, I would love to, but—" She took a deep breath. "I have a problem."

He cocked a brow. "What problem?"

"People who touch me die."

He stared at her. "What?"

"Anyone good dies. I'm . . . like . . . poison. Satan's fault."

"Satan? You're contaminated by Satan?" He looked interested now. "How'd that happen?"

"You believe me?"

"Well, sure. It explains your black aura."

She felt her heart sag. "My aura's black?"

"Like coal."

"And you still wanted me?"

He shrugged. "You're the only good-looking girl that's looked my way in two hundred years. I was willing to overlook that small flaw."

"Well . . ." She drew her shoulders back. "I'd love to take this thing with us all the way, but I can't. You might die."

"Might?" He looked thoughtful.

"Well, my friend says that an angel who was truly good and truly pure would be able to cleanse me and wouldn't get blown up by me. . . ."

"I'm an all-star," Ralph announced. "Top of the list." He eyed her. "You'd really sleep with me if I could make it safe?"

She took a deep breath, trying to calm her frantically racing heart. "I . . . would." She lifted her chin and forced herself to say the words, "Yes, Ralph, I would have sex with you if you'd save my soul."

Ralph broke into a big grin. "Well, then, let's go."

"Go where?"

"Clean you up." He held out his hand, then dropped it. "Never mind. Follow me."

Fantastic! Was this really going to work? Yeah, she was feeling slightly ill at the thought of having sex with Ralph, but if he could save her . . . wow! She gave Jed a thumbs-up as she weaved through the crowd after Sam. Who knew men could get so desperate for sex?

Then again, she was related to Satan. Need she look further to see the power of sex?

Jed shoved his chair back and started walking after them.

And she suddenly felt even better. Yeah, she wasn't having sex with *Jed,* but if he was around, maybe she could pretend it was him and then she'd be able to make herself do it. Not that she had a problem with sex. It just was that she'd always had a fantasy about who her first time would be with, and this guy wasn't it. Jed was, in all ways. And now that he was in her life, now that she'd kissed him, laughed with him . . . she bit her lip and ordered herself to stop thinking about Jed.

She had a job to do. Just a job. Nothing else. *Get over yourself, Paige.* It's all for a worthy cause: her own humanity.

"Through here." Sam held open a wooden door at the back of the club.

She slipped inside and he let the door shut behind him. It clicked, and she wondered briefly if it was locked.

Not that it mattered.

Jed would have no problem with it.

Sam led her through another door, then down a hall, then up a flight of stairs, and then punched in a seventeen-digit code that Paige lost track of after about eleven digits. Then a heavy steel door swung open, and she stepped through the doorway.

The door slammed shut, and she had no doubt she was locked in, and her heart began to beat a little bit faster. She slid her hand behind her back and flared up a fireball. A white one, that wouldn't be deadly, but would let her get away if she needed to. Would her transport to hell even work in here? She had a bad feeling it wouldn't.

Sam pulled open another door and she followed him inside.

There was nothing in the room but a king-sized bed, and a mirror on the ceiling.

Sam turned toward her. "Clothes off."

She immediately tensed. "You haven't saved me yet."

"I want to see what I'm getting."

"What? No way." She folded her arms over her chest, starting to panic at the thought of actually getting naked in front of him. "You can see enough. Save me first." *I can't go through with this. I can't sleep with him.*

"Show me first." He walked up to her and leaned his face toward hers.

She instinctively pulled back out of his reach. "I don't want to kill you." *Or have sex with you.* She had to, though. To save herself. *Come on, Paige. Be tough!*

"You won't kill me. You can't. I'm angel. Nothing can hurt me."

"I already killed one."

"One what?"

"An angel. I already killed one."

Ralph grinned and stepped back. "And that's all she wrote."

"Wrote? Who wrote what?"

The ceiling mirror slid back to reveal an opening, and a man leaned down into the room.

He was wearing all white. *One of heaven's posse members.* The leader, maybe?

"Paige Darlington, your confession was recorded, digitized, and put on the Internet. My name is Oscar Montefriece. You killed my angel. Prepare to die."

She backed up toward the door, suddenly ice cold. "But—"

Ralph blew her a kiss, hopped up on the bed. "It didn't occur to you that an Angel Alert might have been issued? Everyone in that bar has been watching you all night to see who you decided to go after. Nice try, Paige, but your playtime is over." Then he grabbed the edge of the ceiling opening and swung up through it, and disappeared.

Oscar Montefriece studied her, his hair hanging off his head and pointing toward the floor from his upside-down position. "You have interesting aura. It's like you're half-angel and half-demon. It would be much more interesting to study you than kill you. Too bad for me, right?"

"I'm not in the mood to die, thanks so much for the offer." She flung her fireball at him, clenching her jaw against the sudden twitch of pain in her hip.

Oscar didn't even flinch as it bounced off his forehead. "You can't kill an angel that way. You really think we'd be that vulnerable?" He cocked his head. "How exactly *did* you kill my angel? We all want to know."

She recalled Jerome's warning that heaven's enforcers would kill her immediately if they thought she was Satan's new deadly weapon. "It was a mistake. An accident.

A coming together of over a million cosmic forces that can never be repeated."

"Tell me now and maybe we'll torture you less."

Torture? She didn't like torture. She swallowed hard. "I said it was a mistake. Can't I apologize and do community service work or something? Take serial killers on tours of hell to get them to stop slashing the throats of innocents?"

"What kind of example would we set if we let an angel murderer negotiate herself out of torture and death? Everyone would try to kill angels. It would only be a matter of time until some well-funded lab figured out how to poison them, and then there'd be a mass extermination of angels, and then where would we be?"

"In an angel drought?"

"Precisely. Do you have any idea what that would do to the balance of power in the Otherworld?"

"Um . . . no."

"A world consumed by evil. We can't allow that, you see? So, you need to die a horrible death, plus everyone you care about as well, just to make our point to anyone else thinking of killing an angel."

Oh, God. *Not my friends.* "I'm a Rivka," she said with a dismissive shrug. "I care about no one."

"No? Sadly for you, we have a fantastic information retrieval system in heaven. We think you'd care very much if we killed a certain dragon, her husband, a woman named Dani Rawlings, a former Rivka named Becca Gibbs, and her fiancé."

Paige felt her legs begin to shake. "You could never get them. They're too tough for you."

"Are they? Too tough for an army of angels who can't

be hurt by anything? Who are on a mission to save the world for good? That is a noble mission. The power will be with us. Your friends will have no chance." He snapped his fingers. "Oh, I forgot. We much appreciated your phone call about Rafi Buchanan's plight."

Paige stiffened. *Crud!* It was as she'd voiced to Jed. They'd taken her message about Rafi and the vortex Bandit had predicted, and they'd made their own plans. "What did you do to him?"

Oscar smiled. "We'd forgotten about him, being stashed out of sight and all, but thanks to your hints about how he was ready to be a shadow warrior, we remembered and we took some action. Now we have a fantastic new weapon, and we owe it to you. Just for that, we won't torture you. You get quick death instead. Because we're from heaven, and we're always fair."

Paige frowned. "What are you talking about? Rafi's your new weapon? What kind of weapon?"

Oscar waggled his finger. "You're his first assignment. Make it easy on him, if you will? We have high hopes for his future."

Then he grabbed the edge of the ceiling and yanked himself back out of sight. Paige sprinted after him and leapt up, stretching for the opening in the ceiling. The mirror zipped back into place a split second before she reached it. She slammed a fireball into it, flames exploded all over her, and the mirror stayed intact.

She cursed and whipped out her cell phone and tried to call Theresa.

No signal.

Tried to fade to hell.

Nothing.

"Don't panic, Paige. You can get out of here." She whirled around and fireballed the door, then scowled when it came ricocheting back at her. Ceiling, walls, doors . . . all steel with a hint of Otherworld karma.

Then she saw a flash of gray smoke trickle out from under the door, and elation swept through her. "Jed!"

She jumped back to clear space for him to form. "Thank God you're—"

She gasped as the smoky cloud plunged straight into her heart and clamped down. She clutched her chest and dropped to her knees, doubling over at the pain, as she felt her body seize up.

I'm going to die.

She felt a lurch in her heart, and she knew then that it wasn't Jed who held her life.

It was Rafi.

Heaven's new weapon of death.

And he was here to kill her.

Twenty-one

R aphael Buchanan, you must cease and desist immediately!"

Paige jerked her head up as the steel door exploded off the hinges in an explosion of gold bubbles, and Satan leapt through, his eyes blazing with blue fire. "You will not kill her before she has turned!"

She gasped as Rafi's grip tightened around her heart and her arms began to go numb.

"I command you to stop!" Satan Jr. appeared in the doorway right behind Satan. "She's mine! I recall you to my torture chamber immediately!"

The pressure around her heart increased, and the room blurred.

"Idiot!" Satan shouted. "You have no power to recall him unless his brother breaches the contract. Do you have no idea how to write contracts? You are useless." He dropped to his knees, grabbing Paige's face between his hands. "Find your wraith, former apprentice Rivka. Drive him out! Destroy him! He can be killed by your touch!"

Paige closed her eyes and tried to summon up her darkness, but . . . couldn't think . . . had . . . no . . . will. . . .

"The shadow warrior is pure evil! She can't hurt him in

that form," Junior shrieked. "Dammit to hell! This can't be happening! I want her!"

She felt a sudden prickling over her skin, and recognized it instantly. *Jed. Must. Let. Him. In.* She tried to focus on dropping her shields the way she'd done in the church to let him in, but her mind kept blanking out.

The prickling increased until it felt like thousands of daggers pressing against her skin. She scrunched her eyes against the pain and threw all the last remnants of energy into her shields and suddenly they were down.

Jed slammed into her so hard that her body jerked, and she felt like her skin was going to explode.

"Former Rivka apprentice?" Satan slapped her cheeks. "I will be extremely disappointed if you allow yourself to die. Do you wish to disappoint me? I torture most brutally when I am disappointed."

She felt a rumble in her chest, and suddenly the pressure around her heart eased, and she gasped in a breath as Jed freed her heart from Rafi's grasp.

"Excellent!"

Then pain exploded in her heart again. She couldn't breathe. Couldn't. Inhale.

"Paige!" Satan Jr. dropped next to her. "You're too evil to go this way. Don't die!"

Her heart trembled, and then the pressure eased just enough for her to suck in another gasp of air. Vibrations rocked her chest, and she could feel her heart shuddering, fighting to stay alive, desperately trying to fend off death, while the brothers battled inside her body.

Then there was warmth around her heart, and the muscle burst to light. *Jed.*

There was a shudder in her body, and then Rafi was gone.

She opened her eyes, but didn't see a gray cloud. Too small to be seen?

But she knew he'd fled her body.

She sighed and collapsed back in Satan's lap as she felt Jed work on her heart, breathing strength and life back into it . . . but as he worked, she felt her dark side begin to awaken, creeping up her leg, spreading through her body, gravitating toward Jed's darkness. Seeking to feed on him.

Get out now.

And then he was gone.

She opened her eyes, but she couldn't see him, and she knew he'd gone after his brother.

"She is alive!" Satan crowed and helped her sit up. "Most excellent work, former Rivka apprentice."

She groaned and put her head between her knees, trying to keep from passing out. "I'm way too young for a heart attack."

Satan Jr. was sitting back on his heels, frowning. "How'd you fend off the shadow warrior? I've never seen anyone do that."

"Magic." She clenched her fists as her inner wraith continued to rise, fed by the battle in her own body.

Satan cursed and quickly scrambled to his feet. "Oh, no. You do not go wraith around me. I leave, you turn, all is good. Fruit of my loins, you must leave as well. You cannot be around her either when she turns. Is generous of me to offer advice to keep you alive, no?"

Junior narrowed his eyes. "I'm not letting her change.

She's not loyal enough yet to me." He grabbed her arms. "Fight it."

"Hah." Satan stood up. "You cannot prevail, fruit of my loins. The wraith will not be yours. You cannot control it. It will be mine."

"I'm a *her,* not an it," she muttered. "And I'm right here."

"Shut up," Junior ordered her. "Concentrate on fighting it." He peered down at her. "Or do you love Jed yet? Because if you do, then give me the word and I'll take off so you can change."

Shut up? Paige dragged her eyes up to his face. "Go to hell."

His eyes flashed. "I'll go to hell when I'm powerful enough to claim it. I need you, so you won't change yet. You can't change if you're unconscious, so—" Something hard cracked her on the back of her head, and the room went black.

Jed streamed down the hall faster than he'd ever gone, following the essence Rafi was leaving behind. What the hell was going on? Why was Rafi in the mortal world? How had he gotten out? And what the hell was he doing murdering Paige?

He slipped under the door and into the bar . . . and then lost the trail.

He reformed instantly, and sprinted into the crowd. "Rafi!"

Bolted past the dancers and out into the street.

It was starting to rain, and the streets were shiny, reflecting the fluorescent lights from the strip of bars.

But no Rafi.

Jed cursed and opened his senses, reaching out for his brother.

But Rafi had obviously gone back to human form, because Jed couldn't track him. "Rafi!"

Nothing.

His brother was gone.

Or what was left of his brother.

Rafi would never do what he'd just done to Paige.

What the hell had happened to him?

What had Junior done?

Junior. Satan. With Paige. Who was going wraith.

His gut lurched, and he whirled around and tore back into the building.

Jed burst through the broken door, ready for battle.

But all was still.

Paige was moaning softly, holding her head, curled in a ball on the burned-out carpet. Smoke was rising from the now-blackened walls, the mattress was smoldering, and the mirror had melted right down onto the bed, no doubt from a friendly father-son disagreement.

But Satan and Junior were gone.

He kneeled beside her, and cradled her face in his hands. "Paige? Are you still with me?"

"I feel like hell."

Relief shot through him, and he had to sit down before his legs gave out. "No wraith yet?"

"No wraith ever. I hate it. I refuse to succumb." She allowed him to pull her onto his lap, resting her head on his thigh. "I have to admit, though, I owe Junior. If he hadn't knocked me out, I have a feeling I'd be screaming around here killing everything in sight."

Jed tensed, and suddenly shadows began to swim at the edges of his vision. *"Junior hit you?"*

"Knocked me right out." She twisted so she could look at him. "Jed! You're getting transparent. Stop it! I need you right now."

His form became solid again and he looked down at her, but his eyes were solid black. No white at all. "I'll kill him."

"Would you stop with the macho hero crap? You promised you'd knock me out if I couldn't stop the change. Why is Junior any different?"

Jed's fingers began to trace her head, and she knew he was looking for damage. "Because he didn't care if he hurt you."

"And you do?" She winced when he brushed across the back of her head.

Jed cursed. "What'd he hit you with? A baseball bat?" He sat her up and parted her hair, peering at her head. "You're *bleeding*." His voice was throaty and low, vibrating with low energy she hadn't felt before.

She sat up, gripping his arm hard to keep from tipping over from dizziness, and she looked at him. His eyes were still black, and edges of his head were getting a little fuzzy. She blinked hard several times to try to get rid of the sensation of the room spinning. "If you go shadow right now, you'll call my wraith out. I don't have the strength to stop it, and my head hurts like a mother and I really don't want to be knocked out again."

He continued to fade, and she grabbed his face. "What's wrong with you? You have total control over your inner demon. Why can't you stop it now?"

"Paige," he growled. *"He hurt you."*

Her jaw dropped open. "Omigod. You've lost your leg-endary control of your inner demon because *he hurt me*?" She threw her arms around him and slammed her mouth onto his, kissing him with delight. His lips were cold, his breath tasted like smoke, and his body was rigid.

And she didn't care! "That is the *sweetest* thing anyone has ever done for me! I had no idea you really cared about me like that!" She pressed his hand to her heart. "That gets me right here, Jed. Truly. I'll carry this moment with me forever, or at least for the next couple hours until I turn wraith and lose my mind."

She threw her leg across his lap, and pressed her hands into the front of his shoulders, pinning him to the floor. "Jed Buchanan, you are my hero." His eyes were black, but she was too excited and overwhelmed to care. She simply dropped to his chest and plastered her mouth to his, swirled her tongue over his, dug her fingers into his hair. Kissed him with every fiber of her being, completely unable to control her delight and her happiness . . .

And suddenly he was back. His mouth turned to fire, he tasted of mint, and he smelled like cinnamon and some-thing woodsy and dark. And he was kissing her like he was trying to yank her soul right out of her mouth.

Hooray!

His hands shot to her back and he ripped her dress open, dozens of pearl buttons flying, and then she was on her back, and he was kissing her ribs and her belly button and her collarbone. And then her bra was off and he was kiss-ing her left breast and then her right and then . . . "Slow down," she gasped. "I want to savor this."

He stopped kissing her and lifted his head to look at

her. His eyes were violent and intense, and all Jed. "We can't—"

She grabbed his hair. "We can. Just don't merge your aura with mine."

He cursed. "Paige, there's no way I can make love to you and not merge. It's impossible."

"I don't think I would have been able to sleep with the angel," she whispered.

He said nothing, but he didn't take his eyes off her face.

"All I could think of was you. I want you." She lifted herself up far enough to kiss him. "You're my fantasy man, Jed. Most women don't get to lose their virginity to their fantasy men. I don't want to be one of those women who looks back on their first time and wonders why she didn't hold out for magic." She met his gaze. "You're my magic, Jed."

He closed his eyes for a long moment, his body utterly still.

"Jed?"

He opened them again, his eyes glittering. Without taking his gaze off hers, he placed his left hand on her ankle, then slid it up her leg, under the hem of her dress, and along the inside of her thigh.

"Is that a 'yes'?" she whispered, even as she parted her legs, hoping . . .

His fingers fluttered up the inside of her leg until they brushed against the satin of her underwear and she felt her belly convulse at the touch. "Oh, wow . . . that's . . ."

Still watching her, and still saying nothing, he slipped his fingers underneath the skimpy material and sank them deep inside her.

"Holy hell." Paige dropped her head back as her body quivered as his thumb began to rub against some sensitive spot. "Jed—"

Then he flipped the skirt of her dress up, trailing kisses down her belly and over her thighs and then his mouth found her core.

"Holy *hell*. That's the most amaz—" She forgot to talk as pressure started to build inside her. Hot, vibrating, teasing, trembling. His whiskers scraped her inner thigh, and she reached down to entwine her fingers in his hair. In Jed's hair. *Jed.*

The orgasm slammed through her so hard she shouted and came up off the carpet, her body spasming. Jed gripped her tightly, holding her as the tremors spilled through her, taking over her soul, her mind, her spirit, her everything.

She sagged back on the carpet as Jed scooted next to her and wrapped himself around her, pulling her against him so her cheek rested against his biceps. She closed her eyes and let the sensations continue to wash over her, snuggled against the heat of his body. "See?" she whispered. "I knew I was right to hold out for you."

She felt his whiskers press into her face and knew he was grinning. She didn't have to look at him to know it was a macho man sex look, all proud to be introducing a woman to the wonders of intimacy.

He deserved to gloat.

"No intercourse though," he said.

She stretched, grinding her body against him. "Who the hell cares?"

"Spoken like a woman who's never had sex." He traced his fingers over her hip.

"And whose fault is that? Yours." She sighed. "I wish

we didn't have all this crap to deal with. I wish we could go back to your place and you could rock my world until I went insane from orgasm overload."

His hand stilled on her hip. "You need to stop talking like that."

"Oh." She sat up eagerly and started unbuttoning his jeans. "You need me to do you, don't you? I didn't even think of that."

"No." He peeled himself off her and stood up. "I think it's better if you don't get me started." He adjusted the front of his pants.

She eyed the bulge. "You're already started."

"Not hardly, darling. Not hardly." He grabbed her hand and pulled her up.

"Darling? You called me darling. I love it when you call me things like that."

His eyes narrowed, and she thought he was going to tell her to stop thinking of him like that, like he did every time he thought she was starting to like him too much.

But he didn't.

He ignored her instead.

Excellent. They were making progress. Failure to deny was a good step forward. Especially now that she knew the truth about how he felt. He might not love her, but he cared enough to lose control.

And that was enough for her.

Twenty-two

He shrugged off his shirt and handed it to her. "Put this on. We need to get out of here."

There were too many buttons on the floor to hope that her dress was going to stay up around her chest, so she pulled on his shirt, and let it drape over her hips, where her dress was resting. "A T-shirt and a silk skirt. Theresa would be disgust—"

She suddenly remembered Oscar's threat against Theresa and stumbled.

Jed caught her arm, then hauled her up against his side as they headed down the hall. "Talk. Tell me what happened before I got there." He grip tightened on her. "Before my brother tried to murder you."

The pain in her head began to subside somewhat, and the ache in her chest from Rafi's attack was starting to ease. "He went into me in shadow form. I thought you said that shadow warriors couldn't enter Rivkas without permission."

Jed shoved open a heavy steel door so hard it slammed against the wall and got stuck. "They can't." Jed stepped through the door into the bar. "My brother isn't a pure shadow warrior. I felt it when I was battling him inside you. He's shadow warrior, but also something else."

She frowned. "What else is he?"

"Hell if I know." He let the door slam shut behind her, and cupped her waist as he began to move them through the crowd. "But he's not my brother anymore. Something happened to him, and he's . . . twisted."

She'd felt that searing evil inside her, and knew he was right.

"And he intends to murder both of us. I could feel it." Jed's voice was bitter, and she looked sharply at him as they stepped out of the club into the rainy street.

"You'd let him kill you, wouldn't you?"

Jed said nothing, but before she could think of what to say, her new phone rang. She nearly dropped with relief when she saw who was calling. "Theresa? Are you okay?"

"It's a trap! The angels are onto you! Get out! They're sending a shadow warrior to kill you!"

"I'm already out. No sex."

"Thank God. You virgins can be so gullible, I was afraid he'd nail you before you realized what he was up to. Zeke was on the Internet looking for Beatrice McFleet, and he stumbled across this big warning about you on all the Angel websites, but I'd turned my phone off at the bar, so he couldn't reach me until I got home. Angels are out, girlfriend. They're all on the alert for you."

"That's okay." After her orgasm with Jed, she knew there was no way she could ever bring herself to have sex with an angel. "I wasn't into the angel thing anyway."

Jed put his arm around her shoulder and squeezed.

"The shadow warrior," he said into the phone. "How did Zeke know about the shadow warrior?"

"Because he hacked into the Council server after that to see what their plans were for Paige. Apparently, they have a shadow warrior on the payroll now, hired for the sole purpose of killing her. Aren't you honored, Paige? It's quite the cachet these days to have a personal assassin—Hang on, Zeke's telling me something."

"Theresa! Wait! The Men in White are coming after you guys, and Dani and Becca and Nick to set an example for other people planning to kill angels."

"Zeke says they're here now. Gotta run. We'll find Dani, and no one knows where Becca is, so she's safe." There was a crash and the sound of wind rushing, as if Theresa had taken to the air. "You have a meeting with Justine and Derek in two hours. They'll call you to tell you where to meet, and Zeke found the scientist. She's located in the basement of the Lamborghini dealership in Midtown. Gotta run. We'll talk later. Zeke, stop complaining. I'm a perfectly safe flier—" And then the phone clicked off.

Paige looked at Jed in shock. "What did she just say?" She grabbed his shirt. "Did you hear what I just heard? Tell me I'm not delusional. Tell me!"

"You're not delusional." He grinned and covered her fists with his hands. "Zeke found the scientist. He found her."

"Oh, God." Tears filled her eyes and she sat heavily on the ground, her legs suddenly giving out. "He found the scientist."

Jed grabbed her arms, pulled her to her feet, and gave her a big hug. Then he kissed her hair, tucked her under his arm, and waved for a cab. "No time for curb-sitting, sweetheart. Let's go find her." The cab sailed past and he scowled.

"Find her. Find the scientist. How awesome does that sound?" She sighed and leaned against him as he unsuccessfully tried to flag down another cab, blinking at him when he cursed.

His face was tense, and she suddenly remembered that even if she'd finally gotten a break on her issue, he was still dealing with the fact that his brother had turned into a murderer. She immediately pulled out her phone and dialed her old cell phone number.

Bandit answered on the sixth ring. "Bandit? Hi, this is Paige."

There was the roar of loud music over the phone. "Rock on, girlfriend! I'm free! Time for retirement!"

"What happened?" She could barely hear him over the noise of a crowd. "Do you know?"

"No idea! All of a sudden, everything clicked and I was free. Thanks for the clothes, though. The chicks are digging them. Do you still need me to testify?"

"No. No vortex issue. Have fun."

"Will do, babe!" He howled like a wolf, then hung up.

Paige shut the phone just as Jed stepped in front of a cab, which screeched to a halt. He walked to the passenger door and yanked it open, glowering at the occupants. "You were getting out here?"

A man in a suit leapt out. "Absolutely. Your cab."

Jed held the door open for Paige. "Coming?"

"Well, yeah." She ducked past the displaced man. "Sorry about this. We're in kind of a rush."

She told the driver to take them to the Lamborghini

dealership, then flopped next to Jed, who had his arms folded across his chest. He was staring out the window, his jaw tense, his face impassive.

"Jed? You okay?"

"My brother hated what I became to keep him safe from Junior, and now he's become worse than I ever was. Something happened to him to turn him into his worst nightmare, and he's still going to get sucked back into Junior's hell if I don't turn you by tomorrow." He slammed his fist against the cushions. "This is my fault, and I can't fix it. It just keeps getting worse."

She put her hand on his, and he flipped his hand over and tangled his fingers with hers. "You keep saying it's your fault, but you haven't convinced me of it. What aren't you telling me?"

He ground his jaw, leaned back against the seat, and wrapped his hands around her right hand, his thumbs rubbing against the underside of her wrist. Then, to her surprise, he started to talk. "My dad died when I was little, and my mom got remarried to some asshole who liked to practice his kicking techniques on the family. On me, specifically, because I stepped up when he used to turn on Rafi and my mom."

"Oh, Jed. I'm so sorry."

He fiddled with her gold bracelet "I hated him, and plotted how to destroy him. He was a huge guy, bigger than Rafi and I together, so I knew I couldn't beat him." He managed a small grin. "I tried, though."

She smiled. "I can imagine."

"Anyway, I learned about Satan's disenfranchised son, and figured he'd want to make a deal. So, I found him and told him that if he'd kill my stepdad, then I'd work for him when I came into my powers. He was pumped."

Paige raised her brows. "Really? You contacted him?"

Jed snorted. "Oh, I had no intention of working for him. I didn't let Junior rope me into a contract, so he came by and killed my stepdad for me, and then I bailed. Took off to where he'd never find me. Stayed gone for twenty-five years."

"And your stepdad?"

"Junior paid him a visit in hell, and he told Junior that Rafi was my weakness, and to use Rafi to get to me."

"Ah . . ."

"So, Junior took Rafi and tortured him until I got back." He stared out the window. "I was gone for twenty-five years, having a blast, not worrying about home or anything. Just causing trouble and using my powers to impress women into my bed."

She frowned. "So, you were a player?"

He looked at her. "Oh, yeah. Big time." He went back to staring out the window. "Then when I realized what had happened to Rafi, I . . ." He balled his fist and gently punched the door. "All I want is to free him. That's it. Then I'm going after Junior. One of us will die, probably both of us. As long as I take Junior out, I don't care what else happens. I owe Rafi that much."

"Wow." She sat back in her seat.

He raised his eyebrows at her.

"What?" she asked.

"Aren't you going to tell me it's not my fault? That I'm being a martyr? That I shouldn't give up my life for him? Something positive like that?"

"Hell, no. It is your fault. Of course, you were trying

to save the family in the beginning, so that's admirable, and I'd probably run away from a deal with Junior too, but yeah, all that bad stuff that's happened to Rafi is your fault."

He frowned. "But—"

"And I totally agree that Junior should die for what he did to Rafi, and I think it's so awesome that you can love Rafi so much that you'd give your life for him." She sighed. "Love like that is so amazing. It makes the world a place I want to be."

He was still scowling at her.

"Oh . . ." She understood his cranky expression. "You wanted someone to tell you that you're an okay guy, right? That all the guilt you've been living with for so long isn't right?" She sighed. "I hear you, Jed. You're in a sucky position. You did what you thought was right, and it all turned out badly and keeps getting worse. And you feel bad, rightfully, because it *is* your fault he's in this position. If you'd stayed around the family until you came into your powers, you could have just killed your stepdad yourself and saved everyone a lot of grief."

He gave her a long look and turned to stare out the window again.

"But everything you did was out of love, to protect your brother, and I just think that's the most awesome thing ever. I'd love to love someone so much that I'd forfeit my eternal soul to save them. That's . . . it's . . ." She pressed her hand to her chest. "It makes me feel whole right here. In my heart."

He was watching her again, his eyes intent.

"See, when I killed the assassins who were after Becca, I did it to save her, yeah, but I also did it because I wanted

to kill them. Because it was fun to harvest their evil souls."
She sighed. "I did it for the wrong reasons." She pulled
her knees up to her chest. "Listening to your story . . . it's
clear that I never really did love Becca. I mean, I thought
I did, but would I give my entire soul up for her?"

She paused to imagine accepting her future as an inner
wraith in order to save Becca, and shook her head. "No,
I'd try to find a way to save myself and her. But you didn't.
You gave yourself over to Junior one hundred percent
for your brother, and that's just the most amazing thing
ever. You're still not trying to find a way to save yourself.
Just him. And me. You don't want to kill me either." She
looked at him, realizing he was still staring at her. "I wish
I was like you. I wish I could love like you do. I know it
sucks, but I want my life to suck like that. I really do." She
snorted. "See? You keep saying I'm all sunshine. I'm not.
You are. You're the sunshine around here. Yeah, you're
damned, but you're also sunshine. Damned sunshine, I
guess."

For a long time, he said nothing.

And she didn't expect him to. She hadn't exactly comforted him. Hadn't comforted herself either.

After a while he lifted his arm, set it around her shoulders, and pulled her up against him. "Thank you," he
whispered.

Then he kissed the top of her head, leaned his head
back, and closed his eyes.

Twenty-three

Jed woke up when Paige's phone rang. She was nestled against him in the backseat of the cab, gripping his shirt even in her sleep.

He slipped the phone out of her purse and answered it. "Paige's phone."

"Is this Jed?" a woman's voice asked.

"Yeah. Who's this?"

Paige mumbled something and shifted, and he stroked her hair.

"Justine Bennett. Theresa said you needed help. What's up?"

He let his head drop back against the seat, willing himself not to get excited as he detailed the situation.

When he finished explaining that they needed to find a way out of the contract so Junior wouldn't be able to recall Rafi to his torture chamber if Jed failed to convert Paige, Justine got off the phone and he could hear her consulting with two male voices. Then she came back on. "E-mail the contract over. We'll look at it, but quite honestly, it doesn't sound like anything we'll be able to help with. But you never know." She rattled off her e-mail address, gave him directions to her condo, and then hung up.

Jed pulled out his own phone and e-mailed the contract, then set his phone on his lap, just breathing in the scent that was Paige. "I'm not sunshine," he whispered. "If I was, you wouldn't be able to touch me."

But damn, she made him want to be.

He sighed and dialed Rafi's cell phone.

As he suspected, it went right into voice mail. Phones didn't work when warriors were in shadow form, and he had a feeling Rafi wasn't going to reform anytime soon. Too much time spent in shadow form changed a man. He became the evil that the shadow had to be. "Rafi. It's Jed. Call me."

He snapped his phone shut and ground his teeth. How had Rafi gotten mixed up with the Men in White? Paige's phone rang and he answered it. "Paige's phone."

"This is Jerome, returning her call. Who's this?"

"Jed Buchanan. What happened to Rafi? How'd he get out? What did you guys do to him?"

Silence.

There was a rustle, and then Jerome came back on, his voice a whisper. "I can't talk here. We'll meet somewhere else."

"My place." Jed gave the address. "Ten minutes."

"Three hours. It's the best I can do." Then he hung up.

Jed cursed and snapped the phone shut. *Three hours?*

"Jerome?" Paige mumbled against his chest as the cab rolled to a stop.

"Yeah." Jed handed Paige's phone back to her as she sat up and rubbed her eyes. "I know it'll endanger you to be near him, so I'll go by myself. I need to find out what happened to Rafi, and see if Jerome can leverage the Council into breaking our three-way contract with Junior."

She snorted, tossed some money at the cabbie, then shoved the door open. "Yeah, *right*, you'll leave me behind. I need to have a word with him as well. Sending a shadow warrior after me. Stalking my friends. Reprehensible behavior for a man who purports to love my best friend. That man does not know the meaning of love. Unlike you. As long as the Men in White aren't with him, we can deal with him."

Unlike you. Her words reverberating in his mind, Jed followed her out of the car, standing on the street next to the Lamborghini dealership. The sun was just starting to come out, and the dawn light was turning the puddles on the street orange.

Orange like hell.

Or orange like the sunrise.

He was picking sunrise.

Five minutes and a few blown-up doors later, Paige was standing over the bed of a woman who looked like she was in her late twenties. She had dark brown hair spread out over her pillow, and her cheeks were pale. Too pale.

Paige reached out and let her hand hover over the woman's chest. "She still has a soul." Paige squatted next to the cot. It was stashed in the corner of a huge basement filled with more lab equipment than she'd ever seen. Paige had no idea what any of it was for, but it looked impressive. "Hello? Beatrice? Wake up?"

The woman didn't even shift.

"Beatrice. Your lab is on fire."

Still nothing.

She looked up at Jed. "I can't touch her."

He kneeled next to Paige and lifted the woman's hand. "Bea—"

"I'm working! I'm working!" She leapt out of bed, shot over their heads, and landed without a flicker of sound in front of the computer, where she yanked a set of noise reduction headphones onto her head, shoved a pair of blue-rimmed glasses on her face, and started pounding away at the keys. "I'm on it!"

Paige frowned. "Was it just me, or did she actually vault over our heads?"

"She did." Jed was frowning too. "Not human."

"No." Paige and Jed stood up and walked over to the computer.

Beatrice's hair was going out in all directions, and she still had a line on her cheek from the sheets. Her eyes were rapidly moving over the screen, and her mouth was moving, as if she were singing along to a song, or discussing whatever it was she was typing.

Paige waved her hand in front of Beatrice's face, and the woman's gaze jerked up. She stared at Paige for a second, then looked at Jed. Then she turned and looked behind her, above her, and under the desk, then back at them again.

Beatrice yanked the headphones off her head. "You work for Satan?"

"Nope."

"Satan around?"

"Nope."

Beatrice glanced back and forth between them, searching their faces, then she sagged back in her seat, dropping her headphones on the keyboard, and pulling the glasses off her face. "You scared the hell out of me." She picked up a pen and levered it at them. "Never, *ever,* sneak up on me again. Got it?"

Paige grinned. "Or you'll what? Shoot ink all over me?"

Beatrice gave her a dangerous look that immediately wiped the grin off Paige's face. "Yeah, okay, I give," Paige said. "What are you?"

"Who are you, and why are you in my lab? My house, my questions."

Paige pulled up a chair and sat next to her, very much liking Beatrice's attitude. "I'm Paige Darlington. I'm—"

"You? You're Paige?" Beatrice picked her glasses back up and leaned forward to inspect Paige. "How are you doing? You look all right." She frowned. "You should be a wraith by now. Satan said you were a spineless wench who wouldn't be able to resist more than an hour or so."

Paige scowled. "I'm not spineless, and I'm not succumbing." She glanced up to see that Jed was wandering around the lab, opening cabinets and peering into bubbling vats. "You're Beatrice McFleet?"

"Beatrice?" Beatrice looked surprised. "Of course not. I'm Rita Halperston."

"But . . . did you do the thing that's turning me into a wraith?"

"Of course I did. Who else could do that?"

"Satan lied about her name," Jed said as he pulled open a door to a stainless-steel freezer. "No wonder Zeke had trouble finding her." He disappeared into what was apparently a walk-in freezer, and the door slammed shut behind him.

Rita stared at him. "Who is he? Why is he in my freezer?"

"Jed Buchanan. Gorgeous, isn't he?"

"You bet he is. Yours?"

Paige didn't even hesitate. "Mine," she said firmly. "But I'm here because I wanted to know how to avoid becoming a wraith. Surely you put in a back door or something."

Rita pulled her gaze off the freezer door and gave Paige a calculating look. "Of course I did."

Paige caught her breath and she leaned forward. "What is it? How do I stop it?"

Rita gave her a sympathetic look. "Oh, girlfriend, I'd love to help you, but you know how Satan is. I can't mess with him."

"Why not? He doesn't have your soul, so why do you have to make him happy? Make me happy instead. I'm a lot nicer."

Rita grimaced and shook her head. "I'm sorry. I really can't. I can't afford to."

Paige felt herself starting to panic. "Please. What can I do to convince you to help me? You want Satan off your case? I'll get him off your case. Anything. *Please.*"

Rita gave her a sharp glance. "Don't make promises you can't keep. The only two people who could control him at all were Becca Gibbs and the former love of his life, Iris Bennett. Now that he's shacking up with all these women in an attempt to forget Iris, he's out of control. Ruthless." She looked at Paige. "He's turning into the Satan that everyone thought he was all along. Look at you. He's destroying you for no reason. Would the old Satan have done that? No. He would have talked about it, but he wouldn't have. Because he was trying to be good to win Iris's love, and because Becca kept him in line. But now . . ." She shuddered. "You'll be lucky to be a wraith when he finally snaps. You'll be oblivious."

Paige suddenly got cold. "You think he's going to snap?"

Rita gave her a look that made Paige feel really young. "Don't you?"

"I hadn't thought about—"

Jed opened the door to the freezer, and stepped back into the room, his gaze on Rita. "I found the second room."

Rita sucked in her breath and sat up. "How? It's sealed off. It's impossible—"

"Help Paige, and I'll keep your secret. Don't help her and . . ." He shrugged. "You know what I'll do."

Rita looked sick, and Paige almost reached out to hug her. "Jed. You're upsetting her."

He didn't look away from Rita. "I don't care."

Rita drew in a shaky breath. "But if you—"

"I have nothing to lose," Jed interrupted. "I don't give a shit. Help Paige. That's your only option."

Rita pressed her lips together, and Paige could see her hands shaking. Paige shot Jed a frown, but he gave her a warning look that kept her from protesting.

Finally Rita said, "I truly can't tell you—" She held up her hand as Jed started to speak. "But if you go to the third gateway, you will know."

"The third gateway?" Paige repeated. "You mean, between heaven and hell?"

Jed immediately stiffened as Rita nodded. "That's all I can say. Find the gate." She looked at Jed. "You can find it."

"No, I can't. I've never been able to—"

"You can." Rita stood up. "You must leave now."

Jed didn't move. "Do you know where the gate is?"

"No."

"Who does?"

"You do." Rita spread her hands. "Don't ask me for more, or you both lose. You must do the rest on your own."

Jed studied her for a long moment. "I don't know where the gate is."

Rita shot Paige a look of exasperation. "Open your mind. The world is not always as you think it is." She waved at them. "You both must leave now. You *must*. Satan's coming."

Paige stood up quickly, not wanting to deal with the Lord of About-to-Snap. "Let's go, Jed."

He stood still, as if he had no intention of moving.

"Loophole meeting, Jed. If I'm going to be saved from being a wraith, we have to find out how to break your contract with Junior so he can't recall Rafi."

Jed cursed, grabbed her arm, and strode toward the exit.

Paige jogged next to him, and shot a glance over her shoulder at Rita, then stumbled when she saw Rita's eyes were glowing silver as she watched them leave. Then Paige was jerked against Jed's body and slammed into a corner. "Rafi's here. He's hunting you. Be silent."

Twenty-four

Jed's mind was still reeling as he backed Paige into the dark corner, putting himself in front of her. Find a gate? How the hell was he supposed to do that?

"Is he in shadow form?" Paige whispered.

He pressed his body against hers, pinning her to the wall. "Yes."

She let out a low breath, then dropped her head to his back.

"Raise your shields," he whispered.

"Already on it," she muttered. She grabbed his waist, her fingers digging into his skin as she concentrated.

Jed felt the hum of his brother's shadow in the dealership above their heads, then felt him focus on Paige's essence and start bolting toward them. *Shit.* He was going to have to kill Rafi to save Paige. One or the other would die.

He couldn't make that choice. "Paige. Take us to hell. Now."

She didn't even ask. She simply did it.

They landed in Satan's bedroom, where Satan was sitting on his bed, wearing gold silk pajamas and thick glasses. He was reading a book titled *Too Many Women*,

Not Enough Beds: Why You Should Forget about "The One" and Move On. He had *Dirty Dancing* playing on his plasma television and a stack of romance novels on the floor by his fireplace, several of which were already burning in the flames. And he was wearing a LOVE SUCKS button on his left lapel and a SEX ROCKS one on his right.

He jerked his gaze out of the book, his eyes wide with surprise as he stared at them.

Paige sucked in her breath and instantly transported them back out of hell.

This time, they landed in the middle of Fifth Avenue, with traffic screaming around them.

Jed cursed and yanked Paige across the street, slamming his foot into the bumper of a yellow cab that was gunning for them. The bumper collapsed under his force, and the car slammed to a stop, its entire front end dented.

And then they were on the sidewalk.

Paige sighed and leaned on a lamppost. "That was close."

"No one can drive a car through me."

She rolled her eyes. "No, when we landed in Satan's bedroom. He would have killed us for sure if we'd stayed. He can't afford to be seen like that." She rubbed her palm over her forehead. "He's reading self-help books on how to forget about love. That can't be good. Love's all that kept him sane. Next time he sees us, we're both dead."

He grimaced and looked up to check where they were. "So, why'd you put us here?"

"I have no control. Satan gave me this bracelet, and it's probably set to land in random locations in the Underworld and the mortal world. You think I would have dumped us in Yankee Stadium on purpose?"

"I did wonder about that. I thought maybe you were a groupie." He realized they were only a few blocks from where they were meeting with Justine and Derek, and he grabbed Paige's hand and started walking.

"A groupie is so undignified. I'd never be a *groupie*." She sighed. "Who am I kidding? To be a groupie, you have to really love the group, and we've both determined that I can't love."

He glanced over at her as he strode down the sidewalk. She was biting her lower lip, and her eyes were sad. Not out of self-pity, but loneliness. "Of course you can love. You love Becca."

"Not enough to sacrifice myself for her." Paige sighed. "Maybe my self-preservation instinct is too strong. She was willing to give up her eternal soul for Nick. That's love right there. I wouldn't do that."

He shot her a glance as they jogged across the street. "I think you would."

"Nope. Nope, I wouldn't."

He reached the doorway of their building and pulled the door open. "You never know how far you'd go in a situation until you're actually faced with it. I never in my life would have thought I'd give up my soul for Rafi. I couldn't stand him as a kid." He nodded at a large black man in a gilded doorman's suit, then looked back at him. *That man is not an ordinary doorman.*

"Penthouse," the man said. "They're expecting you."

Paige glanced at Jed as they walked across the plush carpet. "You said that earlier, but how could you have *really* hated him? Especially since you love him now."

He punched the elevator button. "Oh, trust me, I hated him." He recalled how much anger he'd had when he'd walked out when he was fifteen. Stupid anger. If only . . . No. It was what it was. There were no "if onlys." "But yeah, I tried to save him. Who knew?" He was suddenly aware that Paige was staring at him with a soft look on his face. He slanted a glance at her as the elevator door slid open. "What?"

She smiled, hopped up on her tiptoes to plant a soft kiss on his mouth, then skipped into the elevator and propped herself up against the back rail. "You make me want to be a better person."

He scowled as he stepped into the elevator and punched the button for the thirty-seventh floor. "You're already fine as you are."

She held up her arms. "Kiss me."

He wasn't in the mood to kiss. He was worried he wouldn't be able to find the gateway for Paige. He was also worried he *would* find it and Rafi would die because Paige would be saved. He groaned and pressed his palm to his forehead. What if there wasn't a way for them both to win? Then what? "Can't."

"You can't?" She levered herself off the railing, walked up to him, and slipped her arms around his waist. "Playing the martyr again? Too consumed by your darkness to allow yourself a minute of pleasure?" She lifted her face to his. "We have about thirty seconds until the doors open and real life returns. I want to taste your mouth, feel your body against mine, bask in the hardness that's you. Don't you—"

He cut her off with a kiss that he couldn't stop himself from doing. He closed his eyes, tasted the softness of her lips, the feel of her tongue brushing against his. He wrapped his arms around her, tugging her as tightly as he could against him, drinking in the warmth of her essence, basking in the feel of her hands gripping his waist, in her mouth seeking his, burning for him. Utter and complete trust from her. Her body was his, her soul was his, and she was offering all that she was, for that one kiss.

He growled and slid his hands up her back, cupping her shoulder blades and crushing her breasts against his chest. She was soft, she was firm, she was light, and she was *his*.

She leaned into him, opening herself to him, taking all that he would give, offering all that she had, in a kiss that left him breathless and overwhelmed. He dropped his hands to the lush curves of her bottom, kneading the flesh as she made a small noise and wiggled her belly against the front of his jeans, drawing his heat south so fast he nearly staggered from the impact.

He tugged the silk skirt upward, until there was nothing between his hands and her skin. He shuddered at the feel of her warm skin against his hands, so soft compared to the roughness of his palms. He bit the lobe of her ear, and grinned when she trembled against him.

"Make love to me, Jed. *Please*."

He lifted his head to look at her, at the need in her eyes. It wasn't just lust, it was wanting for *him*. Only him. It was too overwhelming, and he cursed. "I can't make love to you. What if I have to choose between you and Rafi?" He took a deep breath, and said the truth as he knew it had to be. "I'll have to turn you. That's a lot worse than not calling you the next day. You've waited this long. Wait for the right situation. For the right guy."

She waved her hand in dismissal. "I'll choose myself over your brother, if it comes to that. What difference does that make now? I won't take offense, and you won't take offense. We both have priorities. But now . . ." She stood on her tiptoes to kiss him again, and his knees nearly gave out at the taste of her mouth. She pulled back, her gaze fixed on him. "Now is our time. It might be our only time. Please, Jed? Make love to me? You're the right guy. And now's the right time."

He felt her earnestness, knew she believed every word she spoke, and suddenly, he couldn't hold out any longer. He wanted to know what it would be like to be held by her, to be embraced on all levels by someone who knew what he was, and still thought he had value. He needed it more than she did, and he wasn't going to deny it anymore. He couldn't.

But he gave one last effort to be honorable. "What about your virginity keeping the wraith at bay?"

She rolled her eyes. "You were right. This wraith is far beyond anything that superficial. It won't matter, as long as we don't merge." She met his gaze. "What do you say?"

He knew he was lost even before he spoke. "Okay."

She blinked, and then a smile burst over her face. "Really?"

He couldn't help but smile back. "Really."

Then the elevator dinged, and he tugged her skirt back down over her body just as the elevator door slid open.

She didn't even glance toward the door. "When? Name a time, Jed. I'll be there with my clothes off ready for—"

"I don't think I want to hear this."

They both turned their head toward the doorway. A woman was leaning against the doorjamb of the apartment that the elevator opened directly into. She was wear-

ing jeans and a soft cotton sweater and she was holding a
dagger in her right hand.

Paige grinned as her cheeks flushed red with embarrassment. "You must be Justine! It's so fantastic to meet
you!" She raised her arms and fluttered her hands. "Long
distance hug!"

Justine held up her hand. "And you are?"

"Paige Darlington and Jed Buchanan," Jed said.

"Theresa sent us," Paige added.

"Great." The woman smiled and tossed the dagger out
of sight with a clatter. "Yes, I'm Justine. Derek and his
brother Quincy are in the kitchen, working on the contract. Come on in. We have hot pretzels and coffee. It's
such fun to have guests. We don't get many visitors." She
eyed Jed as she stepped back to allow room for them to
pass by. "Has Theresa met you?"

"Yeah, why?"

"You look dangerous." She picked up her dagger off
the table she'd tossed it on and shoved it in a sheath under
her arm. "I'll just keep this handy."

Paige immediately stepped in front of Jed. "You touch
him, and I'll kill you. He's mine."

Justine raised her brows at Jed, and he shrugged. "She's
my bodyguard."

"*Your* bodyguard?" Justine snorted. "Hah."

But she seemed to relax and headed off toward the
back of what was apparently a loft apartment that took up
the entire top floor of the building. It was huge, airy, and
smelled of fresh paint and new wood.

"Did some redecorating lately?" Jed asked.

"Yeah." Justine shot a look at Paige. "Your former
mentor shot up the place with machine guns. Hope

you're not feeling so inclined. We just moved back in last week."

Paige held out her hands. "You're perfectly safe as long as you don't mess with Jed."

Jed realized that her dark side was starting to flare up. Justine's warning to him had fired Paige up that much? He grinned, even as he reached out and took her hands in his. "Keep those down, killer. We're guests."

Paige bit her lip and looked at him, then she nodded, and took a deep breath.

He put his arm around her shoulder and she snuggled right up next to him. He felt a faint tingling on that side of his body, and he realized he could feel the darkness she was pushing into him. He frowned and looked down at her. "You all right?"

"Other than being a boiling cauldron of death and evil? I'm fantastic."

"Derek and Quincy, meet Paige Darlington and Jed Buchanan," Justine said as they stepped into the kitchen. "Paige and Jed, meet Derek and Quincy LaValle." She raised her eyebrows at Paige. "You guys want some clothes?"

Jed realized that Paige was wearing his shirt and the torn dress, and he had no shirt on at all. "Yeah, thanks."

Justine nodded and walked out of the room.

Derek inclined his head. "Hey."

"Hey." Jed tightened his arm around Paige as he inspected the brothers. Derek was taller, a little wider, and he carried a strong confidence and sense of purpose. Quincy was still a big guy, but not as large as Derek. He hadn't even bothered to look up; instead, he was bent over the computer, frowning at the screen.

Paige looked around the room. "So, this is where the Goblet lives, huh?" Her gaze came to rest on the espresso machine. "Last time I saw her, she was a crystal around Theresa's neck. That's a pretty impressive switch."

The espresso machine promptly turned into a punch bowl, filled with a pale pink punch and a crystal ladle.

Jed blinked. "Damn."

The punch bowl flashed brightly, then turned into a container labeled CREATINE.

Jed grinned. "Thanks, but I'm clean."

"But he does have a nice bod, doesn't he?" Paige patted his chest. "You should feel his muscles. Rock hard."

"Oh stop, already." Justine walked into the kitchen, thrust a pair of jeans and a shirt at Paige and a T-shirt at Jed, then she dropped a dish towel over the CREATINE container, as if Mona were a chatty parrot she wanted to shush. "Ever since Theresa took her and she got to visit hell and run around the city, she hasn't been the same. No longer satisfied to live in my kitchen."

The dish towel burst into the air and floated gently down to the floor, revealing that Mona had transformed yet again, this time into a bottle of vanilla scented massage oil, according to the label.

"Nice one, but we're all set," Paige said, as she tugged the jeans over her legs and ditched the torn dress. "Thanks for the pants."

Jed noticed that she left his shirt on instead of putting on the one Justine had brought her. He grinned as he tugged the T-shirt over his head. A little small, but it would do.

Quincy spun the computer screen so Jed and Paige

could see it. "See here? This faint lettering at the end of the contract you sent us?"

Jed and Paige both leaned forward and Jed noticed some shadows after the last paragraph. "What's that?"

"Words. He used a template he must have stolen from somewhere," Justine said, as she sat on Derek's lap, not appearing to mind that all four chairs were already taken. "He didn't do a good job deleting it."

Jed frowned. "What do you mean?"

"Oh, I know this." Paige banged her fist on the table. "Satan uses a boilerplate to start all his contracts, but it's pretty tight since he's got awesome lawyers on his staff. I bet Junior got his off the Internet or something, huh?"

"Probably." Quincy pointed to the shadowed letters. "But with an Otherworld contract, even though it's in a Word document, it's really three dimensional. So, Junior just got in there and fixed the Word document, but he didn't take it 3D to fully address the issue."

Jed's heart starting beating a little faster. "So, what did he leave in there?"

Quincy nodded. "Most boilerplate Otherworld contracts have a clause that says if either side breaches the contract, then the contract is void. Junior thought he took out any repercussions for him violating the contract. . . ." Quincy got a very smug look on his face. "But he didn't go deep enough. It's still in there."

Jed sat back in his seat. "So, if I can get him to breach the contract, then it automatically voids?"

Quincy nodded. "It voids."

"Well, that rocks! Let's get him to breach, then." Paige grabbed the computer and tried to yank it closer so she could read it, but Quincy swept it out of her hands.

Jed set his hand on her shoulder. "How do we get him to breach? Isn't his only obligation to leave Rafi alone?"

"Yep." Quincy sat back. "So, you're going to have to piss Junior off enough that he takes Rafi back without you having violated your obligations to him."

"No." Jed sat back. "I can't send him back to Junior's hell. Not even for a minute."

Justine was playing with Derek's hair. "One minute of hell for freedom? I think you might underestimate your brother and what he can handle."

"It's, um, actually, about five minutes," Paige spoke up. "That's how long it takes for all the neurons to fire, or whatever happens, for the powers that be to realize that the contract needs to be voided and to actually have it happen. But I don't think it'll work anyway, because Satan told Junior that he couldn't recall Rafi unless he violates the contract."

"Recall him as part of the contract, no, he can't do that. But he could simply steal his soul. It would be no different than stealing anyone else's." Quincy grinned. "Junior's not the brightest, so I can't imagine you'd have too much difficulty tricking him into stealing Rafi."

Jed stood up. "Thanks for your help. We're leaving."

"Don't be a fool."

Jed turned to look at Derek. "Don't judge me."

Derek shifted Justine off his lap and walked over to Jed, blocking his path. "Sometimes you have to take a risk to save those you care about. Quin found your loophole. Don't be too stupid to use it."

Take a risk? Not when his brother had already lost what little sanity he still had. Give him back to Junior for five minutes? Even if Rafi's soul was free, Rafi would never be alive again. "Get out of my way."

"Theresa told me that if you choose to save Rafi, then Paige dies. Is that true? You'd trade her for your brother, when you could save both of them? Five minutes of torture?" Derek's eyes flashed. "I thought you loved her. You'd kill her? Just like that?"

Jed felt his fists curl into tight balls. "Get the *hell* out of my way."

"Okay, boys." Justine was suddenly between them, a hand on each of their chests. "Derek, let him go. Jed, I see something in your eyes that I don't like, so you'd better walk out that door before I have to kill you."

Paige jumped between them to peer at his face. "Oh, that's bad. His eyes are black." She grabbed his hand. "Derek, you don't understand the situation. Jed can't put Rafi back in Junior's hands. He can't. It's not an option." She tugged at his hand. "Come on, Jed. You're getting a little too malevolent, and I would hate to have to kill Theresa's best friend to save your evil butt, as nice as it is."

Justine stepped aside, using her body to make Derek back up. He put his hands on her shoulders and whispered something in her ear. She smiled and patted his hand, and suddenly Jed stopped to face Derek.

Derek's eyes narrowed. "What?"

"If you had to choose between your brother and Justine, who would *you* choose? How would you choose?"

"I did have to choose."

Jed blinked. He hadn't expected that. "How did you choose?"

Derek wrapped his arm around Justine's neck, cradling her against him. "I made the only choice I could, because it was the only chance of everyone surviving." He kissed Justine's hair and nodded at his brother. "Any other choice, and one would have lived, but the other would have died. With the choice I made, we all had a chance."

"Dammit, man! But who would have died if you'd been wrong? How did you choose?"

"We were all in it together," Quincy said.

"Team decision," Justine agreed. "Whatever happened, we all took responsibility."

Derek looked at him. "Have faith."

" 'Faith'?" Jed spit out the word. "I lost that a long time ago."

Derek shrugged. "Find it again. It's not that hard."

"Not that hard? Are you—" He stopped as Paige slid her arm around his waist.

"Jed," she whispered. "You're starting to go fuzzy around the edges. Let's leave before we both end up killing people, okay? These are my friend's friends, and I don't want them to be hurt. And if I kill them, then no more decisions will need to be made because my fate will be a foregone conclusion." She tugged at his waist, and he again felt a tingling from her touch. "Come on."

He let Paige drag him to the elevator. Not because he was concerned he couldn't control his shadow warrior, but because his entire left side was starting to go numb from her touch. Something was happening to Paige, and it wasn't good.

Twenty-five

Paige turned on Jed the instant the elevator door shut behind him. "Okay, so that was a bust. New plan: We need to find a gate like really, really soon. I'm totally starting to wig out here." She smacked his chest. "And you *cannot* go all evil on me! You practically call my dark side right out of my body when you do that."

He cupped her face between his hands and kissed her, trying to soothe her wraith.

She sighed and kissed him back, gripping his wrists.

After way too short a time, he stopped kissing her and pulled back just enough to see her face. "You're not doing well, are you?"

"No, not really." She tightened her grip on his wrists, in case he was thinking about letting go. "You have to find the gate."

He cursed, and rubbed his thumb over her lips. "I don't—"

"Yes, you do! Rita knows things. Couldn't you tell? She *knows*."

"I got that feeling too."

"What did you find in her closet?"

"Can't tell." He kissed her jaw, feathering kisses along it. "Not worth the risk."

She tilted her head so he had better access as the desire pulsing through her distracted the wraith, which, apparently, was rumbling but willing to be distracted for the moment. Probably still had a full stomach, and who can destroy the world on a full stomach? "If you find the gate, then, according to Rita, we'll know how to save me. Which means that you won't be able to convert me for Junior. Is that why you don't know where the gates are? Because you don't *want* to know?"

His mouth froze on the side of her neck, then he lifted her head to look at her, a look of startled surprise. "It can't be that easy, can it?"

"What can't?"

"I hate being a shadow warrior. The thought of being trapped guarding a gate is like a nightmare." He met her gaze. "I've never wanted to know where the gates are. I don't want to get trapped."

"And you don't want to know now either, do you? Not really." She shrugged. "I mean, I know if it was just about me, you would, but that will end Rafi's life." She felt his sudden frustration. "No, no, I understand. Rafi wouldn't survive the torture chamber for another minute, let alone five. I *know* that. I'm not asking you to trade him for me." She cursed and let her head flop back against the elevator wall. "I don't know what I'm asking you for."

He cupped her neck with his hands, his gaze intense. "You're asking me to find a way to keep you alive."

She nodded. "I guess I am, if there was a way. But maybe there isn't." She looked at him, appalled to discover her eyes were starting to sting. "Maybe it's time to walk away from you."

The elevator doors slid open, but neither of them moved.

Jed slid his thumbs along her throat. "We still have Jerome. He might have answers."

She felt a flicker of understanding, of hope. "You're actually hoping for a team win, like Derek and Justine got? You've come over to the other side?"

He managed a half smile. "Not a team win. A win for the two of you."

She scowled. "Why not a win for you?"

He lifted her hand to his mouth and pressed his lips against her skin. "Because there is no win for me. I'm damned."

She saw the sadness in his eyes, and she immediately wrapped herself around him and buried her face in his chest. "I don't care if you're damned. I lo—"

Jed slammed his hand over her mouth, his face raw with emotion. "Don't say it. If you say it, Junior wins." His voice fell to a whisper. A plea. "I beg you, please don't say it."

Her throat tightened. "If I say it, Rafi's free. But you don't want me to say it?"

"Not yet." He leaned his forehead against hers. "Not yet."

The elevator doors began to slide shut, and he thrust his foot between them, not breaking eye contact. He twisted his fingers in her hair, tugging her close so his breath was warming her lips. "Tomorrow night, we run out of time. Tomorrow night, Junior calls in his marker on my brother."

"I don't know if I've even got that long."

He kissed her hard, and then let go of her. "Let's go meet with Jerome." He grabbed her hand and pulled her out of the elevator. "With any luck, he'll void the contract and we can go after that gateway."

She managed a smile. "Look at you, sounding so optimistic. I'm rubbing off on you, aren't I?"

"Yeah." He gripped her hand. "More than I can afford."

Jed leaned against the wall as he watched Paige walk around his apartment. Inspecting it. They'd come straight to his place and they were waiting for Jerome.

Jerome was their last chance for a win-win. If he wouldn't void the contract and free Jed and Rafi from Junior, then Jed had a choice to make. The gate to try to save Paige, or convert Paige to save his brother.

Hell.

Paige came out of his bedroom and set her hands on her hips. "It's awfully barren."

It felt right to have her in his space. "It's a place to crash."

"But it's not home. You live here, but it doesn't have any of you in it. You need some personal touches to make it home."

Home. Now there was a word he hadn't thought about in a long time. But seeing Paige standing there, in his house, made him think of things like roots and belonging. Things he hadn't considered in years. Or maybe ever.

The buzzer rang and he reached over his shoulder and punched the intercom. "Yeah."

"Jerome here."

He and Paige stared at each other, and he felt his adrenaline kick in. *This was it.* "You bring anyone with you?"

"No."

"Good. Come on up." He buzzed Jerome through, and then resumed watching Paige, who had tied his shirt in a knot around her waist to get it up off her thighs. The style revealed curvy hips and a flat stomach that he wanted to touch. To taste. To—

Paige noticed him watching her, and raised her brows, then slowly untied the knot, sliding the shirt up over her ribs, letting her skin peek out.

He groaned, and she smiled, a seductive smile that she had no right torturing him with.

Then she slipped her hand under the shirt, raising it ever so slightly so he caught a glimpse of the underside of her breast, braless after he'd torn off the one she'd been wearing. He thought of how they tasted, and his body began to pulse.

She cupped her breast with her hand and flicked her thumb over her nipple, a small noise of surprise popping out of her mouth.

He levered himself off the wall, and grabbed her, slamming his mouth onto hers, sliding his hand to cup her breast. "Teasing me is a bad idea," he growled. "Not with my bed twenty feet away and at least three minutes to kill until Jerome gets up here, thanks to the slow elevators in this building."

"Three whole minutes? So much time." She grabbed the waist of his jeans and slipped her hand down the front.

His whole body jerked when she wrapped her hand around his arousal, her fingers warm against him. She lifted her face to his, her face radiating her need, her openness, her trust. "I want you. You said okay."

"Three minutes isn't enough time to give you what you deserve." He grabbed the bottom of her shirt and tore it off over her head, then felt his gut clench at the sight of her body before him. "You're a virgin, for hell's sake."

Her only reply was to wrap her legs around his waist, flatten her breasts against his chest, and plunder his mouth with a kiss that was so fierce he felt like she was tearing his guts out. She grabbed his hair so he had to look at her. "I love your damned blackness and your evil shadow warrior and your guilt and your self-hate and all the shit you've done for your brother. You're too hot for words."

And suddenly, he couldn't stop himself anymore. He just couldn't. His hands went to her butt and she crushed herself against his body. He staggered over to the couch and dropped them both on it. "I can't merge my aura with you," he gasped as her hands went to the front of his jeans, yanking at the zipper.

"I have faith in your ability to restrain yourself," she sighed as she parted his pants and he burst free. "You're beautiful." She scooted down and feathered soft kisses over him.

Jed held himself over her, his arms rigid, his body hard as he felt her tongue flicker against his skin, her fingers cup his balls, gently, tentatively, but with a conviction that had his muscles tighten. *"Jesus."*

He closed his eyes and drank in the sensations of her exploration, her innocent wonder at his body. Then her mouth closed over him, and he shuddered and pulled himself out her reach, nearly smiling at her protests. "Come on, darling. This is about you." He wrapped his arm around her waist and tossed her on her back.

He landed on her and kissed her hard as he quickly undid her jeans and slid them over her hips. She clung to him, her arms so tight around his neck that he couldn't have gotten free if he'd wanted to.

And he sure as hell didn't. Not anymore. He was committed all the way.

A knock sounded at the door, and Jed felt a surge of resentment, and finally understood Bandit's position about "a last hurrah." Five minutes with Paige, to last them forever. Five minutes of escape before everything came crashing down. He needed it too desperately to walk away. *Five minutes.*

Jerome knocked again. "Hello? Paige?"

Jed skimmed his fingers down over her belly and tangled them in her curls. "You bring coffee?" he called out, and he slid his fingers along the crease of her legs, so close, teasing her.

"What? Coffee? What are you talking about?" Jerome sounded annoyed. "I just got here." He rattled the door. "Open up."

"Coffee, Jerome. I'm extremely cranky before I get my coffee, and trust me, you don't want to see me cranky." He dropped his head and trailed light kisses over her breasts, grinning as she twisted under him, whispering his name.

"Coffee? You're serious."

"There's a Starbucks on the corner." He slipped his finger inside her and nearly groaned at how ready for him she was. "I'm a shadow warrior, Jerome. Coffee or you see me at my worst."

Jerome cursed, and then there was the sound of feet running down the hall.

Paige moaned softly, lifting her face to kiss him. "That was mean, scaring him."

"Fuck him. I need more time." He kissed her again, hard, his tongue mating with hers as he slid another finger into her body, stretching her. "Five minutes to last an eternity. I have to have this moment."

"That is so sweet!" Paige broke the kiss with a gasp, her fingers digging into his butt. "Do that again."

He slid down her body, letting his skin rub over hers, grazing his teeth over her nipples, over her belly, then kissing her hard at her core, while his fingers continued to slide, to caress. He wanted to do this right. He'd never really cared before, but now, he had to know, had to make it good for her; not good, amazing. . . . "How are you doing, sweetheart? Is this okay?"

She groaned and grabbed his shoulders so hard that it hurt. "God, yes." She lifted her hips off the couch, driving his fingers deeper inside her. "Make love to me, now, Jed. That's all I want. You inside me. Now."

He hesitated. "I have to run to my room and get protection."

"I can't get any diseases. I'm immortal."

"Can you get pregnant?"

"No. Maybe. Yes. I don't know. Good question."

He scooped her up, wrapped her legs around his waist so his arousal was rubbing up against her. "Come on, sweetheart." He shot to his feet, kissing her hard, continuing to caress her as he took them into the bedroom.

Paige made a small noise and started shifting her hips,

rubbing against him, her body so slippery that she glided easily. "This feels amazing."

All he could manage was a groan in response as he dropped her on the bed, yanked open the nightstand drawer, and sheathed himself. Paige pushed him onto his back and threw her leg over him. "This way."

"Any way you want." He caught her hips, directing her as she eased down onto him, groaning as her body enveloped his, her hot warmth drawing him in deep.

She flattened her palms on his chest as she began to move, and he gripped her hips tighter, driving his hips upward into her. Wanting more. Needing more. Intensity began to build inside him, and he felt her brightness reaching out. Enveloping him. Spearing his core.

Shit. They were merging. He slammed up his shields, as she began to move faster, whispering his name, clutching him, and he felt her need for him. Not just for his body, but for *him*.

Something rose deep inside him, and he felt her soul rise in response, answering his call. Reaching for him. Embracing him.

I need you, Paige.

No. He needed to stay in control. He gritted his teeth against the call of her soul, yearning for him, felt his own ache for completeness. His soul began to respond, and he instantly felt a darkness rise in her.

"Jed—" There was a slight rise to her voice, as her hips slowed.

"Don't worry. I've got it under control." He cupped her breasts and flicked his thumb over her nipples. "Let it go."

"Jed . . ." There was such relief in her voice, and he felt

her body commit, felt her trust as she did exactly as he said and dropped all her guards and opened herself to the moment, to every sensation, to the feel of his body driving deep into hers.

He groaned and lifted his hips, moving with her, rising to meet her with each move of her pelvis, fighting against his need to commit with his soul and his heart and his spirit. He closed his eyes against the urge building in him, not physically, but spiritually, needing her, needing the completion of the merge unlike he ever had before.

Paige began to move faster, and there were trickles of sweat on her chest, sliding down her stomach. "Jed—"

"I'm with you. I'm right here—"

And then her body tensed, and her muscles clenched around him and the force of her orgasm slammed into his gut, into his soul, and he felt his own body respond, catapulting over the edge. Darkness rose around them, and he knew he was about to merge with her.

I can't do this to her. He threw all his energy into his shields and pulled himself out of his body. Not quite into shadow form, but close. He pulled his spirit into a protective shell as his physical body exploded with the force of the orgasm, driving into Paige as she clung to him. But it wasn't real to him. It was a distant echo, kept from his senses by the shields he had erected. He was there, but not there. Not at all, and it was breaking him. *God, I want to be in this moment.*

But he held back. Had to hold back.

He could feel the sensations pressing at him, but they couldn't reach him. His heart ached as he felt her soul reaching for him, crying for completion, but he didn't release his shields. The tremors subsided from their bodies, and he gradually allowed himself to reenter himself, drinking in the residual tremors of the moment, opening himself up to what was left between them, desperate to feel what he'd removed himself from.

Paige slumped onto his chest and kissed his collarbone. "You left."

He wrapped his arms around her and hugged her, pressing his face into her hair. "I had to."

"It felt different when you left. Empty. Lonely."

He cursed. "I'm sorry. I wanted it to be perfect—"

"Oh, it was." She lifted her head to look at him. "It was. When you were there, I felt . . ." She trailed her finger over the stubble in his chin. "I felt complete for the first time in my life." She frowned. "It wasn't just sex, was it? It was more. Or it was until you left."

He kissed her softly. "Yeah, it was."

She cocked her head to look at him. "Did you . . . were you able to . . . did you stay long enough?"

"I stayed long enough." Long enough to know that he'd never, ever wanted to leave.

She narrowed her eyes. "You didn't, did you?"

He sighed and smoothed her hair back from her face. "I stayed as long as I could. Any longer, and you'd be a wraith." He studied her face. "I'm sorry I ruined it by leaving. I wanted it to be so amazing—"

"It was amazing." Her eyes were bright, and he sensed her honesty. "It was just that when you were there, it was so much more than amazing. So, when you left, I felt it."

He frowned, and trailed his fingers through the rivulets of sweat on her chest, humbled by the fact she'd trusted him with her life.

She snuggled against him. "You know, I was thinking about what I almost said earlier, that I loved you?"

His breath caught in his chest. "Yeah?"

"Well, I was thinking that I was wrong."

He closed his eyes against an unexpected wave of pain. "You don't love me?"

"Well, yes and no." She propped her elbows up on his chest, and he opened his eyes to see her staring down at him. "See, I love you . . ."

Something blossomed in his chest, something he didn't recognize.

". . . but it's like how I love Becca. It's love, but it's not Love."

The light died and he frowned. "You mean, you love me like a friend?"

"Oh, no." She grinned. "I love you like a hot manly man who makes my womanly parts soar."

He heard the unspoken hesitation. "But . . . ?"

"But I was thinking that I love you, but if it comes down to tomorrow night, and you're trying to convert me to save your brother, I'm going to fight you to save myself." She rested her chin on his chest and eyed him. "That's not true love. That's not the kind of love I want. I want the kind of love where I love you more than I love myself, where I'd sacrifice myself for you." She grimaced. "I don't see that happening. I could never just walk into the darkness. It's against my instinct, and everything that I believe in. I want to live, you know?"

He hugged her tightly, pressing his face into her hair. "I *know*." God, he knew.

"See?" She sighed and pulled back from him. "I know nothing about love. I want to Love, dammit, and I don't have it in me! I throw around words like that, but it's nothing. I love you, but would it transcend being a wraith? No. Because it's not Love."

He grabbed her face. "You do have it in you; you're just smart enough not to waste it on me."

She pursed her lips, then said, "If you hadn't been ruined by your life, if you weren't damned and evil, do you think you might have loved me? Like the kind of love where you'd dive into a vat of hell acid to retrieve a lock of my hair? That kind of love?"

There was a vulnerability in her eyes, but also a strength. A conviction that didn't need him to tell her he loved her just because they'd made love. She just wanted to know. His throat tightened, but he shook his head. "I'm not capable of that."

"But if you were, would it have been me?"

He hesitated, then gave her the truth. "Yeah, I think it might've."

Twenty-six

A high-voltage smile lit up Paige's face, and zapped him right in the chest.

He groaned. "Paige—"

She put her hand over his mouth. "No. Don't say anything else. That's enough for me. I'm going to tuck it into my heart and keep it with me no matter what happens. Don't take it back. Don't qualify it. Just let it be."

He cupped her face and kissed her, unable to articulate a response.

She smiled and returned the kiss, her tongue dancing with his, searching for him, needing him as much as he needed her.

A heavy pounding sounded through the apartment and she jerked to a sitting position. "Damn him for interrupting me just when I've got you where I want you."

He frowned at the sudden hostility in her voice. "Paige? You all right?"

"The rat bastard Jerome's back," she said. The smile had dropped off her face, replaced with a slow fury, and he felt his body begin to tingle everywhere she was touching him.

The wraith was back, and it was strong. And suddenly,

as if it had jumped on the chance to ride the wave of her hostility toward Jerome.

Jed grabbed her wrist as she started to get off him, ignoring the fact that his hand went numb almost instantly. "Keep it together, Paige. I'm not giving up on you yet."

"He almost killed Dani, he allowed the Men in White to try to murder me, and he did something horrible to your brother," she growled. "He deserves to die."

"Not at the expense of your life." He sat up, so he was level with her. "You have to shield your emotions. Forget that you don't like him. Think of him only as a man with possible answers." His thigh was now completely numb where she was sitting on it, and he gripped her wrist more tightly. "Paige! Look at me!"

She did, and he cursed when he saw that her eyes had gone black.

He pulled her back down on the bed and wrapped himself around her, touching skin to skin everywhere he could reach. He bent his head so his lips were against her ear. "What does love feel like?"

"What?" She gripped his forearm where he had it wrapped around her chest.

"What does it feel like?" His entire body was beginning to go numb, but he didn't release her.

"Love?" She sounded confused, but it was a step up from murderous, so that was good.

"Yes." Little zings of pain began to shoot through his muscles from her wraith invading his body. "What does love feel like? Your love for me. What's it like?"

She was quiet for a minute, and he willed Jerome not to knock again, not to remind Paige of his presence until she'd gotten herself back under control. "I feel this ache in my heart," she said. "It feels like sunshine, and like pain at the same time."

"Can you make the sunshine touch other parts of your body?" His quad began to twitch, and he gritted his teeth against the pain.

"Maybe." She fell silent, and gradually he began to feel her body relax.

"Good job," he whispered. "Focus on that."

"I'm focusing."

Jerome knocked again, and Paige didn't flinch. "Sunshine. Love," she said. "I'm feeling the love. Not Love, but love."

"Good girl." He kissed her forehead and then tried to release her, but couldn't get his muscles to work. "Let's get dressed."

She carefully eased out of his grip, ran out into the living room to grab their clothes, and brought them back. She tossed him his jeans and yanked on her own pants.

Jed lay on the bed, waiting for his body to come back to him.

Paige frowned as she pulled her shirt over her head. "Are you coming?"

"I think so."

She narrowed her eyes and peered at him. "What's wrong?"

"Nothing." He gritted his teeth and tried to move again. This time, his body responded, and he sat up, excruciating pain blasting through every muscle in his body. "I just wanted to watch you get dressed."

She grinned. "That's so cute."

Jerome pounded on the door again. "Hello? Are you in there?"

"Coming!" Jed yelled.

Her smile faded. "You should probably get that. I'll hover in the distant background."

"Right." He leaned over to pick up his jeans and bit his lip to keep from groaning. He stood up slowly, trying not to wince as he made his body bend over so he could put his jeans on.

Paige stood watching him, with her hands on her hips.

After a second, she walked over and helped him get dressed, chewing on her lower lip as she did so. Neither of them commented on the assistance, but he had a feeling she'd figured out that her wraith had taken a serious toll on him.

Once his jeans were zipped, he brushed off the shirt. "Forget it. Let's go." There was no way he was going to be able to lift his arms over his head yet.

"Okay." She dropped the shirt on the bed and stepped back to make sure she didn't brush against him as he headed toward the door.

So he caught her hand in his and took her with him.

Paige hugged her knees to her chest as she sat on the couch next to Jed, across from Jerome.

To his credit, Jerome did look like hell. His clothes were dirty and rumpled, his hair was messy, and he had a frazzled glaze in his eyes. And he was so restless he was making her dizzy. Tapping his foot, shifting his weight, glancing at the big windows, picking at the lid to his coffee.

The guy was a strung-out mess, and she was glad to see it.

He hadn't met her eyes since he'd come in, and that

was helping her ego as well. Nice to see him cowed before her. Made her feel a little less driven to destroy him.

She slanted a glance at Jed, who looked fairly recovered from the incident in the bedroom. He'd saved her, she knew he had. She'd been so mad at Jerome for interrupting their moment after Jed had made that amazing declaration, and she'd nearly lost control. But Jed had taken the hit: enough blackness to have killed a regular human for sure.

Was she getting that much worse? She flexed her hand, felt the pain even at that slight movement. Yes, she was.

Jed draped his forearm over her knees, drumming his fingers on her thigh. She smiled and entwined her fingers in his. Even if she went wraith, she'd remember making love with him. She'd always be able to recall his supreme effort when he'd pulled himself back to keep them from merging.

She knew that Jed would do his absolute best to keep from turning her. And if he *did* turn her, he'd be destroyed forever, even if he saved his brother. She rubbed her fingers over the back of his hand, tracing the veins. *I will not let Jed suffer anymore.* She had to find a way to save all of them. Had to.

"Is Raphael working for the Council?" Jed asked.

Jerome nodded, and took a drag of his coffee. "Since angels are completely unkillable, the Men in White were stressing about how Paige had managed to kill one. They finally decided that it didn't matter, and that she was too dangerous to be kept alive." His gaze finally went to Paige. "I told them you were an innocent, and they didn't care."

Despite her animosity toward Jerome, she almost smiled at him in appreciation. After all she'd done, he could still consider her an innocent? Two men who thought she was good. Somehow, after looking into the bleakness of her wraith future, being considered an innocent . . . well . . . it just didn't sound so bad anymore. Jed had made it sound like an okay thing to be.

"Since you're a Rivka *and* had some kind of deadly killing technique, no one wanted to risk their enforcers by trying to kill you," Jerome continued. "So they decided to recruit outside talent."

Jed's body tensed. "Rafi."

Jerome nodded. "It's my fault, and I'm sorry. When I got your message, I immediately called an emergency meeting to see if anyone could verify Bandit's claim. Unfortunately, when they heard about Rafi getting tapped and realized how badly he needed to get free, they knew they could coerce him into agreeing to anything in exchange for his freedom. Sadly, I doubt he had any idea what he was agreeing to when he took the deal, but that didn't matter."

"Rafi was *alive*," Jed growled. "How could they put him in the Afterlife?"

Jerome took another drink, and Paige realized his hands were shaking. "Satan Jr. bribed the Council originally. And since they're the ones who locked him up, it was simply a matter of unlocking the door to let him out." A bitter smile curved Jerome's lips. "It was easy to reverse it."

Jed dropped his head to his hands. "Easy. It was *easy*. And I was going to let him *die*."

Paige scooted next to Jed and slipped her arm under his so she could nestle against him. He pulled Paige onto his lap, wrapping his arms around her waist as if he was afraid she'd fly away. His body was hard with tension, his muscles like rocks. "So, what did you do to him? He's not pure shadow warrior right now."

"Well, no. He couldn't kill Paige if he was pure shadow warrior. We enhanced him."

"How?"

"A little bit of this, a little bit of that. He's now a deadly killing machine. A joint venture by the Council and the Men in White." To his credit, Jerome sounded disgusted by it. "I tried to stop them, and they locked me out. I don't know exactly what they did to him."

"Or how to undo it?"

Jerome shook his head. "I'm working on it, but I'm currently on administrative leave as of two hours ago." He tightened his grip on his coffee. "I thought I could clean things up, but I'm buying my own ticket to hell instead."

Jed pressed his face into Paige's hair for a minute, then lifted his head, his voice deceptively calm; she could feel the tension radiating everywhere they were touching. "So, how do we break my contract with Satan Jr.?"

Jerome drained his coffee, tossed his cup aside, and grabbed another one. "You can't. Those things are impossible." He looked at them both, and Paige saw him gather his resolution. "I've learned a lot more about Paige's condition, and I came here tonight to talk to you guys."

Paige sat up. "You know how to stop it?"

Jerome shook his head. "You can't stop it. You're going to turn. It's inevitable." He leaned forward. "I know this is personal to both of you, but you have to understand that this situation is bigger than both of you. All mortals and Otherworld beings will be in serious trouble if Paige goes wraith, no matter who she's loyal to." He looked at both of them, his gaze intense. "The greater good must take priority here. Paige, you have to die before you change."

"But—"

Jed's arms tightened around her. "No."

Jerome gave a dismissive wave of his hand. "I know, I know. If you kill her, then she'll be dead, because she was created as part of the Afterlife, so she has nowhere else to go. And Jed's brother will be recalled to Junior's hell for an eternity of torture, as will Jed. I get it. It sucks for all three of you. But I've looked at all the scenarios and there is no way out of it." He looked at them both. "Three lives sacrificed to save millions, to preserve the fragile balance between heaven and hell, is nothing. It may be personal to you, but in the grand scheme of good and evil, you three can't look at yourselves as individuals. You're part of the big picture, and like the thousands who have given their lives to preserve our freedoms, you three must do the same."

Paige swallowed the lump in her throat. "But if I can get into heaven and purify myself . . ."

Jerome snorted. "No chance. You can't get in, and even if you could, the cleansing moat is under armed guard. Not to keep you from saving yourself, but to keep you from *trying* to save yourself and blowing up heaven in the process." He gave her a challenging look. "There's no way to stop the change, but once you change, you'll be unstoppable. You *have* to die before you change. Do the right thing."

"But Rita said if we got to the third gate—"

"Who's Rita?" Jerome interrupted.

Paige sagged with sudden realization. "She's working

for Satan," she admitted. "She'd have incentive to want me to destroy heaven."

Jerome reached out to touch her, then dropped his hand before he got too close. "I'm sorry, Paige. I know you don't like me, but you're Dani's best friend, and I would do anything I could to save you." He looked at Jed. "You have to kill her."

"No." There was so much force in that one word that Paige actually turned to look at Jed. His face was hard, his gaze unwavering, and he looked scary as hell.

And she loved it.

"No?" Jerome shot him a look of disgust. "Then you're going to turn Paige wraith? What exactly do you think the world will become if Paige is turned?"

Jed cursed under his breath.

Her heart tightened and she tugged on his hand. "Jed?"

He turned his head to look at her, his eyes bleak. "I've felt your power. Jerome is right. If you're allowed to change . . . it will potentially destroy the world."

"Well, crap." Paige pushed to her feet and paced away from the couch. "This sucks. It sucks!" She whirled toward them. "This is so unfair! I didn't ask to be the key to the end of the world!"

"No, but you did embrace your dark side," Jerome said.

"Not like this!" She flared up a fireball and hurled it at Jerome, who barely ducked in time. "Dammit! I'm not ready to die! I will not give up!"

Jerome stood up. "Which is why you have to be killed. If you won't do it, then I'm going to have to let the Men in White take care of you."

Jed jumped up and slammed Jerome in the chest hard

enough to throw him into the coffee table with a loud crack. "You stay away from her," Jed snapped as Jerome groaned and rolled onto his stomach in the pile of splintered boards.

Then Jed turned to Paige and headed toward her, his voice softening. "You need to calm down, love. Jerome isn't worth it." He grabbed her hands. "I'm not going to let him kill you, okay?"

There was a noise at the window, then a man's voice said, "Jerome's not going to kill you. I am."

Paige's heart stuttered and she spun around to see Rafi standing by the window, in a shadowy human form, nearly transparent. She immediately started backing up, throwing all her energy into her shields, even as a feeling of dread seized her.

His eyes were black, blacker than Jed's had ever been. There was no humanity in there. Nothing left of Rafi. No sanity. No mercy. Just pure, killing evil.

And he was there for her.

Twenty-seven

It's the way it has to be," Jerome groaned as he pulled himself to his feet. "I know this will destroy any chance I have with Dani, but I'm willing to sacrifice my love for the greater good." He staggered toward the front door and opened it. "You should do the same and accept your fate." Then he disappeared through it and was gone.

Paige couldn't spare more than a split second to think about how much she hated him and how she wanted to go after him and harvest him for hell, and then Jed moved in front of her, blocking Rafi's path toward her heart. "Rafi. You don't want to kill her."

"She dies."

"No, I don't!" Paige stepped out from behind Jed and hurled a fireball at Rafi. It sizzled right through him and burned a hole in Jed's wall. "Oh, hell." She backpedaled, tripping over the couch, her heart pounding.

"Wait." Jed grabbed her arm and pulled her to her feet. "Rafi. It's Jed. Come back to human form."

The image that was Rafi became even more faint, and Jed cursed. "Raphael! This isn't you! Find yourself and come back, dammit!"

Rafi became nothing but a gray cloud, then whirled and speared right for them.

Paige yelped and sent them to hell. They popped up in the middle of Satan's torture chamber, which was fortunately not occupied.

Jed sat down heavily on the king-sized bed, nicely accessorized with handcuffs and heavy chains at the footboard and the headboard. They clanged as he sat down. "Fuck."

She hugged herself. "I don't want to die. And I don't want to turn wraith. But I also don't want to destroy the world. I really don't." She couldn't keep the tremble out of her voice.

He looked up, then held out his arms.

She immediately crawled onto his lap, pulling her feet up under her, curling into the smallest ball she could. He wrapped his arms around her and tugged her close, resting his chin on the top of her head.

"Do you really think I need to die? Am I that bad?"

His arms tightened, and he didn't answer.

A lump formed in her throat at his response. "That's a 'yes,'" she whispered. Then she closed her eyes and tried to think. "How do we know Jerome's right? Maybe Rita's the one who is telling the truth. Who do we believe? Try Rita's suggestion first?"

Jed said nothing.

She pressed her face into his chest. "But is it worth risking the entire world on the word of one woman with a secret?" She lifted her head suddenly, bumping Jed's chin. "What was her secret?"

He shook his head. "I don't know. I couldn't get in the room."

"But—"

"I bluffed."

"So, maybe she knew you were bluffing and bluffed back? A double bluff?"

"Or maybe she didn't and she was telling the truth."

The hackles on the back of her neck suddenly popped up and she jumped up and spun around as Jed stood up next to her. Rafi was inside the door, barely visible again.

"How'd you find us so fast?" Jed asked.

"The Council gave me extra powers. Still learning how to use them." Rafi fluttered into focus slightly, his voice shadowed and dark.

"Rafi." Jed was across the floor and in front of his brother in an instant. "If you kill Paige before she shifts, you'll return to Junior's dungeon, because I won't be able to meet my obligations to Junior. Do you realize that? This is your future."

Rafi flickered out of sight, then back again, and that's when Paige saw the torment in his eyes. "I can't help it. I have to do it."

"No." Jed started to fade. "I won't let you kill her. You'll never survive it."

Rafi began to fade as well. "I'll kill you to get to her. But you won't kill me to stop me. That's why they chose me."

"Jed!"

He glanced over his shoulder at her, and his face was full of such anguish, she couldn't stop herself. She lunged at him, grabbed his arm, and took them back to the mortal world.

They formed inside Central Park, near the skating rink,

but before Jed had even taken full form, Rafi appeared behind him, his eyes black, so black. He said nothing, but Paige began to feel a pressure around her heart . . . even though he was twenty feet away. "Jed—"

He grabbed her arm as she dropped to the grass, gasping.

"Rafi!" he shouted. "Stop it! Not this way!"

"It's the only way."

Then there was flash of gold bubbles and Satan leapt between them. "No! You will not kill my weapon!" He threw a blue firebolt at Rafi, slamming him into a tree trunk, his solid human form hitting with a loud crash.

Then Satan whirled on Paige as she coughed air back into her lungs. "You will turn now, wraith! Now!" He was holding the arm of a hot tamale who'd apparently won girlfriend-of-the-week honors and thrust her at Paige. "One more death will be enough."

The girl shrieked and Paige scrambled backward. "No, no, no! Don't touch me!"

Jed lunged for Satan, who threw a firebolt into his chest, and Jed fell to the ground next to his brother, gasping for breath.

"No more protectors." Satan stood before her, holding the girl's arm. His eyes were glowing red, and there was a black aura surrounding him. Black smoke was billowing out of his head, and the ends of his hair were actually on fire. His face was dark and contorted, and he'd ditched his custom Italian suit and white shirt for a solid black leather ensemble. Even his lips were black.

He looked every bit like the scary-as-shit leader of hell that he'd never been before.

"Wait!" Paige threw a trash can between them, and

jumped over a park bench. "What about Iris? You'll lose all chance with her if you turn me wraith. She wouldn't approve! Do you really want to give up like that? I mean, you lose her forever, and there's no hope! What's life without hope?"

Satan paused, hanging onto the now screaming girl by her left arm. "There is no hope! Hope is gone! I must avenge her destruction to my ego by destroying the world! There is no other way!"

"Love transcends all," Paige shouted as she reached Jed and touched him with her toe. He groaned and rolled onto his side. Still alive. She nearly sagged with relief. "You haven't lost her yet. She loves you, for hell's sake. All relationships take work. You just have to put some effort into it, but destroying the world will be one of those deal breakers."

Satan stood still, staring at her. "She does love me. I know she does. But she wants me to be other than I am. There is no solution."

"Of course there is. Don't give up." She grabbed Jed by the ankles and hauled him behind the tree that Rafi had crashed into, out of direct line of another firebolt. "You can always destroy the world later, right? It's not going anywhere."

Satan frowned, and his black aura began to fade. "Perhaps you are correct. Perhaps I have been too hasty. Perhaps if I kidnap her and lock her in my bedroom, I will be able to show her that I am perfect as I am. Do you think?"

"Definitely. Go kidnap her."

"Excellent idea." He looked at the girl. "I break up

with you now. It is not me. It is you. Farewell." And then he was gone, leaving the girl behind.

Paige dropped to her knees, grabbing Jed's shoulders and ignoring the shrieking of the girl as she streaked across the park. "Jed? You okay?"

"That hurt like shit." He groaned and rolled onto his back. His shirt was charred, and there was an oozing red burn on his chest.

She let out a shaky breath. *He was okay.*

"Rafi?" Jed asked.

She looked up, then tensed. Rafi was on his hands and knees, trying to stand up, looking at her with the same black eyes he'd had before. She cursed, and Jed lifted his head to look at his brother. He groaned and struggled to sit up. "Dammit, Rafi, get out of that form and use your mind!"

"No."

"Stop!" Satan Jr. appeared next to Rafi. "You must stop!"

Rafi's head jerked toward Junior, then his entire body shuddered and his skin went white. "You," he whispered, the terror and hate so deep in his voice that Paige felt her own skin crawl.

"Me." Junior squatted next to Rafi and gazed at him. "You're trying to take my prize." He turned an assessing gaze on Paige and Jed, and Paige quickly took her hand off Jed's shoulder. "The loyalty's there, but not enough to transcend the wraith. And you don't have much time. I'll show you exactly how much you love him."

Jed turned his head slightly, his mouth near her ear. "Run."

She wrapped her hand around his arm to take him with her, and then suddenly there was an explosion of light, and then darkness, and then she couldn't move. Couldn't see. Couldn't feel. She was trapped in darkness. Silent, oppressive, brutally hot darkness.

Twenty-eight

"Jed?"

Silence.

Paige strained to see into the blackness, but there was nothing. "Rafi?"

Silence.

She licked her suddenly dry lips. "Hello?" Her voice cracked as sweat trickled down between her shoulder blades. She started to yank at her arms, at her legs, but she couldn't move anything. She was immobile. Totally unable to move. "Jed!"

Her scream echoed around her like evil laughter, and she shuddered.

Then she tried to transport herself to hell, but nothing happened.

She was trapped, physically and metaphysically.

Her heart began to race, and she closed her eyes and took deep breaths. "I'm not trapped. I'm not in darkness. I can handle this."

Then there was a flash of light, and she jerked her eyes open, blinking against the sudden brightness.

The first thing she saw was Jed, in irons, hanging from a wall directly across from her. He was in full human form, stripped naked, his muscles bulging as he fought the iron, trying to break free.

"Jed!"

He jerked his head in her direction, his gaze desperate until he found her. "Paige? Are you all right?"

She tried to nod, but couldn't move her head. "I can't move. What did he do to me?"

"You're wrapped in chains. Nothing permanent." His voice was calm, soothing. "You're all right."

Okay. I'm okay. "What about you? Are you okay?"

He nodded. "Fine, but we need to get out of here before he comes back." He paused. "This is where Junior held Rafi."

She suddenly got really cold. "Where Rafi went crazy?"

"Yeah . . ." His face darkened and he snapped his mouth shut as he looked over her shoulder.

Oh, God. What was behind her? She tried to twist around, but chains held her immobile.

"Good evening, darlings." She jumped at the sound of Satan Jr.'s voice, but she didn't see him anywhere. As far as she could tell, they were in a round stone room made of black rock. And it was just them.

"I feel your pain," Junior said.

She felt a tickle of fingers over her cheek and she flinched, even as Junior chuckled. "It hurts to see Jed suffering, doesn't it?" Suddenly Junior's grinning face was right in front of hers. "You'll realize exactly how much you love him when you see him suffer."

She glared at him. "You don't have the power to do this kind of thing. Your mom was your only source of power."

"Is that so?" Junior smiled wider, revealing perfect white teeth. "Too bad so many people have underestimated me, don't you think?" He moved next to her, resting his arm around her shoulders. "It took me a while to figure out how to tap into my powers, since they're different than my dad's. Didn't quite know what I could do. Still learning."

Jed had stopped fighting and was looking around the room, studying everything, but she knew he was listening to the exchange.

"Why can't Jed go into shadow form and escape?"

"Magic, my dear. Magic." Satan Jr. chuckled. "Same reason you can't escape to hell. Did you really think I'd have brought the two of you to a place that couldn't keep you?"

Paige grimaced, her brain whirling as she tried to think. Jed was calm, clearly assessing, and she tried to do the same. Satan Jr. was arrogant. Surely there was something he hadn't thought of?

"Keep an eye on Jed." Junior smiled, a nasty smile that made her stomach turn. "There's nothing like seeing someone you love suffer to make you realize how much you love them."

Jed looked right at her. "He won't let you change until he knows you love me enough. Don't watch." Jed's jaw suddenly clenched and his arms spasmed.

Tears filled her eyes. "Oh, God. Jed? Are you all right?"

His gaze went cold as he stared at her, his jaw flexing. "Close. Your. Eyes. We have time. Don't give in. Close them. Do it for me."

She hesitated, then shut her eyes.

"No, no, you must watch." Junior tried to pull her eyelids open, and she slammed her darkness at him the way she'd done to Jed in the restaurant. He yelped and snatched his hands away. "Bitch."

She scrunched her eyes shut, then there was a shout from Jed, followed by silence.

What was happening? Was he dead? Her heart started pounding, and she willed herself not to look. *I can't give Junior the power.*

"No! You must scream with pain so she can hear you!" Junior yelled.

There was silence. Not even the sound of Jed breathing.

What was happening to him? Her breath got tight in her chest, and she started to feel dizzy, as images of Jed's bloodied body flashed in her mind.

"Scream, you bastard!"

More silence.

She willed her eyes shut, just as she knew Jed was willing himself not to make a sound. She forced herself to think about when they'd made love. About what an amazing moment it was. How great the sex was. The sex. The orgasm. *Don't think about how much it meant to you emotionally.*

She thought about how Jed had distanced himself from his body when they'd made love. *He's doing that now. He's not feeling any pain. He's gone.* Relief made her body sag, even though she still couldn't move. She focused on that thought, repeating it until that's all that she could think of, all that she could focus on. Until it consumed her every thought, every fiber of her being, blocking everything else.

She had no idea how long she held the image, no concept of how much time had passed before Junior finally put her in another room, and released her body from the chains. She felt soft carpet beneath her feet, and crumbled to the floor, finally allowing her eyes to open.

And that's when she saw what they'd done to Jed.

Twenty-nine

J ed became aware of warm hands on his face, of his
name whispered, so soothing, so soft, of a cool cloth
on his chest. "Paige?" His voice came out a gnarled mess,
and he winced at the pain in his throat.

"Don't talk. I'm here." Her voice was broken, strained,
and he forced his eyes to open, blinking at the bright light,
at the stinging in his eyes.

She was bent over him, her hair brushing against his
chest. Her face was streaked with tears, and she was biting her lower lip. Her eyes were focused on his chest, and
he winced as she touched him.

"Paige."

Her gaze flicked to his, and she gave him a tremulous
smile. "You know, I thought you were more indestructible
than this."

"I'm fine."

"Yeah, fine. That's why it's taken me twenty minutes
to wash off enough blood to be able to tell exactly what
he did to you."

He closed his eyes again, unable to deal with the pain
of keeping them open. "What did he do?"

"Looks like he flayed all the skin off you . . ." She

paused, and he opened his eyes again to see her pressing her hand over her mouth.

He dragged his hand off the floor, unable to keep from groaning. She immediately grabbed his hand and pressed it to her heart. "You'll be okay, right?"

He winced at the pain in his wrist and hand where she held him, but he didn't tell her to let go. Pain or not, he needed her touch. Badly. "Eventually. Hopefully. Depends."

"Depends? On what?"

He kept looking at her face, at her bright blue eyes, not letting himself think about anything else, like the excruciating torment he was in. "It depends on whether Junior lets me heal or not. It depends what kind of power he used to hurt me."

Her hands tightened on his. "He might . . . take you back in there?"

"Yeah."

Tears filled her eyes. "I can't handle that. I'll let him turn me. I'll—"

"No." He tried to sit up and failed. "Come down here."

She immediately laid down next to him, curled up against his side, barely touching him, but even that hurt. Not that he cared. He needed to feel her touch. "Closer."

"But I'll hurt—"

"Closer."

She grimaced, but she moved up against him, until he could feel her breasts against his side, and her head was resting on the front of his shoulder. She carefully draped her leg over his, and he gritted his teeth to keep from groaning when she laid her arm over his chest. "Is that okay?"

"Just don't move." He turned his head slightly so he could smell her hair. "You smell like sunshine."

"Sunshine doesn't have a smell."

"Sure it does." He closed his eyes and let her scent drift into his mind, into his body, giving him peace.

"Jed?"

"Yeah."

"I was thinking about what Jerome said. About the greater good."

"Forget Jerome."

He felt her smile, and then she kissed his cheek. "Jed—"

"Kiss me."

She shifted, and he winced at how much that slight movement hurt, then forgot about it when he felt her mouth brush against his, but she was gone too quickly.

"Again," he commanded.

She didn't argue. She simply moved closer and kissed him. But this time, she kissed him the way he wanted to be kissed. With her heart, her soul, and everything that made her who she was. God, he wanted to hold her, but he couldn't. Couldn't even lift his damn head off the floor. But she kissed him deeply, thoroughly, with a completeness that eased the pain in his body ever so slightly.

She finally pulled back. "I want to touch you."

"So do it."

"No. It'll hurt too much." She settled back down against his side, and he couldn't keep himself from gasping from the pain.

But she didn't mention it, and didn't back away.

And once she stopped moving, once she settled herself against him, the pain subsided to a level just below excruciating.

"I think he broke most of your bones," she said. "Maybe your back too."

He cursed.

"But inside . . . they did something inside. I can tell. When I was cleaning you off, while you were still unconscious, I could feel something inside you. Something was wrong. There's something wrong with your soul, or your spirit or something."

"Wouldn't surprise me." *Damn.* Junior had gone all out on him.

"How did you not scream? Why didn't you scream? I would have looked and then he would have stopped—"

"No." He concentrated on the feel of her breathing, on the movement of her breasts against his side, blocking out all other sensations. "He can't win."

"But he will win. I know now why you can't let Rafi go through this again. I can't let him do it to you again—"

"No!" His voice was sharp, and his quick intake of breath sent pain spiraling through him again. "Dammit, Paige. Don't say it. He's probably listening."

"But—"

"Come where I can see you." He had to look into her eyes. Had to let her know how much he meant it.

She sighed, then carefully raised herself up on her elbow and leaned over him, so he could see her. "What?"

His throat tightened at the sight of her face. "God, you're beautiful."

She smiled. "Don't try to distract me. What annoying male ego thing are you going to try to order me to do?"

"My contract with Junior isn't triggered until tomorrow night."

"Tonight. It's almost noon. You've been out for hours."

He felt a flicker of tension. They had only twelve hours? "I want it all, Paige. I want you fine, and I want my brother fine."

She narrowed her eyes. "And you're going to sacrifice yourself, aren't you?"

He ignored the question. "We need to get out of here, get you to the third gate. Rafi will show up to get you, and then—"

"How are we going to get out of here? We're in a dungeon."

"Call Satan."

"Call him? Sorry. but Junior didn't let me keep my cell phone."

"No. You're part Satan. He always seems to be able to find you when you're about to be turned. He has a connection to you and shows up when it's convenient for him. Open up those lines and tell him to come save you."

She frowned. "And then what?"

"I have no idea. But we've got twelve hours to figure it out." All he knew was that he couldn't let Paige turn wraith, and he couldn't let his brother return to Junior.

There had to be a way to win. He almost grinned when he realized the direction of his thoughts. Paige had finally gotten to him. Her optimism, her belief in a happy ending. His body was decimated, he was in pain more excruciating than anything he'd ever felt, and he was actually latching onto hope and wasn't going to let go. Because of Paige. "Call Satan. Call him before Junior comes back."

She brushed her hand through his hair, and he closed his eyes at her touch, trying to lose himself in it.

Then he felt a vibration in the air and he knew she was calling the man who'd created her, whose life force still vibrated deep in her soul.

Paige was so startled when Satan exploded through the wall in a mass of gold bubbles that she actually yelped and threw herself over Jed's body to protect him from the attack.

He let out a small shout of pain and his hands went to her back, to try to lift her off his chest, off his broken ribs.

"Shit, shit, shit. I'm sorry." She scrambled back off him, trying to be gentle. "Jed? Are you all right?"

"Yeah, fine," he gritted out. "Don't leave me."

"I'm here." She clasped his hand and looked up at Satan, who was circling the room, running his hands over the stone walls, and staring up at the endless blackness that was above their heads. "Satan?"

"Most interesting torture chamber. Very mundane, but dreary. Excellent for mental torture."

"It's the recovery room," Jed said.

"Recovery? Ah . . . interesting." Satan was wearing a dashing tuxedo with a gold cummerbund and bow tie, with a black vest and a rose in his pocket, looking much more like his usual dapper self instead of a deranged leader of hell. "To prolong the torture? I like it. My son is brilliant, is he not?"

"He's trying to turn me into a wraith," Paige said.

Satan whirled around to face her. "We decided that it would be best to postpone destroying the world, did we not? Why are you not resisting? Do you threaten me? Is that your plan?" He smiled. "I like your spunk. Most fun. I miss spunk now that my best Rivka has left." He squatted next to her. "You would like her job, would you not? I give it to you. Welcome to the team."

"No, it's not like that," she interrupted. "Junior's going to force the change and he's going to force my loyalty to him. You have to get us out of the torture chamber, or he'll make me change."

Satan's smile widened. "My son is a worthy opponent, is he not? I am much impressed that he abducted you and tortured your man friend to gain your cooperation."

"So, that means you going to let him win?"

Satan's smile faded. "Sadly, though I love and support the fruit of my loins, territorial battles must take priority. I cannot give him my domain, so I must thwart his plans." He eyed Paige. "The easiest to do would be to simply kill you, no?"

"No." Jed's voice was cold.

Satan gave Jed an amused look. "Yes, I fear you greatly, man who is so weak he cannot lift his head. Do you see me tremble?"

Jed lifted his head, and propped himself up on his elbows, without even grimacing, but Paige knew how much it must have hurt. "I'm Jed Buchanan."

Satan's eyes widened. "Oh. *Oh.* I am most pleased to meet you. You have killed many, many, many, including some of my finest employees. Very impressive résumé. Have you slept with as many women, as well?"

Paige didn't want to hear the answer to that. "Satan, I need a focus in my life. I'll come work for you as your number one Rivka, as an independent contractor, if you help us. If you don't help us, then I'll have no choice but to go wraith and ruin your life, your dreams and your hopes. Or I'll die, and then you'll have no one to be your closest confidante and enforcer."

"Paige—" Jed started to protest, but she shook her head at him, and he fell silent, trusting her to know what she was doing.

Satan eyed her, and she saw the gleam in his eye, and she knew how lost he'd been since Becca had left him, as if the wraith thing and the new girlfriend auditions hadn't been enough of an indication. "Will you be submissive and obey all my commands?" he asked.

"Of course not. I'll consider all your requests and negotiate payment for the ones I want to do. I'm not supported by your life force, like Becca was, so it's going to be a different kind of relationship."

He beamed. "That is right answer! It is deal! I agree! Let us remove ourselves from this hovel and reconvene in the splendor to which I have become accustomed."

At that moment, a heavy stone door swung open with a crash, and Junior walked in, wearing a muscle shirt and spandex shorts. "Get out of here. This is my world, Dad."

"Of course." Satan bowed deeply, and then the room filled with golden bubbles, and an explosion rattled the room.

A split second later, Paige, Jed, and Satan were in a gilded room filled with naked statues of men and women, doing all sorts of interesting sexual things. She and Jed were on a massive, plush bed with a gold quilt and dozens of pillows, and Satan was sitting in an armchair, watching them, wearing furry gold slippers on his feet.

He smiled at them. "Welcome to hell, my esteemed

guests. You are mine now." He waved at them. "Have sex while I watch, and then we will begin discussion." He sat back in his seat and clasped his hands on his lap, his gaze eager. "Begin."

Paige winced at Jed's groan. "I'd love to put on a show for you, but Junior pretty much broke all the bones in Jed's body. He's too injured for sex."

"Too injured? Never." Satan hopped and peered at Jed, then his mouth turned into a frown. "Well, this is unfortunate. Shadow warriors are indestructible. My son must have figured out new way of torture." He stood up and rubbed his chin. "Most interesting. My son must be watched. Need spy." He waved at them. "Must be off to assign spy to Junior's camp—"

"Wait!" Paige grabbed his arm. "But what about stopping Junior? What about the contract, or purifying me?"

Satan frowned. "That is your job. I simply removed you." He set his hands on his hips. "Do you mean to say you have no plan? Because then I will sadly be forced to kill you—"

"We have a plan," Jed said. "We're fine. Go."

"Good." Satan smiled cheerfully at Jed. "You are damned, are you not? I offer you hell when you die instead of service with my son. I have much better benefits. Consider the offer."

Jed frowned. "But I'm contractually obligated—"

Satan frowned again. "But I thought you had way to break contract. Do I need to kill you as well? I do not like my son having lethal assassin shadow warrior on payroll."

"No, we're good," Jed said.

Satan beamed at them both. "Fabulous. I see you both

later. Have an excellent day while I set up extensive and undetectable spy network inside my son's miserable and pathetic but increasingly interesting operation."

Then he vanished, and Paige looked at Jed. "So, what now?"

"The Goblet."

She frowned. "What about her?"

"Junior did some sort of metaphysical torture, and I'm having trouble healing it. We need Mona, because I don't have time to heal on my own." He tried to shift his position and winced. "When you get us out of hell this time, picture Justine and Derek's apartment. I have to think that you should be able to control where you land with that thing."

She bit her lip. "Theresa would kill me if she knew I was abusing the Goblet."

He looked at her.

"Yeah, right, everyone else will kill me anyway. Let's go." She grabbed his wrist, and they both flinched as the bones mushed under her grip, then she closed her eyes and pictured Justine and Derek's apartment.

And then they were there.

And five seconds later, Justine and Derek had guns aimed at their heads and were wearing looks on their faces that said it was time to die.

Thirty

Paige slowly eased back from Jed and put her hands up in the air, hoping Justine and Derek wouldn't take them out before she had a chance to remind them who she was. "It's us. Theresa's friends. Paige and Jed? Remember? Breaking the contract with Junior and all that?"

Justine looked all too comfortable holding the gun. "You weren't invited this time. What's up?"

Derek was pointing a machine gun at Jed's head. "I like you, but if you even start to go shadow, I'm taking you out."

Paige flared up a sword made of flames and had it at Justine's throat before the other woman could flinch. "Checkmate."

Justine's brows went up. "Jed dies if you try to kill me."

Paige gave her an unblinking gaze. "I don't care."

"No? I don't believe you."

Shit. She didn't believe herself either. She glanced at Jed. His eyes were closed, his skin was sallow, and his breaths were so shallow she could barely see his chest move. Dying, or trying to heal? She didn't know enough about shadow warriors to know! "Jed? You with me?"

"Yeah. Just taking a nap."

"Hey, guys." There was a door slam and they all jumped as Quincy walked into the room, holding his computer. He nearly tripped over Jed's feet, then looked up, his gaze taking in all the weaponry, Jed's prone body, and the flaming sword at Justine's throat. He blinked, then said, "I'm glad you two are back. I found something out."

He walked right past the guns and sat down at the table with his computer.

No one dropped their weapons or even looked at him. Well, Paige was trying to watch him out of the corner of her eye without taking her attention off Justine.

"I'm listening," Jed said.

"Good. You're the one who matters." Quincy frowned, then got up from the table and walked over and sat down next to Jed, pushing the nose of Derek's machine gun slightly to the side so it wasn't in his face. "See, you didn't tell us that the contract we were looking at was the old one."

Jed opened his eyes a crack. "What do you mean?"

"Well, I was searching the online databases of similar contracts to see if I could find precedent, and I found that the contract you gave me was replaced by a new one." He shook his head at Jed. "It's far easier to do this with complete information, you know?"

Jed turned his head enough to see Quincy. "That's not a new one. It's just the latest incarnation of the old one, with the new conditions of Rafi's freedom."

"No, it's not. Did Junior say your previous one had been breached?"

Jed's face darkened. "Yeah. That's why he was able to recall Rafi."

"Well, if it's breached, and he calls in the marker, then it's done. Over. History. Keeps him from calling in the marker again and again. You must have agreed to a new one, right?"

Jed studied Quincy, a slow awareness dawning on his face. "I did, actually. To get Rafi out."

Quincy grinned and spun the computer toward Jed, so he could read the screen. "Did you ever actually read it after it got automatically codified?"

"No." Jed tried to lift his head, but couldn't.

Paige grimaced and then looked at Justine. "Truce so I can help him? He did get hurt saving me."

"You're welcome to drop your sword at any time."

She hesitated, then extinguished the flaming sword and ran over to sit behind Jed. She lifted his head onto her lap, then helped position the computer, trying to ignore the two guns pointed at her head. Did they know that although Rivkas would never age or grow old, they were completely susceptible to any injury a human was, except fire? That a bullet to the brain would do her in like anyone else?

She eyed Justine, and got a cold smile.

Yeah, they knew.

"Read it," Quincy said, clearly not caring about all the guns aimed at his head. Or maybe he hadn't noticed. He seemed to be the kind of guy who was a little obsessive about his work.

Paige bent down and they both read the contract. She frowned when she finished. "So?"

But Jed was grinning. "Junior forgot to bargain for future services. This contract, your conversion, is the end of this contract. There's nothing else." He looked up at

Paige. "Don't you get it? It's over. After midnight tonight, he doesn't own me anymore, or Rafi. It'll all be over. No more servitude." Awe dawned on his face. "I'll be free. We'll all be free. God, I never thought the day would come."

Oh, hell. She so didn't want to be the one to wipe that look of total disbelieving joy off his face. Her fingers tightened in his hair. "Um, Jed? If you fail to convert me, then he'll get Rafi forever, right? Even if the contract ends tonight."

His smile faded. "Yeah, there is that."

Quin scowled at them. "So, this isn't great news? I thought it was great news."

"It is," Jed sighed. "Thanks."

"You don't look impressed." Quin stood up, tucking his computer under his arm. "I'm going back to work, where they actually appreciate my genius." He stomped out of the room, and they heard the door slam on his way out.

"Well." Justine adjusted her grip on the gun. "What do you want?"

Jed looked at her. "Mona."

She sighed, and looked at Derek. "This pisses me off. Why do people keep trying to take her? Theresa will be so unhappy if I kill them."

"Just a sip," Paige said. "He's already immortal. He's just having trouble healing due to the nature of his injuries."

"No."

Derek eyed Paige. "Why do you want him healed? Isn't he the enemy?"

"Well, yeah."

"So, why do you want to save him?"

She looked at him. "I need his help if we have a chance of winning."

Justine scowled. "Derek, let it go. We have to kill them."

He held up his hand. "Hang on a sec, hon." He turned to Paige again. "Why do you want to save him?"

She sat back and put her hands on her knees. "Because I'm not giving up. We have ten hours left to find an answer and I need Jed—"

Derek shook his head. "That's not what I'm asking. Why not leave him there, and walk away? He won't recover in ten hours to convert you, then the contract will be over and he'll be free, even if his brother isn't. Why would you even think about trying to save him right now?"

There was something in his eyes that made her sit back and look at him.

He raised one eyebrow.

She opened her mouth to reply, then shut it again, her heart tightening. *Because I love him?*

Derek moved the machine gun slightly, so he could look at Jed. "You going to convert her to save your brother, or are you going to let your brother die? Either way, you go free at midnight, so it's no longer about you. Who do you love more?"

Jed opened his eyes to glare at Derek. "You're enjoying this, aren't you?"

"No." Derek set the machine gun over his shoulder and squatted next to Jed. "I'm just trying to understand the situation. What are you going to do if we save you?"

"We aren't going to save him," Justine said. "We can't. The Council—"

"The Council is in disarray right now. They aren't paying any attention to us," Derek said softly. "This is our choice now."

"But my Oath—"

He looked up at his wife. "You broke it for me."

Her face softened, and she looked at Paige and Jed. "He's already immortal, right?"

Paige nodded. "He just needs some healing."

Justine looked at her husband again. He smiled at her, and she finally smiled back.

Then she tossed the gun on the kitchen table, stepped over Jed, and scooped up a ladle of punch from the crystal punch bowl that Mona was currently masquerading as. She hesitated, then walked over to Jed and kneeled down next to him. "You tell anyone we did this, and I'll shoot you."

"You got it."

She eyed Paige.

"Ditto."

Justine hesitated, then Derek put his hand on her shoulder and squeezed. She glanced at him, then gritted her teeth and poured the punch into Jed's mouth.

None of them spoke while Jed drank three times, then Justine sat back on her heels, looking drained. "I can't believe I just did that. I'm getting soft."

Derek put his arm around her and hugged her against his side. "You're modernizing. It's all good."

Jed closed his eyes and let his head rest against Paige's lap. She bit her lip and stroked his hair. "How soon will this work?"

"A few minutes." Justine stood up as sparks began to burst off Jed's skin. Blues, reds, gold sparkers. "Fireworks are a good sign, but I'm going in the other room. I need some space."

Derek hopped up as she disappeared through the swinging door. "I need to check on her. You guys okay if I leave?"

Paige was suddenly envious of their relationship. "Derek? Can I ask you a personal question?"

He raised his brows. "What is it?"

"Would you give your life, your eternal soul, for Justine?"

He got a tender expression on his face and he nodded. "Yeah, I would. I almost did, in fact."

"And what about her? Would she do it for you?"

"Absolutely."

She sighed, and tightened her fingers in Jed's hair. "That's so romantic."

He gave her a sympathetic smile. "It didn't feel romantic at the time. It felt like hell."

"It felt like love, though, huh?"

"Wouldn't have done it otherwise." He hesitated. "Good luck tonight. Hope it works out for you guys." Then he turned and followed his wife out of the room.

Paige stared after him. *How do you know when to do it? How do you know when it's worth it?*

Jed shifted, and she looked down at him.

His eyes were open and alert, and they were bright violet. No blackness at all, as he looked at her.

"Feeling better?"

He reached up and twisted his fingers in her hair, tugging her down. "Yeah." He pulled her until her lips touched his, and he kissed her. "Thanks for taking care of me."

"Yeah, well, fat lot of good it's doing for us, huh?"

He touched her mouth, tracing her frown with his fingers. "Since when are you the pessimist? You're not giving up on me, are you?"

"Well, it does seem kind of dire . . ."

He sat up with a groan, and rolled to his knees, and grabbed her shoulders. "You're the one who's all bright and optimistic, who brings light into every dark spot she enters. Do *not* let this shit get you down! I need you to be who you are." His fingers dug into her shoulders. "Do you hear me?" His eyes were bright violet, the brightest she'd ever seen. "I need you to be my anchor, Paige. I need you." His hands slipped to the sides of her neck, to her cheeks. "God, I need you," he whispered.

Her heart tightened at the intensity on his face. "You do, don't you? You really need me?"

"Hell, yes." He closed his eyes for a long moment, then opened them again, a look on his face she couldn't quite decipher. He grabbed the edge of the table and slowly pulled himself to his feet. "Grab Mona."

"What? Why?"

"Since she heals metaphysical harm, then maybe she can heal what's wrong with Rafi, at least enough for us to talk to him . . ." He paused. "Maybe she can heal you."

"Me?" She caught her breath and looked at Mona, who flashed bright red and then changed into a sports water bottle with a Velcro carry-strap.

"Let's go, before they come back."

"Oh, Theresa is so going to kill me . . ." But she jumped up, grabbed Mona, and strapped her around her waist. "How will we find Rafi?"

Jed just took her hand. "He'll find us. Just get us out of here before Derek and Justine return—"

He paused and frowned, and Paige looked over her shoulder in time to see Rafi stream under the door, like a black cloud. Already? The Men in White had hired a very competent and persistent assassin.

She scowled and turned to face him. "Take form, man. I'm tired of you skulking around behind your vapory mask."

To her surprise, he did take human form . . . all except his eyes. So black.

"Drink this." Jed tossed the water bottle at his brother. "Maybe it'll help."

Rafi took the water bottle between both hands, and ripped it into two pieces. The tearing plastic made a heart-rending wail that made all three of them cover their ears as clear liquid poured all over the floor. Rafi dropped the two pieces as the door flew open and Justine came bounding through the door. "What did you do? What happened?"

Her gaze went to the floor, and she paled and fell to her knees. "Oh, no. Mona!" She grabbed the two parts of the plastic and scooped up what liquid she could, as fast she could. "Derek!"

Paige ran over to help, grabbing one half of the cup from Justine to scoop the liquid back up, then froze as her hand got covered in water. *Holy shit.* She looked at Justine. "Mona's got a soul."

Justine snapped her gaze to her. *"What?"*

"She has a soul. She's alive. I can feel it."

Justine dropped her gaze to the puddle at their knees. "Oh, God, Mona," she whispered. "I had no idea."

Paige could feel Mona weakening. "She's dying,

though. I think Rafi—" She suddenly realized her hands were still in the puddle and she yanked them out with a gasp of horror, stumbling back. "I touched her. Oh, no! She's dying. I can feel it. I'm killing her."

"You can't. She's immortal." Justine kept scooping, trying to round up as much liquid as possible. "I just need to get her back in her containers. Then she'll be fine. Oh, please be fine, baby."

"I can kill immortals." Paige watched in horror as the puddle began to turn black. "I killed her."

"Watch out for Rafi," Jed warned, as his brother began to fade. "Rafi! The contract only goes until tonight. Then you're free. Free!"

Something flickered in Rafi's face, something human and alive, and Jed lunged for his brother, grabbing his shoulders. "You only have to survive until tonight. Then you're free."

"Jed?" Rafi took solid form again, his eyes still black, but there were flecks of brown in them. The strain it was taking to surface, to find himself, was evident, in the tension of his body, in the anguished lines around his mouth. "It's too late. I made a deal."

Jed tightened his grip on his brother. "No. It's not too late. Come back to me, Rafi. Now."

Rafi shook his head. "No. I can't—"

"Drink from Mona. She might heal you," Jed said, the pain in his voice so brittle that Paige's heart almost snapped. "Bring you back from whatever the Council did to you."

A flare of hope showed on Rafi's face, and they both looked down at Mona.

Paige realized the water was getting blacker in the

white cup Justine held, and she pressed her hands to her chest. "She's dying. Mona's dying. I killed her."

Derek slammed the door open, carrying his machine gun. He aimed it at Rafi. "Who are you?"

Justine held up Mona. "Paige said she has a soul, but now . . . she may be dying." She looked around the room, her face a combination of pain and defiance. "Mona is more than a drink of immortality. In order to give her life, she was created by taking life from the three worlds around her: the Afterlife, the mortal world and the Other-world. She holds the final piece to life in her. All life."

Paige felt her mouth drop open. "So, if she dies, the world dies?"

Justine met her gaze. "Yes."

Her knees started to tremble. "Oh, hell."

Derek cursed and raised the gun to aim it at Rafi. "You killed her?"

"No." Paige stepped forward. "I did." She blinked hard. "It was me."

"You didn't kill her." Jed was suddenly beside her. "You didn't kill her. Look at her."

They all leaned forward to look, and Paige realized the water was less black than it had been. Still gray, but definitely improving. Mona was healing herself. "Oh, thank God."

Justine breathed a deep sigh of relief, then glared around the room. "None of you are welcome here again. Derek, do something with them." Then she turned and walked out of the room, cradling the two parts of the water bottle against her chest.

Derek leveled the gun at them. "Out. All of you. Now."

"No." Jed shoved his brother behind him and marched up to Derek. "Rafi needs to drink from Mona. Now."

Paige realized from the look on Derek's face that he was ready to shoot all of them, right there. She set her hands on Jed's arm. "Jed. Your priority is Rafi's soul. His sanity can wait."

Jed hesitated and then nodded. "Take us to the west towers of hell." He reached out and grabbed Rafi's arm. "All of us."

"The west towers? Why?"

"That's where the third gate is."

"The third gate? But I thought you didn't know—"

"It's there. I'm certain." Rafi began to fade into shadow form. "Do it now, Paige. I can't hold him for much longer."

Derek raised his gun. "Now."

So she took them to the only part of hell that was forbidden even to Rivkas. And when they got there, she found out why.

Thirty-one

Jed couldn't believe it when he saw the black towers rising above their heads. Eleven of them, black as night, with fire stacks on the top of each one. It was exactly what he'd envisioned when he'd told Paige to take them here. Inhuman screams were screeching through the black night, and his skin crawled at the sounds. Black shapes darted over their heads, a high-pitched shriek emanating from them as they streaked past, leaving behind the foul stench of sulfur and rot. And death.

The ground was mushy, bubbling with acid geysers, and he could see gaunt faces of people just below the surface. All of them screaming, clawing at the ground, trying to get free. He looked around, suddenly realizing Rafi hadn't made the trip with them. *Dammit.* Where the hell was he?

Paige was staring up at the towers, her mouth open. "This is it."

"'It' what?"

"The bowels of hell. Where no one goes. Ever." She pulled her shirt up over her nose, and glanced down at the ground, then paled. "I recognize them. That woman there . . ." She walked over and squatted, laying her palm in a pool of bubbling acid, hand-to-hand with a woman trapped beneath the pool. "She used to be Satan's head researcher." The woman screamed, a soundless noise that made Jed's hackles rise.

"What did she do to get trapped in there?"

"She murdered Satan's wife."

Jed blinked. "Satan had a wife?"

"A long time ago. He totally lost his mind for like five millenniums after she was murdered." Paige stood up, and wiped her hand on her jeans. "He created this place just for his wife's murderer. And others like her." She shivered. "Satan never comes here, and he's forbidden anyone else to. I think it freaks out even him."

"I can see why." He nudged the ground with his toe, feeling sick at the sight of all the tortured faces. "Can we get them out?"

"Oh, no." Paige shook her head quickly. "You don't want to do that. These people are really bad. Like, true, true evil. To release them would be to destroy the world."

"Kind of like your wraith?"

Paige frowned at him. "Was that a nice thing to say? I'm vulnerable right now."

"Sorry. I didn't mean it like that. I was just assimilating." He took her hand and studied the towers. He could feel a humming coming from the second tower, calling for him. He pointed to it. "There. The gateway's in there."

"So . . . what now? Do we go through it? Rita said we'd know what to do when we got here."

"Hell if I know. Let's go check it out."

Paige led the way, climbing over the rocks that blocked the entrance to the tower.

Jed's hands burned from the hot rock, but not enough

to stop either of them. Paige flared up a fireball for a
torch, so they could see where they were going. It took
almost an hour, but they finally made it to the bottom of
a curving staircase that disappeared into the black void
above their heads.

"Up there?"

Jed could still feel a vibration coming from above.
"Yeah. I think."

"Let's go."

They started to climb, and the vibration became stronger, until suddenly Jed stopped, placing his hand on
Paige's arm. "Wait."

"What?"

"We've got a problem."

"We've got many problems. Do we have a new one?"

"Hang here for a sec." He moved past her and took a
few more steps, and then he stopped and placed his hands
on the stone wall. It was cold under his touch.

"Is this it?" Paige came to stand next to him and pressed
her palm against the rock.

Jed immediately felt something simmer inside him,
something dark. "Step back." The voice that came out
of him was deep and hollow, unlike any sound he'd ever
made.

Paige immediately dropped her hands and moved away
from the wall.

But still, the vibration inside him continued, building
strength, building darkness. He turned to face Paige, leaning his back against the cold stone. "You need to go back
to the bottom of the stairs. Now."

She stared at him, her eyes wide. "You're one seriously
scary-looking dude right now. Your eyes are black, your

hair's standing out on end, and you've got this total murderous look on your face."

"You're a threat to the gate," he ground out. "Get. Back."

"Your shadow warrior's going to kill me because I'm trying to go through the gate? I didn't think of *that*." She started backing down the stairs. "No problem. I'll just wait downstairs while you think on it, okay?"

Jed watched her go, fighting against every instinct in his body to go shadow and destroy her instantly. It wasn't until she disappeared from sight, until he could no longer hear her footsteps on the stone, that he felt the humming subside ever so slightly.

Then he turned and looked at the stone again. Studied it for a long minute. Then he laid his palms on the wall again, moved them around, sliding them over the rough stone until he knew they were in the right place.

Then he pressed them against the stone.

And it worked.

The gate opened.

Paige hopped over the last black boulder and landed on the acid pool ground, then lifted her foot when she realized that Satan's ex–head researcher was under her feet again.

She frowned and squatted so she could look at the woman. Her eyes were wide, and she was screaming, but her mouth was moving as if she were screaming specific words, instead of just random expressions of intolerable pain and misery. Paige frowned. "What are you saying?"

She leaned closer, and put her ear against the ground to see if she could hear, but there was no sound. But she felt better just being that close to her . . . not just better . . . complete.

Which immediately made her sit back up.

Then she saw another face had joined Satan's ex-researcher. This one was a man with red hair and two empty sockets where his eyes should have been.

Recognition flared inside her, and she knew who he was too. She knew his name, his age, what kind of Otherworld being he was, and what he'd done to get himself locked under the ground.

Without thinking, she smiled and laid her hand on the ground.

He lifted his and placed his hand against hers, on the other side of the invisible plane, and he smiled back. *We have been waiting for you.*

She started in surprise when his words rang clearly in her mind. He hadn't said them aloud, but she'd known what he said.

Then another face joined the other two, and she instantly knew who that old lady was, with her gray hair and beady eyes. *Welcome, wraith.*

Paige frowned as the crackly voice sounded in her mind. "How do you know me?"

All three faces smiled at her, but none of them replied.

"How do I know you?" Because she did. She'd never heard about Satan's wife being murdered, but she knew this woman's story. She knew every detail about all of them. As if she *were* them . . . "Oh, shit." She jerked to her feet, suddenly realizing that her whole body was tingling, with pain, with a swirling dark energy.

As she stood there, more faces appeared at her feet, their hands pressed to the ground, gazing up at her. All of them were waiting. She could feel their expectation, their anticipation of . . . getting out.

She thought suddenly of how Mona had been created by harvesting life force from the three worlds, and then she knew what Rita had done. She'd taken parts of the worst evil in hell, and put them in Paige, and when Paige went wraith, all of them would be free, inside her. She stared down at her feet, at the growing crowd. "That's so not a good thing, I'm thinking."

No wonder she was going to destroy the world. There was no way she could control them. No way her love for Zed would withstand that kind of evil. Junior was wrong, so wrong. No one would control them. No one could control her.

"Oh, *God*." She sat down hard on a rock, pulling her feet up off the ground as far away from the people as she could get. "Jerome was right."

"About what?"

She looked up to see Jed vault down off a nearby rock. His eyes were violet again, and he seemed to have regained control of his shadow warrior. His hair was messed up, his body was lithe and muscular as he wove his way down the rocks. He was beautiful, and she could see the pain in his eyes, the anguish of his choices. "What did you find?"

He smiled at her as he reached her side. "Heaven. I opened the gate for you." He hopped up next to her and sat down. "The moat runs around the perimeter of heaven. You can't get into heaven without going through it, but there are heavily armed Men in White lining the shores." He took her hand and played with her fingers absently. "I'm going to go up there first, and try to convince my shadow warrior that the Men in White are trying to get through the gate. Then my shadow form will destroy all of them." He looked at her. "Then all you need to do is go through the gate and hop in before my shadow form notices. The river is huge and powerful. I think it'll work."

She knew it wouldn't. Not with the kind of evil that was inside her.

Jed stared across the barren landscape, gently tapping her hand against his chin. "Don't come near me, though, once you're through, or I'll kill you for going through the gate. I won't be able to stop myself."

"What about Rafi?"

Jed closed his eyes for a long moment, and she realized he'd made his choice.

He'd chosen her.

Her heart suddenly swelled and her eyes filled with tears. "But—"

He spun toward her and grabbed her shoulders. "No." His voice was sharp, and then his face softened as he looked at her. "Don't you understand? I never had a choice. It's always been you, since the first moment. I've been holding out, hoping I could find a way to save Rafi as well, but in the end, it was always going to be you." His hands slid to the sides of her neck, his thumbs rubbing her throat. "It's always been you," he whispered.

She searched his face, the earnestness in it, and felt her whole body warm under his scrutiny. "You Love me," she whispered.

"Hell, yes. I can't live without you." He dropped his head and kissed her, ever so softly, almost reverently, then he lifted his head. "Junior will take my soul when he realizes I failed to hold up my end of the contract, but you'll be free, and that's all I need."

Her throat tightened as she realized the implications of his words. They would be separated forever. She would be free, and alone, and he'd be tortured, along with his brother.

"No, don't look at me like that," Jed said. "It's okay. I'm fine with it." He stroked her hair. "Knowing you'll be safe, it'll be enough for me."

But it won't be for me. "Will you promise me something?"

"Anything. Anything you want." He kissed her again, his mouth so warm and soft against hers, that she wanted to melt into him and live these last minutes with him.

But she pulled back and met his gaze. "If I turn wraith, promise me you'll kill me."

His face grew hard. "It'll work."

"Promise me you'll kill me." She grabbed his hands, desperate to make him agree. "I realized that Jerome was right. I'll destroy the world if I'm allowed to turn wraith. We both know I will, and that can't be allowed to happen. Please, if you can't promise me that you'll kill me if I turn wraith, then I'll kill myself first. It's that important." She couldn't believe she was saying it, but it was true. The beings trapped beneath the acid pool could never be released.

Jed stared at her for a long moment, and then he finally nodded. "I promise I'll kill you if you turn wraith."

"You swear?"

He cupped her face. "I swear."

She felt his conviction and knew he would. "Thank you."

"Just don't turn wraith, okay?"

Instead of answering, she linked her arms behind his

neck. "Before all hell breaks loose, before Junior recalls you and I try to destroy the moat with my evil . . ." She tugged him down toward her and kissed him. "Before our lives fall apart . . ." She kissed him again, and smiled to herself when he groaned and kissed her back, sliding his hands under her shirt. "Make love to me, Jed."

And when his response was to pull her onto his lap and crush her against him, she almost cried.

Because she Loved him.

And that changed everything.

Thirty-two

*D*rink from the Goblet, Rafi. The words vibrated in Rafi's head, cycling again and again, until it was all he could think of, until it had penetrated the darkness that remained of his mind.

Rafi slid under the door to the living room where he'd seen the woman take the Goblet.

Drink from the Goblet, Rafi.

He didn't even know what the phrase meant anymore, didn't know whose words he was hearing, but they comforted him, made him feel safe. Made him want that white plastic cup, and the liquid inside.

The woman was sitting on the couch, holding the white plastic jug that Rafi vaguely recalled tearing apart. Or had he? Didn't know. Everything was fuzzy. There was a man next to her, and Rafi registered the threat. He needed to kill them. . . .

Drink from the Goblet, Rafi.

He knew those words were for him. They would help him. Someone wanted to help him, and he had to drink from the Goblet. He fixed his gaze on the white object and misted toward them, until he was so small he was invisible. *Rafi.* The word sounded familiar. Felt right in his head.

He drifted through the woman's hair, over her skin, circled over her heart.

She coughed and brushed her hand through his mist, and he felt the tingle of her heat, and felt himself refocusing, to find her heart. To stop it.

Drink from the Goblet, Rafi.

His head reverberated with pain, but he whirled around and speared toward the bottle, unable to resist the orders, bursting through the plastic into the grayish liquid inside.

The relief was almost instant, and he slowed down, let his mist mix with the molecules, felt the murmur of life, of recognition of his presence in the liquid. *She was female.* She wrapped herself around him, and he drank her into his being, mixing with her, feeling her loneliness, her call, her need for his touch.

God, he needed her too. Needed her healing.

And she gave it to him, imbuing him with warmth, with light, with life, and suddenly his mind was clear again. His mind was his own, no longer twisted by thoughts he hated. Elation swept through him and he shared it with her, let her feel his joy. He felt her delight, her pleasure at helping him.

They swirled together, until he could no longer tell what thoughts were his, what emotions were hers. They were one, and she clung to him, whispering her secrets to him, the secrets she'd never been able to share with anyone.

And he listened, and he wept for her, and he promised

her she would be alone no longer. He would find a way to release her from the prison that contained her.

Then, suddenly, she kicked him out.

Rafi fell hard on the wooden floor, his shoulder slamming into the marble fireplace as he rolled across the floor.

"Who the hell are you?"

He blinked, and found himself staring down the barrel of a machine gun.

No, make it two.

Rafi grinned, seeing in color for the first time since he'd been yanked out of his prison by the Council, and he knew his eyes were no longer black. "God, it's good to be back."

The woman pressed the gun against his forehead. "Identify yourself, or I'll have to kill you."

"I'm Jed's brother." Rafi sat up, rubbing his shoulder as he suddenly recalled the incident in the kitchen with total clarity. Recalled the midnight deadline. "What time is it?"

The man glanced at his watch. "Ten thirty."

Shit. Less than an hour and a half. His gut lurched at the thought of being sucked back into Junior's hell, and he shoved it aside. Screw that. He wasn't going back. He had to find Jed. Now. "Where's my brother? Do you know where he went?"

Derek lowered his gun. "He and Paige went to the west towers of hell."

The third gate. He knew without even thinking that the gate was there. He blinked, and he realized he knew where all the gates were. And he knew how to get there. "Thanks."

Justine didn't lower her gun. "You're leaving?"

"Yeah." He glanced at the couch, saw the white sports bottle propped up against the cushions. *Mona.* "Sorry about ripping her apart."

"You're not forgiven."

Oh, but he knew he was, by the one who mattered. *I'll be back for you.* The bottle flashed white once, and Justine shot a quick glance at it. "Mona? You're back? Derek! She's back." Justine tossed the gun at her husband and dove back onto the couch, cradling the Goblet to her chest. "Oh, sweetie, I'm so sorry. I swear I won't let Rafi near you again, or anyone else."

Rafi frowned at the implication that he wouldn't be allowed access to her. That could make things more difficult.

"You were leaving?" Derek reminded him.

"Yeah." Rafi tore his gaze away from Mona. He had to save himself before he could rescue her. "Can I have one of the guns?"

Derek shrugged and tossed him one. "Try not to shoot yourself."

"We can't. Not here. I can't make love to you in the bowels of hell—" Jed's protest died as Paige yanked her shirt over her head and sank her mouth onto his. Her lips were warm, hot, her tongue desperate, reaching inside him as if she could never get enough. Her breasts were crushed against his body so hard he could feel her heart racing in his chest.

"Now. Here." Her hands were desperate, tugging at his shirt, touching his chest, his stomach, his shoulders, everywhere, as if she couldn't get enough, as if she was afraid he'd disappear before she had her fill. "Wherever you are, it's the right place to be."

Her desperation, her need, her desire leapt into him, and suddenly he couldn't think. Couldn't stop. He needed her skin against his. The softness of her body, wrapped around his.

His shirt landed in an acid pool, his jeans hit the deck next to hers, and then there was nothing between them. Just slippery skin and heat. She bit his nipple and his body jerked in response, wanting more. Needing more. "It'll never be enough," he whispered. "If I had you for eternity, it still wouldn't be enough."

And he knew it was true. Every kiss, every touch, every place where he felt her body against his, he felt lightness, sunshine, peace. He felt forgiven. "You saved me, Paige." His eyes suddenly began to sting and he rolled her over, his mouth closing over her breast.

She arched off the rock, her fingers digging into his shoulders. "No," she gasped. "You saved me. You showed me who I was."

"Sunshine?" He grazed his teeth over her nipple, laved the firm peak, awed that she could be responding to him so completely. *Him.*

Her fingernails raked his back, and he basked in the pain, in the knowledge that she was losing control. That she was at his mercy. "You made me want to be a better person."

"Oh, hell, Paige." He pulled back long enough to look at her face. "You've got it backwards. It's you who makes the world a better place." He kissed her hard. "Don't you get it? That's why it's always been you. Because the world can't survive without you. Not just me, the world. It needs you. It needs your light, your optimism, your spirit."

She smiled, and her eyes filled with tears. "See? That's what I'm talking about. You think I'm so amazing, and you make me want to be that person, not some evil murderer who slaughters innocents."

"But that's who you are." He trailed his fingers over her cheeks, and began moving slowly between her legs, rubbing his arousal over her most intimate place, teasing, caressing. "You are sunshine. Don't you understand that by now?"

She shifted under him to part her legs farther, allowing him to sink more deeply between her thighs as she lifted her head to press a kiss against the hollow of his throat. "I do." She lifted her lashes to look at him, and he found himself sinking into the depths of her passion, of the love buried within her gaze. Her love was so intense, it burned through him.

"God, Paige. I didn't realize—" He was humbled, cowed by the extent of her feelings for him. Something broke inside him, and he felt a light blossoming through him, awakening him, and suddenly he forgot his past. He forgot his life. He forgot all the shit he'd done. Paige was his world. His existence. *His everything*. He dropped his head and tore into her mouth with a ferocity he couldn't control, didn't want to control.

She met him with equal force, driving him with her need, her love, her *soul*. He felt her reach for him, and he groaned as she shifted under him again, and he moved with her, and then she found him and he drove inside her, never lifting his mouth from hers, *unable* to lift his mouth from hers. He had to taste her, swallow her gasp of pleasure with each move, deeper, harder. *Need to get closer.*

Pressure began to build deep inside him, and he felt her soul searching for him, coaxing him out of the prison he'd kept himself locked away in for so long.

No. Don't merge, Jed, he told himself.

He tried to pull back, and she followed him, her mouth devouring his, her fingernails digging into his shoulders, keeping him with her. "Don't leave. Kiss me harder," she whispered. "I need more. Give it all to me, Jed."

"But—" His hips continued to drive of their own accord, deeper, harder, and he had to clench his jaw to keep from shouting.

"No! Dammit! You will not make me spend eternity wondering what it would be like if you gave all of yourself to me! I love you, Jed Buchanan. Please, give me this one night of all of you." Her voice was thick with emotion that made his throat suddenly clog up.

He couldn't hold back anymore. Her kisses were too demanding, her body calling for him, her soul reaching for him, demanding he join her. He felt his spirit swell up and meet hers, and they met and meshed, and suddenly he knew he would never be complete without her. She was his other half, his destiny, his being. "I love you, Paige." He shouted the words as the orgasm overtook him, and she screamed his name, her body convulsing under his, and his final shields fell and he plunged into her with his body and his spirit and his entity, and she was there to meet him, and sunshine exploded around him, blinding him and searing his body as the final tremors faded from their bodies.

"Oh, God, Jed. I love you. I did this on purpose. Never blame yourself, okay?"

He snapped his head up at the tension in her voice. "Did what?" Then he saw the blackness of her eyes, and felt the cold blast of true evil everywhere they were touching. "Jesus, Paige. *Your wraith*." He started to scramble off her, then froze when she clutched him.

"This is how I wanted to go," she whispered, her voice raspy and harsh.

Her body convulsed and he grabbed her. "Fight it! Don't let this happen."

Her fingers dug into his arms as her back arched and smoke rose off her body. "I want this. You. Rafi. Need to live." She screamed with pain, and he grabbed her arms, his hands shaking.

"Dammit, Paige! I was sacrificing for you! Not you for me! I'm not worth it. Stop it! Just make it stop!" He glanced around desperately, searching for something living to give her to bleed off the evil, but there was nothing. Nothing but him. He wrapped his arms around her and pulled her against him. "Take me. Take me instead."

Her body twisted and convulsed again, and he tightened his grip as she screamed. "Paige. God, Paige. Stop. Why aren't you taking me?" Her skin was turning gray and her body was shuddering in his arms, and he could feel the vibrations of dark energy bursting from her, rippling the ground beneath them, but nothing was hurting him. It was burning past him, as if he didn't exist. No numbness, no blackness, nothing. "I'm alive. Take me!"

"Love transcended the change. Can't hurt you," she gritted out. "You. Rafi. Saved."

There was an inhuman shriek and he jerked his gaze to

the right in time to see the ground begin to bulge up, hands beating from underneath, trying to break the surface.

Paige screamed again, her body contorting in his lap. "You promised," she rasped out.

"Promised what? God, what did I promise? Tell me what to do."

She lifted her head to look at him, her cheeks sunken, her eyes glittering with an evil that made his skin crawl. "You promised to kill me. Do it now, Jed. You promised."

Oh, Jesus, no.

Thirty-three

Paige's gaze met Jed's, and it was pure evil, nothing left of Paige at all. Then her body crumbled in his arms, until he was holding only black ash. Then it whirled away from him, and spread over the ground, and he saw hands burst from the ground through the black coating, then become absorbed into it, watched the thick layer of sludge that used to be Paige grow and solidify.

"What the hell's that?"

Jed spun around to see Rafi standing to his right, a machine gun aimed at the bubbling blackness of the ground, his eyes a dark brown. No black at all. *"Rafi?"*

His brother flashed him a brief smile. "Took your advice and sampled Mona. Got rid of the shit the Council and the Men in White did to me." His smile faded. "I can't go back to Junior's hell. I'm not going. He can claim me, but that doesn't mean I'm going."

Jed's brief moment of relief disappeared, consumed by his worry for Paige. "You're good. Paige turned herself, loves me. Contract satisfied." He gestured at the bubbling ground. "That's her."

Rafi sat down hard on a stone. "I'm free? I'm really

free?" He pressed his hands to his face, and his shoulders shook.

Jed felt his own throat tighten, but he shrugged it off. No time. "Give me your gun."

Rafi lifted his head, and his eyes were bright. "Why?"

"I have to kill Paige." *Oh,* God.

Rafi slid the strap off his shoulder and tossed it at Jed as the black sludge began to rise up, solidifying, taking the shape of a human. Jed caught it, then fumbled it and nearly dropped it in the black sludge. His hands were shaking, his chest ached, he felt sick. He lifted the gun and aimed it at the figure taking shape. "I love you," he whispered, as he slid his finger over the trigger. "I always will."

"Wait," Rafi said.

Jed's finger froze, but he didn't avert the gun from the figure forming before him. "What?"

"Why are you killing her?"

"Because she'll destroy the world as a wraith. I promised her I wouldn't let her do that. I promised I'd kill her first."

Rafi cursed under his breath. "What about heaven?"

"The moat?"

"Yeah."

"Too late." He realized suddenly that the figure was taking the shape of Paige again. Her golden hair appeared, then the curves of her body, the tilt of her lips as if she were about to smile. He dropped the gun in disbelief. "Paige?"

"Look at her eyes," Rafi said.

He did.

They were bottomless pits of blackness, of raging evil.

He cursed and raised the gun up again, his hands shaking as he sighted for where her heart should be.

For a long moment, neither of them moved. *Pull the trigger, Jed. You have to.*

But he couldn't.

He put down the gun and looked at his brother. "I know you owe me nothing, but will you help me?"

Rafi stood up instantly. "What do you need?"

"It might blow up heaven."

Rafi shrugged. "I'm not a fan of anything related to heaven these days. Count me in. What's up?"

Jed eyed Paige as she raised her hands skyward and let out an ear-splitting shriek that had them slamming their hands over their ears and cringing as the pain knifed through their heads.

She stopped suddenly and looked at Jed. Or rather, the bottomless pits of hell that used to be her eyes stared at him.

"Holy crap." Rafi dropped his hands from his ears. "You love that thing?"

"Yeah. I do." Jed clenched his fists. "We need to get her through the third gate and into the moat."

Rafi grimaced. "I can't let her through. I know I won't be able to."

"I know. We'll go up there, and you let me knock you out as we reach the gate, and I'll take her through."

"You think you can make yourself do that? Go against your true nature?"

Jed watched Paige as she started to look around, scanning for something—hell only knew what. Then she saw

Rafi, and turned toward him, a hiss leaking out of her mouth. He thought of how he'd almost killed her earlier when she'd gotten too close to the gate. "Yeah, I'll take her through." *I have to.*

"But you'll forfeit your destiny." Rafi sounded incredulous. "By violating the most basic tenet of being a shadow warrior, you'll be wiped from the tables. Your shadow warrior legacy will be stripped from you and passed on to someone else. You won't even be *immortal*. You'll be cannon fodder when Junior comes calling, all pissed off because he lost us both."

"Doesn't matter."

"It's like suicide. If losing your destiny doesn't kill you, Junior will. You'd really do that for her?"

"Yeah." He watched Paige stalk Rafi. "Yeah, I will."

"Is she still going to want you when you're not a harbinger of death? I mean, she's a Rivka. A human male isn't going to be much of a match for her."

"Don't care. I'm doing it anyway."

"Well, shit, man. It was good knowing you." Rafi backed up a step as Paige started to head toward him. "So, what's your grand plan, here?"

"I can't enter a Rivka without permission, but you can. I'll merge with you, and you'll take me inside with you, and then we'll try to take over her and get her up to the gate."

"Inside *her*?"

Jed nodded. "I'm guessing she can't hurt us if we're both in shadow form, but I don't know. She might kill us." He looked at Rafi. "I'm sorry for screwing up your life, and you don't owe me this."

"Damn right. I owe you nothing. Remember that. But you get it anyway, brother." And then he went shadow.

Jed was momentarily stunned by his brother's response, then he too went shadow, and he moved next to his brother.

Paige had stopped when Rafi had disappeared, and she was turning her head, searching for him, searching for her victim.

Ready? Jed spoke into his brother's mind, sharing the link they'd been destined for since birth. Warrior to warrior. He couldn't believe how right it felt.

Hell, yeah.

Then they moved together, mixing their molecules in the way of shadow warriors of ages past, gaining strength from each other, becoming a force more than twice that of their individual selves. Jed linked himself to Rafi, becoming one with his brother.

Go.

They speared toward Paige and slammed into her body, Rafi bursting through her defenses, dragging Jed with him. Together they attacked her body, her spirit, slicing through the evil that consumed her, matching their own evil with hers, fighting it out. Jed could hear her screaming, felt her deadly fury raging, felt his shadow warrior rise to the challenge, fighting her with Rafi beside him.

Start heading her toward the gate. Jed felt himself beginning to weaken, a numbness starting to build. *I don't know how much longer we'll be able to hold out.*

No shit. This is one nasty bitch.

Anger roared through Jed and he slammed it into the wraith, momentarily stunning it. *Don't call the woman I love a bitch.* Jed forced her to turn, to begin climbing the rocks toward the third gate.

This thing we're inside right now isn't the woman you love.

Rafi was right. What if there was nothing left of Paige? What if the moat wiped out the wraith, and there was nothing left?

She loves you, bro. That's still there.

Jed clung to his brother's words as they forced the wraith up the steps, to the gaping hole in the stone wall, battling death and evil with every step. Never had he been so happy to be evil, to be a match for the worst darkness he'd ever encountered.

Rafi stopped just inside the gate. *Take me out, now. I can't let her through.*

Thank you. Then he swung hard with all his darkness and knocked out his brother. He felt Rafi drift from Paige's body, and then he was alone inside her.

Her evil swelled and slammed him hard, and he faltered, momentarily overwhelmed by how powerful she was. Then he pulled himself together and smacked her hard with his own energy. *Forget it, sweetheart. This is one battle you aren't winning.* He thrust her through the gate and she stumbled into a Man in White, who screamed and exploded. Jed shoved her forward as Men in White shouted at her, trying to get their machine guns working. Bullets began to spray, and Jed felt them slice through Paige. She jerked with each blow, but didn't stop. Didn't falter. Was she literally unstoppable?

Jed could feel her focus, her burning lust to kill, realized she'd stopped fighting him so she could focus on her prey. So he grabbed her by the heart and threw her over the edge of the moat before she could fight back, and they plunged into the cool water.

He pulled himself out of her as the water churned and bubbled around them, turning black, steam rising from it. He sucked in a lungful of water as he took human form, too exhausted to swim, felt himself sinking toward the bottom.

Then hands grabbed him and pulled him out, and dumped him on the shore. He coughed, spewing water, then rolled over, leaning over the edge, smacking away hands that tried to touch him, to pull him back. "Paige! Can you hear me? Paige!" He coughed again, his body aching, his lungs seizing in his chest, his soul trembling from the battle. "Paige! I love you!"

The water rose higher, spilling over the banks, and Jed found himself yanked backward by the Men in White, away from the cascading black liquid, bubbling, steaming, hissing rising into the air until a black cloud shut out all the light and darkness descended. Jed jerked himself free of their grasp and walked forward into the water, letting it swirl around his legs, wincing as it burned his skin. "Paige Darlington, I know you're in there! I demand you come back to me! I need you, dammit!"

The water slowly stopped bubbling, faded back to a brilliant blue and subsided back within its banks.

But no Paige.

He stood hip deep in water, staring in stunned disbelief at the clear river, flowing gently past. *There was nothing left*.

"Down here!"

He jerked his head up and saw a Man in White downstream. He was waving his arms as another Man in White emerged from the water, the naked body of a woman draped over his shoulder.

"Paige!" Jed sprinted down the riverbank, sliding in the mud as he raced toward her. He reached the man and pulled Paige off his shoulder, cradling her to his chest as he set her down in the sand. "Paige? Are you there? Sweetheart?"

"Jed?" Her eyelids fluttered, and then her eyes were open.

Blue eyes.

Paige's blue eyes. No wraith. "You broke your promise," she whispered.

"Yeah, I did."

She smiled. "Thanks."

And suddenly, he couldn't talk. So he wrapped his arms around her and hauled her against him, and didn't even try to keep the tears from sliding down his cheeks.

Thirty-four

Rafi was standing at the gate, his hair dark and wild, his body language aggressive and confident as Jed and Paige walked up to the gate. They'd both been given clothes by the Men in White, and looked like a couple of delinquent angels.

Jed stopped in front of his brother, ignoring the sounds of frenzied debate as the Men in White argued over what do with Paige, now that she was no longer the being that had killed the angel. Jerome had finally arrived, and he was leading the Council and the delegates from heaven toward the conclusion that they couldn't legally hold her responsible for actions done while she'd been possessed by the souls of the most evil beings that had ever existed. Jerome had nodded at Jed as he'd guided Paige out of there, and he knew Jerome would prevail.

Not that he would ever like the guy, but keeping the Men in White off Paige's tail would start his redemption.

They reached Rafi, and he stopped, but Paige tugged her hand out of Jed's and threw herself at Rafi. His hands came up to catch her as she thudded against his chest. "Thank you, thank you, thank you, thank you!" She grabbed his face between her hands and planted a kiss squarely on his mouth. "I don't care you almost killed me like eighty times. You're my new favorite person, except of course for Jed." She kissed him again, then jumped out of Rafi's arms.

Jed grinned as Paige skipped back to him and wrapped her arms around his waist, wiggling herself up against his side. "She's a keeper, huh?"

Rafi finally got the stunned look off his face. "A little more appealing than she was an hour ago, yeah."

Paige beamed at both of them. "That's too cool that the estranged brothers came together in a time of strife. This is what family is all about, you know? Always there for each other when needed."

Rafi and Jed exchanged glances, and Jed saw the hesitation on his brother's face. "She's right, you know," Jed said. "About that family bonding stuff."

Rafi's gaze darkened. "I helped you, but I can't forgive—"

Paige grabbed Rafi's wrist and yanked him over to her and shoved a fireball in his chest. "Hey! Since Jed and I are now bonded for all eternity, you're my brother now. You must harass me, throw spitballs at me over the Thanksgiving dinner table, hold my hand when Jed's off chasing down bad guys and I'm worried about him, and you will *always* be there for me. And for him." She grabbed the front of his shirt and pulled him until his face was level with hers. "Do you understand me? I love Jed. I love you. And I expect you to love us both. Got it?"

Rafi stared at her, and Jed saw the damage in his brother's eyes. The rage. And he knew that despite the fact his brother had shaken off some of the effects of the Men in White's experiment, Rafi was still extremely dangerous and volatile. After decades of being unable to fight back, he was now unshackled and brimming with rage and the effects of years of abuse. And who knew what the Men in White had done to him. Jed had no idea what his brother was capable of anymore, and he didn't think Rafi knew either.

"Rafi?" Paige pushed at his chest, completely ignoring the dangerous vibes coming off his brother, and Jed almost wanted to grab her and pull her back from him.

But Paige could handle it, and maybe, just maybe, her sunshine could help Rafi too. She tapped his chin. "Raphael! You got it, or what?"

Rafi gave a visible shudder, then he focused on Paige; his torment was hidden behind a mask once again. "Yeah, I got it," Rafi finally said. "But I'm still pissed at Jed."

She smiled and patted his cheek. "Of course you are. You should be. You're brothers. You should have issues. I expect you and I to develop issues as well, that will, of course, be fully subordinated to our deep familial bond, right?"

Jed laughed as Rafi shot him a look. "Might as well agree, Rafi. She's pretty high on the whole concept of family. You're stuck with her now."

"I'm sure I can drive her away." The edge was back in Rafi's voice again.

"Not a chance, dear brother." Paige reached up and straightened his shirt, then brushed some dirt off it. "But you're welcome to try."

"But not right now." Jed pulled her back into his arms and anchored her against his chest. "I'm taking her with me now. Got some things to discuss."

Rafi caught his tone. "You haven't told her?"

"No. Not yet."

"Told me what?" She pulled out of Jed's arms to face

him. "We've been married for like ten minutes, and you're already holding out on me?"

Jed raised his brows. "We're married?"

"Well, of course. I mean, if you opening a gate for me and me turning myself into a wraith for you isn't enough to join us for all eternity, then I don't know what is." She narrowed her eyes. "Why? You backing out now? After finally teaching me how to truly love?" She threw her hands onto her hips and lifted her chin, giving him her haughtiest look. "And before you answer that, remember that you devirginized me. In many civilizations, you'd be forced to the altar at gunpoint." She flared up a fireball and threw it so it hovered at his throat. "I'm not above using force to get what I want. And I want you. For eternity. Got it?"

Jed tensed and slowly eased back from the fireball. "Be careful with that, sweetheart. I'm not the man I used to be."

She stared at him, and slowly, her face began to get worried. "Jed? What's wrong? What happened?"

Shit. He hadn't wanted to tell her yet. He'd wanted more time, so he could convince her to love him as he was.

"Jed?" Her voice was shaky now, and she extinguished the fireball as she marched up to him. She grabbed his upper arms, her fingers digging in. "What's going on?"

"Just tell her," Rafi said. "She needs to know before she accidentally kills you."

She didn't take her gaze off his face. "Tell me!"

He peeled her hands off his shoulders and entwined her fingers with his, gripping her tighter than he meant to. "When I took you across the gate, I broke the number one rule of a shadow warrior."

She frowned. "So you want a thank you? I appreciate it, but I thought you already knew that—"

"No, you don't understand." He pulled his hands free and clasped them behind his head. "I lost my shadow warrior status."

She smiled with relief. "That's it? That's great. You didn't want to be one anyway. Did those soul remnants leave your body too?"

He hesitated, suddenly realizing his chest was empty, for the first time in decades. He was the only one in there. Him, and Paige, because he could still feel her in there from their merge. "Yes, but I lost it all. I'm an ordinary human now. I'll get old, I'll die in fifty years—"

"If he's lucky. More likely, Junior will kill him first. He's a bad loser."

He glared at Rafi. "Don't you need to go somewhere?"

"Yeah, I do actually." Rafi looked a little frustrated. "I have a promise I need to keep, but I appear to be stuck guarding the gate now that it's open. Can't leave." He rapped a fist on the stone. "Traded one damned prison for another."

Before Jed could ask what the promise was, Paige's hands slid around his waist, and he turned back to find her beaming up at him. "Men are so dense sometimes."

He frowned. "Didn't you hear me? I'm human. I'll die, leaving you alone, and you'll have to be *my* bodyguard."

She grinned. "First of all, you're a total badass in human form, or did you already forget laying out all those men at Yankee Stadium? That was *hot*." She licked her finger, then trailed it down his chest, as if she were setting it on fire. "Shadow warrior thing wasn't so hot, because you were invisible, so how could I appreciate all your manly muscles flexing like that?" Her palm spread over his stomach, drawing heat to the southern parts of his body. "And, you obviously forgot you took three drinks of Mona when we were trying to heal you from Junior's torture, didn't you?"

He stared at her. He *had* forgotten.

She smiled up at him, then stood on her tiptoes so her mouth was hovering over his. "So, basically, not only are you still immortal, but you're also a total badass who doesn't need shadow form to do some major damage." Her breath was warm on his mouth, and he slid his arms around her waist, pulling her tighter against him with a groan. "We both know Junior won't dare come after either of you guys because he's too much of a coward to show his face when you guys are free to kill him." She flicked her tongue over his lips. "And now that I'm embracing my good side, I find I'm strangely attracted to a man who doesn't kill for a living and who isn't damned anymore, now that he got himself purified." She grinned. "Or maybe it's your washboard abs and your unmatched sexual talents. It could simply be a case of mad lust, I suppose."

Rafi groaned. "Okay, you guys can so hit the road now."

Jed couldn't wipe the grin off his face. "So, yeah, I guess I'll let you declare us married then. Since you know what you're getting into and you're okay with it."

She jumped up and wrapped her legs around his waist, and he caught her hips. "Take me to bed, man who I love so much, and I'll show you exactly how okay with it I am."

So he did.

And she did.

And it was perfect.

About the Author

Golden Heart–winner Stephanie Rowe wrote her first novel when she was ten, and sold her first book twenty-three years later. After a brief stint as an attorney, Stephanie decided wearing suits wasn't her style and opted for a more fulfilling career. Stephanie now spends her days immersed in magical worlds creating quirky stories about smart, scrappy women who find true love while braving the insanity of modern life and Otherworldly challenges. When she's not glued to the computer or avoiding housework, Stephanie spends her time reading, playing tennis, and hanging out with her own fantasy man and their two Labradors. You can reach Stephanie on the Web at www.stephanierowe.com.

ENJOY A SNEAK PEEK AT THE
FIRST BOOK IN THE
EXCITING NEW SERIES OF
PARANORMAL SUSPENSE

by Stephanie Rowe!

The Order of the Blade:
The First Seduction

available in Summer 2008.

Please see below
for a preview.

Meghan stood in the middle of the one-room cabin, shoving her hands deep inside her jeans pockets to keep them from shaking. There was a utility kitchen in one corner, and a large braided rug covered most of the floor. It was thick, mostly blues and reds. Cozy in a way she wouldn't have associated with a Calydon warrior.

Taking up one entire wall was a huge stone fireplace, the kind that made her want to curl up under a comforter in front of a roaring fire, sipping hot chocolate and snuggling with . . . Her gaze flicked to Baden as he flicked the rain out of his dark hair with the swipe of his hand.

Not him. There was nothing snuggly about Baden at all.

She pulled her thoughts off him and surveyed the rest of the one-room cabin. A double bed took up most of the remaining space, and a closed door led to what must have been the bathroom. An armoire of roughly hewn boards was shoved in the corner. It looked handmade, and the knotted wood was an extraordinary shade of pine, with almost a hint of red in it. "Did you make that?"

"Yeah." He walked over to the fireplace and knelt, throwing a couple huge logs onto the andirons and wadding up some old newspapers that were yellowed with age.

"It's beautiful."

He lit the fire, and his face glowed as the orange flames leapt into the air, crackling and popping. Then he stood up and turned around to face her, his face hard.

She swallowed at the utter and complete coldness in his eyes, suddenly wanting to bolt for the door. There was no humanity in this man. None at all. She'd been an idiot to think he'd help her, and she'd realized that the moment she'd been able to see his face in the moonlight.

She should have left right then, but she'd been too damn cold and wet. She hugged her arms tighter, trying to stop herself from trembling. But even her belly was aching from shivering. She'd been too cold for too long. Oregon wasn't supposed to be cold in the winter. Warm and rain, not below freezing with the forecast of an ice storm.

She watched him walk over to the double bed wedged

in the corner, a bed made of pine logs lashed together
with rope. The same handiwork as the armoire.

Baden yanked the faded plaid comforter off the bed
and tossed it at her.

She barely caught it with her numb hands, then tugged
off her damp jacket and wrapped the quilt around herself, hugging it tightly. "Thanks." She edged toward the
roaring fire until she felt the heat licking at her back,
penetrating her stiff muscles.

He inclined his head. "You were cold."

Her belly jerked at his admission that he'd noticed her
discomfort, making it impossible to deny the other reason
she hadn't left the minute she'd seen into his eyes: she
simply hadn't been able to force herself to walk away
from him.

He was cold, dangerous, and clearly not happy she was
here . . . but it didn't matter. She was staying. Because she
had no other options, and because she simply couldn't
bring herself to leave his presence. Which rattled her
severely.

Baden walked to the kitchen, helped himself to three
bagels, and a couple bottles of water. He shoved one of
each at her as he walked past, then eased himself onto
the edge of his bed, the only place to sit in the room. The
faded blue blankets were askew from him ripping off the
comforter, and one of the pillows was on the floor.

He opened his water, took a big bite of the bagel, and
leaned back, wincing slightly when his back hit the wall.
His body was solid and well muscled as he hooked his
arm over the pine headboard. The body of a warrior.
There was a scar above his right eye, and his nose looked
like it had been shattered more than once, giving him the

appearance of a soldier who had endured the worst and come out the victor.

His blue eyes regarded her coldly. Waiting.

You have no other options. She willed herself courage, then dragged herself and the comforter across the room and sat down at the other end of the bed. She faced him, tucking her feet up under her to keep her toes from brushing against his heavily muscled thigh. "I'm Meghan Baxter."

He narrowed his eyes. "What do you want?"

She met his gaze, trying to keep the desperation out of her voice. "I need your help."

His face grew hard and unreadable, and she flinched at the sudden thread of warning in the air. *Get the fuck away from me.* The message was clear, and she felt it pushing at her like a hot brand, driving her to jump to her feet and run to the door.

But she had no choice. She dug her toes into the blankets and ordered her body to stay where it was. "No."

He looked confused for a minute. "No, what?"

"I'm not getting the fuck away from you as you so eloquently put it."

Tension snapped through his body, and he jerked upright. "You heard that?"

"Of course. How could I not? I'd have to be dead not to."

He cursed and shoved to his feet with a groan of pain that made her heart tighten. "Are you all right?" she asked.

He ignored her question, running his hand through his hair in agitation. "How the hell did you hear my thoughts?" He leaned over her suddenly, his hands on the blankets on either side of her hips, his face in her space.

"Tell me——" He stopped suddenly, and he bent closer and inhaled. "Fuck. You smell unbelievable."

"Your thoughts?" she echoed. "I can't read thoughts." Her spine curled at the deep rumble of his voice, at the intensity of his voice, stripping right through her and burning her skin. She immediately leaned back, trying to get away from him, even as she wanted to lean into him, to press her nose against his neck, to inhale the scent that was him. *What is wrong with me?*

He cursed and pulled away, jerking his hands back to his sides. His jaw was clenched, with a shaggy beard covering it. It didn't look like he was wearing a beard on purpose; it looked like he hadn't bothered to shave in weeks. He was wearing black jeans, an old gray tee shirt, and a hip-length black leather jacket that was creased, battered and ripped to shreds over his left forearm. It looked like it had been worn so much that it had become part of his body. Like it belonged on him.

He shifted, and a flash of pain crossed his face before he could school them into a neutral expression.

Concern flared inside her, and she grabbed his hand before she could stop herself, her fingers closing over the roughness of his skin "You're hurt?" Shock rattled her as soon as their skin touched, and she felt herself falling——

He growled and yanked his hand out of hers. "You need to get out. Now. I have . . . things I have to do. Someone to find and kill." He added the last as if trying to scare her, then he spun away from her, grabbed a heavy parka from his armoire and held it out. "This will keep you dry and warm. Now, get out."

She stood up and faced him, making no move to take the coat, realizing she probably had about two seconds before he picked her up and tossed her out the door. Here was her moment. Succeed or fail. It was now. "I'm here because I need your help finding my sister." She couldn't keep the pain out of her voice, and Baden visibly winced. "She's missing."

His hand went to her face, and his fingers drifted over her cheek with the lightest touch, making her throat tighten. She froze, afraid any movement from her would destroy the moment, drive him away.

Then he cursed, dropped his hand and strode past her. He swept her backpack off the floor and yanked open the front door. "Out."

She didn't move, digging her fingernails into the palms of her hands at the hostile expression on Baden's face. His eyes were cold and harsh, a reflection of the Calydon warrior he was. A man who had killed many and never cared. She lifted her chin and let him see the truth in her face as to why she was here, why she'd picked *him*. "In case you haven't heard the news out here in the woods, your friend Hecktor was found murdered last night." He sucked in his breath, but she didn't let him answer. "I think my sister did it."

THE DISH

Where authors give you the inside scoop!

♥ ♥ ♥ ♥ ♥ ♥ ♥ ♥ ♥ ♥ ♥ ♥ ♥ ♥ ♥

A Note to Readers from Paige Darlington
(SEX & THE IMMORTAL BAD BOY)
and Marissa Kincaid
(TO CATCH A CHEAT)

Marissa: We want to talk to you about liars and cheats. Wait—no—something more positive.

Paige: Oh, fantastic idea! I'm all about being positive. How about being turned into an evil wraith who answers to Satan? Or about being caught in a turf battle between Satan and his sociopathic son, Satan Junior? No? I guess that still isn't very positive, is it? Tell you what, you tell me something positive about liars and cheats, and I'll tell you something positive about being consumed by evil and groomed to destroy the world.

Marissa: Okay, I've got it. Let's talk about a woman who has been cheated on by every man in her life and is finally going to make them all pay. Yeah, that's a positive spin on it.

Paige: You sound as if you're speaking from experience.

Marissa: Who, me?

Paige: Okay, to make them pay, what exactly does she do? Because my idea of making people pay—well, we're probably talking about two different kinds of making people pay.

Marissa: I—um, *she*—created a cheater database where women could list the guys who've cheated on them in the past and could also check potential dates to see if they'd cheated before.

Paige: Hmm . . . sounds like a database Satan could use. Brilliant idea.

Marissa: Yeah, it would've been, if the first cheater listed had actually cheated. And if he hadn't retaliated with his own Web site identifying women who lie. And if he hadn't put me—I mean, *her*—as the liar of the month.

Paige: Oh, wow. I'm feeling your pain, girlfriend. Is he hot? Because if he is, I'm thinking maybe you could have fun making him pay . . .

Marissa: Anyway, what about something positive about "wraithhood" and Satan?

Paige: Well, I guess that it's helping me organize my career goals. I've crossed being an evil being who kowtows to Satan off my list. But I'm thinking I need to hire someone tough enough to handle me and keep me from turning wraith while I try to get things resolved.

Marissa: Got someone in mind?

Paige: Oh, yeah.

Marissa: Then *your* problems are solved.

Paige: Not exactly. Satan Junior's holding his brother hostage, and Junior won't release his brother until he delivers the goods.

Marissa: The goods . . . as in you?

Paige: As in me.

Wouldn't it be nice if life (and wraithhood) were easy?

So, readers, let our authors know what you think about liars and cheats, Satan (and Satan Jr.), and the men who complicate all of the above or anything else. They love hearing from you!

Sincerely,

Stephanie   *Kelley St. John*

Paige Darlington, of
SEX AND THE IMMORTAL
BAD BOY
By Stephanie Rowe
(Available now)
www.stephanierowe.com

Marissa Kincaid, of
TO CATCH A CHEAT
By Kelley St. John
(Available now)
www.kelleystjohn.com